The 70 recruits waited in silence beneath the white-hot South Carolina sun. In front of them a recruiting poster was spiked onto the lawn. It pictured handsome male and female marines wearing dress blues and standing in church, heads uplifted, a shaft of sunlight brightening their scrubbed faces.

To their left a screen door squeaked, and the recruits clenched themselves more tightly at attention. The door slammed. A staff sergeant came down the steps.

"My name," he said, "is Staff Sergeant Maguire. I am your drill instructor. I have just 12 weeks, no more, to find out which of you pussies got what it takes to be a marine. Now I might have to break your balls to find that out. But I will do it. Understand? Understand that,

MAGGOTS."

MAGGOT

by

Robert Flanagan

WARNER BOOKS

A Warner Communications Company

For my Mother and Father;
for John Brick
who helped me get started,
and Tom Ireland
who helped me ask the right questions.

WARNER BOOKS EDITION

Copyright © 1971 by Robert Flanagan
All rights reserved

Warner Books, Inc., 75 Rockefeller Plaza, New York, N.Y. 10019

 A Warner Communications Company

Printed in the United States of America

First Printing: November, 1971

Reissued: December, 1980

10 9 8

Behold a marine—
a mere shadow and reminiscence of humanity,
a man laid out alive and standing
and already, as one may say,
buried under arms
with funereal accompaniments.

Thoreau

ONE

"GET OUT!"

Get out. Get out. Adamczyk tried, but couldn't rise. Weight pressed down on him, in against his sides. He tried to breathe. Get out. Get out. The weight became a movement inside him, a slight threading movement indefinable as an itch. His eyes, ears, anus, his mouth, his penis were opening. A crawling in him, and then he knew what it was and in an explosion of fear fought to rise and found the threads of movement were like wires stringing him through, holding him fast. He was clawing at the dirt above him, hunting for air. Then he wasn't. He was clawing into, not out of; hunting matter, not air, and small and soft and white he wormed his way through an eye socket of his own body. He did not want to get out. He wanted to hide. He moved over and under soft bodies like small, white rice grains. Lost in the swarm of others, he would be safe; warm in the sweet decay of his own flesh.

"Giddout giddout giddout giddout giddout."

He snapped back his head, waking, hit something hard. Dizzied, tears came against his will. He was sitting on a concrete floor, his back to a concrete wall. He got to one knee.

"Up and out. Let's go. Hey you, carrot-top! You'd best move before I put a boot up your skinny young ass."

Adamczyk moved. His stomach flopping, he pushed in among the others pushing out of the huge, gray room through a screen door. Outside, he leaped the four metal steps onto the concrete walk and scrambled for a place in ranks. He found one, froze at attention.

The first day and he'd dozed off in the lecture. Stupid. Stupid. He had to make himself pay better attention. Yet

7

the room had been so hot, so many others sweating and breathing all around him. Why did they pack people in so close together if they wanted them to listen?

An image of his dream returned, but was too slight to grasp. All he could remember was his fear. Waking hadn't dispelled that.

Adamczyk, tall and thin with worried blue eyes, in gray slacks and a white short sleeve shirt which had been neatly pressed when he'd left home the day before, stood motionless in the front rank of the group of recruits. The recruits wore a rainbow variety of civilian clothes: T shirts, jeans, sport shirts, wash and wear slacks. Their ranks were uneven; their positions of attention, caricatures of military posture.

The recruits waited in silence beneath the white-hot South Carolina sun. They were flanked on one side by the red brick building they had just left, on the other by a palm-lined road. In front of them a recruiting poster was spiked onto the lawn. It pictured handsome male and female marines wearing dress blues and standing in church, heads uplifted, a shaft of sunlight brightening their scrubbed faces.

The screen door squeaked and the recruits clenched themselves more tightly at attention. The door slammed. A staff sergeant came down the steps. He was short-legged with broad shoulders and a short, thick neck. He stopped in front of the men. His polished brass belt buckle glinted in the sun. A man in the rear rank shifted his weight. Another coughed. The sergeant slowly and sadly shook his head.

"My name," he said, "is staff sergeant Maguire. I am your drill instructor." He paced the length of the front rank, folding his hands behind his back and regulating his speech to match his slow, deliberate steps. "I have just twelve weeks, no more, to find out which of you pussies got what it takes to be a marine. Now I might have to break your balls to find that out, maggots. But I will do it. Them that can't cut it, wash out; get shit-canned."

I'll make it, Adamczyk thought. He forced from his mind the heavy fear that the drill instructor was speaking particularly to him, and he promised himself that no mat-

8

ter what, he'd stick it out. He'd work hard and would pray for help and he'd make it.

"Anybody here," the drill instructor asked, "think they got what it takes to make a good marine?"

"Yessir," the group answered.

"I am a peculiar man," Maguire said. He took a deep breath. The stiff shirt collar cut into his neck. His fleshy face reddened, eyes bulging as if popped loose by the collar's pressure. "When I ask a question I want an answer. Do you think you will make good marines?"

"Yessir."

"Your lungs are weak, maggots. But that's all right. That's what we're here for, to build you up. Down on your bellies. Move, goddamit, giddown, giddown."

The men dropped to their stomachs and lay still, waiting. The pavement burnt their palms. They arched their necks to keep their faces from the hot concrete.

"Hands out shoulder width all right push up. Up. Keep your ass out of the air, fat boy. Back straight, Red. Aw right, down on one, up on two. One."

The men lowered their bodies. Sweat dripped from their foreheads to dry on the pavement.

"Two."

They pushed up, locking their elbows. Adamczyk's back was bent like a strung bow. Maguire tapped the boy's wrist with the toe of his shoe.

"Up. You got a name, maggot?"

"Adamczyk, sir. Thomas S., sir."

"You do pushups like an elephant shits, maggot, slow and sloppy. From now on that's your name—shit. Understand?"

"Yessir."

"And when I tell you to sound off, you sound off with 'sir,' you got that? That is always the first word to come out your scuzzy mouth. 'Sir, my name is. . .! Now let's hear it. And it had best come right from your gut."

"Sir, my name is Thomas S. Adamczyk, sir!"

"Your old lady's ass it is! Didn't your drill instructor just tell you your name is shit? You can't do pushups right, you can't say 'sir' right, and now you can't even remember your own name." Maguire stuck his face close to

9

Adamczyk's, the popped eyes widening further, tiny red veins tracing the edges. Adamczyk stared straight ahead. "From now on, maggot, your name is 'Doubleshit,' you got that?

"Yessir."

"And when we get to our squad bay, you and me are gonna have a little talk. You understand, Doubleshit?"

"Yessir."

"Get back down."

Adamczyk dropped to the pushup position, keeping his back straight. Maguire stepped to the second rank.

"One."

The men lowered

"Two."

and raised,

"One."

lowered

"Two."

and raised their bodies.

Maguire finished examining the third rank. "You maggots aren't used to the heat, are you?"

"Nossir."

"Not used to heat, not used to pushups, not used to sounding off so someone can hear you. Believe me, animals, you got one hell of a lot to learn." Maguire returned to the front of the group and stood for a moment listening to the recruits' uneven breathing. "But," he said, "you will learn. In the next twelve weeks on this rock I will teach you everything you need to know to be a good marine. And you will each one of you learn it all because you will do each and every single thing I tell you to do. If I tell you to shit you will shit and if I tell you to smile you will smile and if I tell you not to breathe, then believe me, animals, you will not breathe. Do you understand?"

"Yessir."

"Because until you leave P.I. I am your mother, your father and your God. You forget that once, just once, and you will wish to hell your old man never climbed on top your old lady and screwed you into this world. You understand that?"

"Yessir."

"There are only two ways off this island, maggots. Either you graduate as a member of this platoon, platoon 197, and you march off, or you wash out and are carried off. Do you understand that?"

"Yessir."

Maguire wiped the perspiration from his forehead, then tilted down the brim of his campaign cover to shade his eyes. "Up."

The men staggered to their feet. Near the end of the first rank there was a sudden short outrush of breath and Adamczyk fell forward in a faint. His shoulder grazed the frame of the recruiting poster, his long body thumping onto the neatly-trimmed lawn. Maguire stepped to him and knelt. He felt the recruit's pulse, loosened his belt, thumbed back his eyelids, then stood.

"Any of you other pussies wanna pass out," Maguire said, "do it now and let's get it over with." He spat on the grass and waited. "Aw right then, when we move out I want you two maggots on the end to haul this meat here," his foot tapped against Adamczyk's ribs, "along behind us. Now pick up your ditty bags and turn to your left. Easy-like. Don't stampede. That's it. Aw right now, forward, walk. Let's start getting you people processed."

"Take it all off," Maguire ordered. "Skivvies, socks, rings, watches, glasses, everything. Let's go herd, hurry it up. All of it, all of it. I want you naked as the day you were born."

What would happen to his high school ring? Adamczyk wondered. He thought for a moment of photographs he'd seen of Nazi concentration camps, and the familiar nausea of fear soured his stomach. Then Maguire ordered the platoon to tie up their belongings in the brown wrapping paper he was passing around. Adamczyk inwardly ridiculed himself, trying to shake off his fear.

"You will take a towel from that pile." Maguire pointed to a large stack of folded purple towels. "You will wrap the towel around your waist and you will proceed around that bulkhead to the barber chairs. There you will wait your turn. You will at all times stay at attention. Understand?"

11

"Yessir."

"Soon as you're done there, you will get right back here and take a hot shower. You will use plenty of soap and you will scrub. I don't want any of that civilian scuz left on you when you're done. Understand?"

"Yessir."

"I want each one of you to come out here fresh and clean so we can start fresh and clean and see if somehow we can make something useful out of you. Understand?"

"Yessir."

"All right, git."

Rough purple towels wrapped about their waists, feeling the cool tile against their bare feet, the recruits stood at attention in front of the two rows of barber chairs. Maguire paced up and down the line, watching. A chair emptied and the line moved forward. A fat boy with a mantle of pimples across his rounded shoulders stepped into the chair. He lay his glasses on the lap formed by the towel. The barber jabbed a cigarette into an ashtray and picked up his clippers. The fat boy straightened his head. He smiled.

He was still smiling when Maguire yanked him from the chair. The glasses clattered onto the tiles and the towel fell limply about the boy's ankles.

"What's your name, maggot?"

"Sir, my name is Milton M. Klein, sir."

"Just what in hell were you doing in that chair?" Maguire's face was thrust close to the recruit's and his fingers dug into the boy's fatty white arm. "You tell me, maggot, and it had best be good."

"Sir, nothing. I . . ."

"You mean your drill instructor didn't see you giving everybody here a shit-eating grin?"

The recruit braced his back, trying hopelessly to stiffen dignity into his pose. "Yessir," he yelled, sucking in the quivering belly.

"Yessir, what? You grin or not?"

"Yessir, I did."

Maguire released his hold on the recruit's arm. Blood sprang back to flush the white skin a purplish red.

12

"Listen to me, pig. Someday you are gonna find your young ass up against an enemy. Chinese, Russians, whatever, there's gonna be no time for laughing. We don't want comedians in this man's Corps, pig, so you had best shape up or ship out right now while you're still in one piece. Understand?"

"Yessir."

"What do you understand?"

"Sir?"

"You said you understood. I wanna know just what you understood."

"Sir, you said I shouldn't . . ."

"YOU!" Maguire shouted. "YOU? YOU? You wanna fuck me, pig?"

"Nossir!"

"You know what a ewe is? A ewe is a female sheep and female sheep are for fucking and you got the balls to call me a ewe?"

"Sir, I . . ."

"What's the matter with you, pig? You queer?"

"Nossir."

"How come you wanna fuck your drill instructor?"

"Sir, I don't. I didn't make it that way, sir."

"A recruit never calls his drill instructor anything but drill instructor, understand?"

"Yessir."

"So you had best think twice before you open that scuzzy mouth of yours. And you had best never open it to give your drill instructor one of them shit-eating grins, understand?"

"Yessir."

" 'Cause I got no use for comedians, understand?"

"Yessir."

"Aw right, pig. You take your towel and cover up that little worm of yours before it gets cold and crawls back into its hole. And get back in that chair. We ain't got the whole damn day."

Klein knotted the towel about his waist and bent to pick up his glasses.

"I tell you to retrieve those coke bottles?"

"Nossir."

"Then you had best do what you were told."

"Sir, I can't see without . . ."

Maguire roared "GET IN THAT GODDAM CHAIR!" so suddenly the barber dropped his clippers, catching them against his leg. Klein scrambled into the chair. The barber smiled at Maguire and the drill instructor nodded. "I want'm bald, Eddie. Then let'm get his goggles."

"Sure thing, sergeant." The barber ran the clippers from front to back in smooth, continuous strokes. Klein's thick black hair fell to the floor in clumps of curls, like wool from a sheared sheep.

The barbers' chair rapidly emptying and filling, the line of recruits moved regularly forward. Maguire left the line to look into the shower room. Under a near shower, Klein was washing. He arched his back, letting the hot water run the suds from his head and neck. Eyes closed, he bent back under the tap and Maguire reached into the room to twist the single handle to cold. Klein, gasping, belly out-thrust, jumped forward to collide with another recruit who, his back to Klein, had stooped to wash his feet.

"I saw that!" Maguire shouted. "I saw that. Turn off those showers."

The recruits turned off the showers. The room was quiet except for the nozzles' dripping and the gurgle of the drain. Klein, shivering, rubbed soap from his eyes.

"Don't even try explaining, pig. I saw every bit of it. I should've known right away from the size of those tits just what you were."

"Sir, it wasn't . . ."

"Shuttup. You just be damn glad I'm not gonna file a report on this. Now I want you to stand right there, dead-center, right on that drain, and stay there till everybody else is done. Then you take your shower." Maguire lowered his voice. "And I don't want any complaints from the other fellas that you were bothering them, understand?"

"Sir, honest . . ."

"On the drain."

Leaning on the window sill, Maguire stared out at the parade ground where the wide stretch of asphalt shimmered in the heat. At the far edge of the ground, five concrete figures on a concrete base jutted into the sky's heat-faded blue. An American flag dangled lifelessly from the pole they had halfway raised.

The slapping of the wet, running feet against concrete did not turn Maguire. He stared out the window, hearing recruits, one by one or in sudden clusters, run from the shower to form ranks. When the sound of the barbers' clippers had stopped, Maguire waited a few minutes, then went to the shower room and ordered everyone out on the double, including Klein. Recruits sprinted into the room, pools of water spreading about their bare feet as they stood stock-still in ranks.

"Move out!" Maguire shouted.

Adamczyk, the last recruit from the showers, stumbled into the light, blinking the water from his eyes, his pale skin reddened with scrubbing, his face puzzled as if he had just come into the world.

Maguire grabbed Adamczyk's arm and shoved him into ranks. "All right, herd, drop the towels."

The recruits dropped their towels and, shaven and scrubbed, stood naked under Maguire's stare. Behind them, the open window framed the giant concrete figures of the Mount Surabachi monument.

Adamczyk wrote slowly and neatly on the lined, yellow notebook paper.

Dear Mom and Dad: Well, I'm here alright and there's nothing for you to worry about. We got here yesterday morning, but spent the first day at what they call "processing" and were too awful busy to write any letters. Today our D.I. (drill instructor) brought us to our barracks and we got rifles and all our other "gear" and are settled down now.

I hope you are both feeling good and won't be worrying so much about me being down here. A lot of the other boys act really scared, but I'm glad now Uncle Ted told me something about boot camp and all, so I wasn't so surprised or scared. One of the boys got sick from the heat and passed out its been so hot here. I got a little bit sick too and so did a lot of us. It's sure not much like Ohio, weather-wise. But I'm okay now and they say it's not too long before you get used to the heat here ("acclimated").

We get our shots tomorrow and I just hope they don't give too many. Anyway I'll be here only for twelve weeks and then we're supposed to get a chance to come home so it can't be too bad when you just remember it's only twelve weeks because that's not a long time at all really.

I have to go now because it's 10 to 9 (2050 hours Navy time), that's what we use here—Navy time, and we only have to 9:30 to get ready for bed. We get up early. One of the guys says 4:30 but some guys think it's 5.00.

The Drill Instructor says we can go to Church on Sundays and I was given a Missal (they "issue" out prayer books for all different religions) so you don't have to worry about me there. I hope you'll say some extra prayers for me, and Mom, when you go to St. Stephen's would you please offer up a Mass that I make it through and do alright. I think I will, but the prayers always seem to help. Also please write whenever you can because the days here seem so long it's like you forget you were ever anywhere else but here and a letter sure helps cheer you up.

Please don't worry about me.

Love,

Adamczyk sat on his locker box looking at the letter. He chewed on the pencil's pink eraser and wondered should he write Tommy, what they called him at home, or maybe Tom. Tommy had been all right at home, but here it sounded too much like a little boy's name. Still, he thought Tom would look funny to his parents. Besides, nobody in the squad bay would see the letter. He wrote "Tommy" and folded the letter into an envelope. Checking his notebook, he carefully copied his new return address onto the envelope's upper left hand corner:

Pvt. Thomas S. Adamczyk
Plt. 197, A. Co., 1st Bn., RTR
MCRD
Parris Island, S.C.

He liked the official look his return address gave to the envelope. With all the numbers and abbreviations, it seemed as if he were already a marine. And he was sure it would impress them at home. His parents knew nothing at all about service life and would probably think the address was in some kind of code. They'd have to ask his Uncle Ted to tell them what it meant.

"Private Thomas S. Adamczyk." That was a big difference from maggot or Doubleshit. Seeing it on paper made Adamczyk feel a bit less hopeless about his chances of surviving the twelve weeks of training.

He turned at the nudge in his side. He'd been aware of the recruit beside him reading his guidebook rather than writing, but hadn't noticed him further.

"Got an extra sheet of paper?"

17

"Sure," Adamczyk whispered. "Here."

"Thanks."

"My name's Adamczyk. Tom."

"Joe Waite. You're the guy passed out, right?"

Adamczyk looked down at the envelope. "Yeah." He had hoped that since they were all new to each other nobody would remember who had fainted.

Waite began writing. He wrote quickly in a slanting hand that he was fine and he asked his mother to write to him when and if she had the time. He added the lie that recruits were allowed to write letters on Sundays only, but that he'd be sure to write home every week, then he closed with "your son, Joe." Below he wrote a postscript asking about his brothers and the dry cleaning business. Then he folded the paper.

"Short letter."

"Maybe you got an extra envelope? And a stamp?"

"You didn't bring any with you?"

"I don't plan to do much writing. Here." He handed Adamczyk a dime.

"That's okay." Adamczyk took an envelope and stamp from his notebook.

"Go ahead," Waite said. "Take it."

"Forget it. Next time, maybe you'll do me a favor."

"Suit yourself."

"I didn't eat any breakfast this morning," Adamczyk said.

Waite was licking the stamp. Tongue out, he glanced at Adamczyk, then pressed the moistened stamp onto the envelope. "Yeh?"

"I was hungry. I think maybe that's why I, you know, passed out like that."

"How old are you, Red?"

"Seventeen. That's got nothing to do with it."

"Well," Waite said, opening his guidebook again and leaning back against the rack, "if I were you, I'd make sure from now on I ate regular."

"Oh, I will. You don't have to worry about that."

"I won't."

Waite read his guidebook. Adamczyk sat looking at the pages, his mind drifting. He liked Waite's calling him Red.

That was better than Tommy and didn't sound awkward to him like Tom. It was something more like what he thought one marine ought to call another. Besides, it seemed to fit as it was a new name in a new way of life which was supposed to turn him into a new man, a marine.

"Psst."

"Better button up, Red," Waite whispered, not looking up. "We get caught and it'll be our ass."

Adamczyk looked at the assigned guidebook section on Military Courtesy and Discipline. He found it boring and leafed through the book until he found a section on Marine Corps History and Tradition. Reading about Tripoli, Tarawa and Iwo Jima excited him, even made him feel proud. So what if he was only a recruit, he was still in the marines, wasn't he? He was inside the Corps, not outside looking in. And he felt that made a big difference, though he wasn't sure exactly how.

The recruit nearest the squad bay hatch screamed "Ten-hut!" and the others jumped to their feet and froze, many still holding guidebooks. Maguire stepped into the center of the squad bay. Beside him was a second drill instructor, a buck sergeant, slimmer and a couple of inches taller than Maguire. His hands were clenched behind his back and his straight jaw was set hard.

"This is Sergeant Midberry," Maguire said. "Sergeant Midberry is 197's junior drill instructor. Your J.D.I. He'll be helping me whip you maggots into marines, and you had best do every-fucking-thing he tells you to do, understand?"

"Yessir."

"Aw right, get your letter and hold it out in your right hand. And there had best be one letter per maggot. I don't want any hysterical mamas calling me in the middle of the night to find out what happened to their babies." Maguire nodded to Sergeant Midberry who started down the line of recruits collecting letters.

"Everybody here better have a letter for me," the J.D.I. said. Then, as if he remembered he wasn't speaking to a single man, but to seventy, a platoon, a recruit platoon, he raised his voice sharply. "Everybody here had best have a letter. Everybody!"

As Midberry collected the letters, Maguire faced Adamczyk. "Doubleshit. You're the maggot can't say 'yessir' right, right?"

"YESSIR!" Adamczyk shouted. He felt sweat inside his utility jacket trickle down the small of his back.

"Well, don't start now," Maguire said. "You should've started this morning. From now on whenever I call you, Doubleshit, you just grunt, understand? Let's hear it now."

"Umph."

"Shit! Not even close, maggot. Like this, rrrumpht."

"Rumpht."

"Again."

"Rumpht."

"Don't you know enough to say 'sir' yet, maggot?"

"Sir. Rumpht."

"That's well. Now assume a shitting position."

"Sir?"

"A shitting position, goddamit! Squat!"

Adamczyk squatted, elbows on his knees. Maguire called "Doubleshit" and Adamczyk answered "Sir. Rumpht."

"Real fine. Real fine. You just stay that way."

Midberry came to the rack and took Adamczyk and Waite's letters. He glanced at Adamczyk, then went to the next rack.

Adamczyk imperceptibly lowered his weight until his buttocks rested against his heels. He leaned forward for balance. Above him, Maguire was watching the far end of the squad bay. Adamczyk's eyes flicked up. Maguire's head was turned. His eyes were a very pale blue and to Adamczyk they seemed empty or like a cat's. You couldn't see past them into anything. Adamczyk caught himself and glared again at Maguire's brass belt buckle. He waited, neck muscles tensing, but Maguire didn't move and Adamczyk figured the D.I. must not have noticed. He felt relieved to have escaped still another punishment. He remembered that morning when another recruit had accidently looked Maguire in the eye during inspection and had been made to do pushups until his arms gave out. When a drill instructor faced a recruit, Maguire had explained, that recruit was to stand every bit as still as his rifle and was to look above, not at, the drill instructor.

Recruits could be looked at, but they were not yet fit to exchange looks with their D.I.s. That was one of the many cardinal rules of recruit training, and Maguire warned the platoon that he would enforce that rule, as he did all the others, vigorously.

Pains grew in Adamczyk's knees and calves. He wondered how long he could hold the position, and what Maguire would do when he caved in. His stomach felt rotten. Jesus, but he wished Maguire would let him get up. What did the D.I. expect anyhow—a superman? Adamczyk pressed his forearms against his thighs to take more weight from his legs. He tried to think of home, but could not manage to concentrate on either his parents or the house itself. Beneath him, his left leg quivered. He hoped to God he did not get a cramp. "Hail Mary, full of grace," he began saying to himself. He hoped if he got his mind on something else he wouldn't notice the pain and the time would go more quickly. "Holy Mary, mother of God. . . ."

Maguire crossed to the other side of the passageway. "You," he said. "You three. Yeah, you; one, two, three. One step forward, harch."

Three recruits stepped from their racks.

"You love me, maggot?" Maguire asked the first man. The recruit hesitated.

"Well?"

"Yessir."

"You sure?"

"Yessir."

"Well, la-de-da. Queer for my gear, hey? Well, it don't surprise me none, you fairy-faced fuck." Maguire suddenly drove a fist into the recruit's solar plexus. The recruit doubled, caught himself, straightened. Maguire stepped to the next man.

"What about you, maggot?"

"Sir?"

"You love me?"

"NO SIR!"

"Then you hate me, don't you?"

"Sir, I. . . ."

"Yes or no."

"Nosir."

"You'd like to kill me, wouldn't you?"

"Nosir."

"Don't lie to me, shitbird. Love me or hate me, it's one or the other and you don't love me, right?"

"Yessir. I mean, no. . . ."

Maguire feinted the right to the recruit's stomach and caught him with an open left hand across the ear and cheek. He looked at the recruit's eyes and his upper lip curled back in disgust. "Well, chicken-shit, you gonna bawl about it?"

"NO SIR!"

"You love me?" Maguire asked the third man. He waited. "You gonna answer your drill instructor?"

The recruit swallowed but didn't speak. He stared straight ahead, took two quick rights to the stomach and went to his knees.

"Get up."

When the recruit had gotten to his feet, Maguire ordered the three to return to their racks. He walked to the center of the squad bay. Midberry stood beside the long, green rifle-cleaning table, holding a thick pack of envelopes.

"All these sweethearts turn one in, sergeant?"

"Yess. . ." Midberry started, stopped and said loudly, "right. Every damn one of them."

Maguire watched as Midberry slapped the letters onto the table, then he turned to the platoon. "They don't call this place Parris Island for nothing, maggots. It maybe ain't Paris, but it sure as hell is an island. There ain't no way off and there ain't nobody here is gonna help you, so this ain't one teeny bit like home, children. Here, you are strictly on your own. Here, every maggot pulls his own weight or he gets shit-canned, understand?"

"Yessir."

"Understand, Doubleshit?"

"Sir, rumpht." Adamczyk congratulated himself on having been ready with the right response. He was learning.

"Aw right then, when I say 'get' you got exactly fifteen minutes to get in that head, shit and shower, and be back out here standing tall in front of your racks. Fifteen minutes. Now there's only ten shower heads in there and seventy warm bodies so you'd best be quick about it, animals." Maguire looked at his wristwatch, waiting for the sweephand to touch twelve. "Aw right," he paused, then barked, "Git!" and the recruits stripped quickly and wrapped towels around their waists, bumping and shoving one another as they ran into the head.

The squad bay emptied of recruits, Maguire sat on the corner of the cleaning table. He took out a pack of cigarettes and held it out to Midberry.

"No thanks."

"What a mob." Maguire lit a cigarette. His silver lighter bore a gold eagle, anchor and globe on one side. "But they'll shape up. They always do."

Something in Maguire's look made Midberry uneasy. He felt he ought to say something; to somehow give the senior D.I. confidence that the junior D.I. had confidence.

"How many," Midberry asked, "you think'll wash out?"

"About ten percent."

"Adamczyk, Doubleshit, you think he'll crack?"

"Could. Too early yet to tell. Some of them that fuck-up right away, you jump on them quick enough and they shape up. Unless of course they just can't cut it, in which case they ain't no loss anyhow. There's others though can hide it at first, then just like a tire blowing out they'll go all of a sudden. But what with the injuries, the medicals, and the crack-ups—the psychos—we'll figure to lose about ten percent."

"By now, I guess you can estimate pretty close ahead of time."

"Oh, shit yes," Maguire said. "Not that much to figure. New platoon is just like all the others. It's got sixty- to seventy-odd maggots and one maggot's no different than any other. You process a couple of these herds and you'll see what I mean."

Recruits began straggling back from the head. When all but a few were at attention before their racks, Maguire stood and shouted into the head for the others to get into the squad bay. The sound of showers running stopped. The last four recruits came out on the run, towels thrown about their waists, to take their place in ranks.

"Aw right, animals, it's night-night time and that means time for our prayers. Get your weapons."

The recruits took their rifles from behind their racks and Maguire called "present, harms!", each recruit bringing his rifle up parallel with his chest, butt toward his feet, front sight on a line with his eyes.

"Repeat after me. This is my rifle."

"This is my rifle."

"There are many like it, but this one is mine."

"There are many like it, but this one is mine."

"Louder, herd! My rifle is my best friend."

"My rifle is my best friend."

"It is my life."

"It is my life."

"I must master it as I must master my life."

"I must master it. . ."

"Louder, goddamit! I can't hear you."

"I must. . ."

"Louder!"

"I must master it," the recruits screamed, "as I must master my life."

The rifle prayer continued, Maguire leading and the recruits, their voices beginning to crack, screaming the words after him. When it was finished, Maguire ordered them to put back their rifles and line up beside their racks.

"Prepare to mount. Mount!"

Recruits leaped into upper and lower bunks. They lay still and the creaking of springs slowly subsided.

"Too slow, maggots, too slow, Get out. Aw right, prepare to mount. Mount."

Again the recruits scrambled into their bunks. Maguire ordered them back out. He had them mount and dismount six times. Then, when the recruits were lying in their racks, holding their breath and feeling the fresh sweat clammy on their bodies and dampening their clean skivvies, Maguire walked the length of the passageway and nodded to Midberry to turn off the lights.

24

"Any talking in here," Maguire said to the dark squad bay, "and we do P.T. the rest of the night." He turned and pushed through the wide swinging doors, Midberry behind him.

The doors squeaked back and forth, back and forth, finally stopping. There was a short, listening quiet then, followed by coughs, sighs, farts, the creak of bunksprings and the rustle of mattress pads.

"Woo," said a high-pitched Alabama voice suddenly in the dark. "He sho is one bad ass!"

"He's mean," another voice said. "Mean clean through."

"Mag-wire. Mag-wire. Woo."

There was a soft chorus of laughter and the squad bay quieted.

"Psst, Waite."

"Yeh?"

"It's Red."

"Yeh?"

"You think he's crazy?"

"Who?"

"Maguire."

"How should I know."

"I mean the way he acts. You think he's like a sadist or something?"

"Come off it, Red. It's his job."

"I don't know," Adamczyk whispered to the form outlined on the mattress pad above his head. "I think there's something wrong with him."

"Don't make it into a big thing. The man's doing his job is all."

Adamczyk didn't answer. He lay quietly, thinking how much he'd like to believe Waite, that it was just a routine thing, a job, nothing very important. But he couldn't. Maybe Waite had been brought up differently, Adamczyk didn't know. But his own family, his religion, Father Matuzak, they'd all taught him right from wrong and he felt now that Maguire was clearly wrong.

He remembered from the catechism the phrase about the body being "the temple of the Holy Spirit." And the teaching that therefore it ought to be respected. But the way Maguire treated people—like animals. . . . And the

25

praying to a rifle. Wasn't that wrong too, making fun of prayer? He wondered if Maguire confessed all the things he did to recruits and the way he talked. Suddenly then, Adamczyk realized how stupid it was to even think that someone like Maguire went to church. Maguire was nothing but an animal. That was why he treated other people as animals. Adamczyk could not imagine Maguire in church or having a family or friends. He felt that Maguire must somehow have been born a D.I. and that he had no other life but the one in the squad bay torturing recruits and making fun of what they believed in.

"You asleep?"

"No," Adamczyk said.

Waite leaned over the edge of his bunk, his face pale in the gray night. "Look, Red. Don't go taking this Doubleshit business personally. That's the way a D.I.'s supposed to act. He's just showing us how tough he is."

"How come you know so much about it?"

"My older brother was in the reserves. Harrassing you's the D.I.'s job. There's nothing personal in it."

"Maybe."

Waite turned onto his side, punched his pillow and closed his eyes. He breathed deeply for a minute or so and went to sleep

Adamczyk could hear the other recruits snoring and he saw, above him, that Waite had stopped moving. Probably everyone but himself, he thought, was getting a good night's sleep. Still, he forced himself to stay awake. During the day all the screaming and shouting confused him. He felt he needed the quiet to think things out clearly. He needed some time by himself to remember just what was important and what was not. And to check over the day and see just where he might have gone wrong. Father Matuzak had always advised him to use an examination of conscience at nights as a way to avoid the sin of masturbation. Since then, it had become Adamczyk's habit to think over the day before going to sleep.

He remembered Maguire's mock prayer. Maybe he should have said something. You were supposed to stand up for what you believed in. That's what he had been taught. And he did believe. In fact, he considered himself

26

much more than just an average Catholic. He'd been an altar boy up to the time he'd enlisted, and on the whole he took his religion more seriously, he thought, than most of the other young people in the parish. Yet he had kept his mouth shut, either too ashamed or too afraid to speak out against Maguire. But what was he supposed to do? A recruit was supposed to obey, even respect, his D.I. That was his duty too, wasn't it? What would his parents and his Uncle Ted, especially his Uncle, say if he got sent home the first day because he'd refused to take orders from Maguire? They'd be ashamed of him. And not only them, but the neighbors and his friends too. They'd all of them find out he hadn't been able to make it; that he'd washed out.

Adamczyk wished he was back home. He wished he was in his own bed in his own room where he could close the door and lock it if he wanted to be alone and think.

He jerked awake from a doze and reminded himself that he should be trying to think over his problems. But he was tired and his legs ached and he couldn't keep his mind focused on any particular thought. In the missal he'd been issued there was a guide for examining one's conscience. He knew that was what he needed, some sort of guide. He always had. But here there was no time for the missal during the day, and it was no good to him now in the dark.

Adamczyk took a rosary from beneath his pillow. He crossed himself and kissed the miniature feet of the crucified Christ. Maybe if he prayed he could think, or if not, maybe just the praying itself would somehow and in some way help him. He offered up the rosary that he would have the strength to stay good and stick to his beliefs. His fingers pressed against the small black beads and he moved his lips silently with the memorized words. The monotony of the repeated Hail Marys relaxed him. His mind drifted and, thinking of home again, he dozed.

Later Adamczyk sat up abruptly. He looked about him, his heart beating hard, and was grateful to see it was still dark. He was glad none of the other recruits or Maguire had found him asleep with the rosary. He knew how they were, dumb and foul-mouthed. He knew they wouldn't understand, but would only make a joke out of it.

He twisted about on an elbow. His cartridge belt hung from a front corner of his rack. Adamczyk tucked the rosary into an empty pocket of the belt, then turned onto his side and slept.

THREE

"Sir?" Waite dropped the shoe he'd been shining and stood to attention. Beside him Adamczyk leaped to his feet.

"I call your name, maggot?" Maguire asked.

"Nosir," Adamczyk said.

"Then siddown and mind your own business."

Adamczyk sat.

"I ain't seen you fuck-up yet, maggot," Maguire said, tapping his foot on the toe of Waite's boot. "How come?"

"Sir," Waite said. "I don't know."

"You think you're all squared away?"

"Nosir."

"Maybe you think you don't need this training?"

"Nosir."

"Or that you know so much I can't teach you nothing?"

"Nosir."

"Well let me tell you something, maggot. You don't know shit yet."

"Yessir."

"Yessir, what?"

"Sir, I don't know shit."

"Cause you are nothing but a recruit, a maggot, a boot, and a boot is as low as whale shit on the floor of the ocean, understand?"

"Yessir."

"Gimme a full answer, dammit. Yessir, what?"

"Sir, I'm as low as whale shit on the bottom of the ocean."

Maguire looked over his shoulder at Midberry. He

smiled, still tapping his foot on Waite's boot. "This one think's he's all squared away, sergeant."

"That so," Midberry said. He came to Waite, looked him over slowly and carefully, then pulled at Waite's jacket pocket. He held up a thin, inch-long green thread. "You Irish, boy?"

"Sir, half-Irish."

"Yeh, and half-asshole," Maguire said.

"That give you the right to wear Irish pennants?" Midberry dangled the green thread before Waite's eyes.

"Nosir."

"You know you're supposed to snip all loose threads from your uniform?"

"Yessir. I didn't see it, sir."

"Well, la-de-da," Maguire said.

"Guess you're not squared away yet then, are you?"

"Nosir."

"Still, Sergeant Midberry," Maguire said. "I guess it can't be helped. Not that this maggot is worth rabbit shit, but the others are all so bad they make him look almost passable."

"And he can walk in a straight line without falling down," Midberry said.

"So I guess then we got no choice." Maguire looked at Waite. "You're it, maggot."

"Sir?"

"We need a third squad leader here. You're it."

"Yessir."

"YESSIR!" Maguire said. "Jesus-fucking-Christ, did you get that? He don't even know enough to say thank you."

"Sir, thank..." Waite stopped, Maguire watching him. "Sir, I'm grateful to the drill instructor."

Maguire laughed. "Well, you're pretty damn quick for a maggot. And for your own good, squad leader, you had best stay quick and keep your squad squared away. They screw up and it's not just their ass, but yours too, understand?"

"Yessir."

"Aw right, carry on."

Maguire and Midberry walked down the passageway to

30

the squad bay's far end. Waite sat on the locker box and took up the shoe he'd been polishing.

"Guess I oughtta congratulate you."

Waite looked at Adamczyk's thin, freckled face with its eager, bright blue eyes. Adamczyk smiled.

"Shit," Waite said. "Shine your shoes, will you."

Squad leader, he thought. Now Adamczyk and all the other idiots like him in the third squad would be his responsibility. That was the last thing in the world Waite had wanted. He had tried to keep in step and to do what he was told when he was told to do it, but not for the sake of promotion. He'd thought that if he didn't make mistakes, he wouldn't be noticed. He had wanted to steer as clear as he could of any and all trouble so he would remain not just unnoticed, but apart from the others. Now his plan had backfired. Now as squad leader he would always be in the thick of things—a part of all the squad's petty problems.

"Shit."

"What?" Adamczyk asked.

"Just leave me alone, will you, Red."

"Come on, get it off your chest. Maybe I can help."

"Look, I said shine your shoes, didn't I?"

"What good's a buddy if . . ."

"You're in my squad, you do what I say. Now you shine those goddam shoes and shut your mouth or I'll run you up to Maguire."

Waite watched his right hand mechanically rubbing black polish into the new shoe leather. He knew that Adamczyk was still staring at him, wearing his hurt, dumb look and hoping Waite would say he hadn't really meant it after all, but Waite did not look up. He concentrated on the shoes and, after a few minutes, saw from the corner of his eye Adamczyk had begun to polish his.

"Listen up, herd."

The recruits stood to attention. Maguire was in the squad bay's center with a black recruit named Neal at his side. Sergeant Midberry, cleaning his fingernails with a silver key ring knife, stood behind him.

"Anybody here hate niggers?"

No one spoke up.

31

Maguire had to have no feelings at all, Adamczyk thought. To say something like that in front of everyone and with Neal having to stand right there and hear it. It wasn't Neal's fault he wasn't white. Maguire ought to leave him alone.

"Nobody here hates niggers, huh? Aw right, I don't wanna hear no scuttlebutt then about there being any trouble. Neal here is first squad leader, understand?"

"Yessir."

"I don't care how it was where you came from. Here, nobody's better than anybody else. Understand?"

"Yessir."

Adamczyk was surprised to see Maguire taking anyone's part. Neal being made a squad leader surprised him too. Not that he himself had anything against colored people. He'd heard a lot of talk against them from his aunts and uncles—the neighborhood going black, property values being pulled down—but there were no colored people yet on his block and he'd had no trouble with those he'd gone to high school with. As far as he was concerned everybody was equal and if they left him alone then he'd do the same. Still, it seemed funny to Adamczyk that Maguire would choose a colored boy over white ones for first squad leader.

"Here," Maguire said, "there ain't no niggers, wops, polaks, bohunks, kikes, micks, swamp rats, ridgerunners or anything else. Nothing but maggots. Here you are all equally worthless. You are all nothings, shitbirds, maggots. And you will all remain nothings until your drill instructors make you into something. Understand?"

"Yessir."

Adamczyk had thought for a moment that maybe he'd been wrong about Maguire. But he saw now that Neal had been picked only to downgrade the whole platoon. His first opinion of Maguire had been right. Maguire was nothing but an animal that got its kicks hurting people.

"Everyone of you is a worthless maggot. Don't forget it. You will be treated like maggots till you show me you're men. And as far as your drill instructors are concerned, that won't happen till you make it as marines. A marine

32

is a man, herd, and a man is a marine. It's just that simple. Understand?"

"Yessir."

Anyhow, Adamczyk thought, he was glad in a way he himself hadn't been made a squad leader. Not that he'd thought there was any chance he would. But when Waite was picked, Adamczyk had found himself wishing Maguire would pick him too. He decided now it was better the way it was. If he wasn't going to openly resist Maguire, then the least he could do was not to cooperate any further than he absolutely had to. Maybe that was why he'd been doing everything wrong. Maybe subconsiously he'd been resisting Maguire right from the start. He'd read of things like that happening—a person doing something and not knowing until later why he'd done it. Even though he hadn't thought of it in exactly the same way before, now that he had thought of it Adamczyk was almost positive that subconscious resistance was the reason for his mistakes. They were his way of fighting back. It wasn't that he couldn't measure up. Deep down he didn't want to.

"Aw right," Maguire said. "Get your weapons." He turned to Midberry. "I got some paperwork's got to get done. You drill'm on the manual. For about a half hour."

"Right,"

"When you're done have'm get ready for the sack."

"Right."

Maguire left the squad bay. The recruits, at attention before their racks, their rifles at the order, lined both sides of the long passageway. Midberry let them endure the silence for a full minute, then put his hands on his hips and stepped forward.

"Listen up, people. When you move those weapons I want you to do it sharp. Put a little snap into it. Show me some pride."

Walking the passageway's length, Midberry called the commands and watched closely as the recruits executed the movements. He saw they were very weak on the move from left to right shoulder arms, and he drilled them on it, calling the command again and again until the sound of the seventy hands slapping stocks came close to sound-

33

ing as one hand. He stopped every so often to correct a recruit's position. "Up some, boy." "That's no loaf of bread you got there. Hold it straight. Straight." Then he moved along, pushing a rifle up or down, straightening a recruit's head or arm, checking the position of a hand or stock.

The thirty minutes went quickly for Midberry. Watching the platoon getting ready for the sack, he felt pleased with himself. His first time in charge of the platoon had seemed to go rather well.

At the end of the second half hour, Maguire returned. He and Midberry put the platoon to bed, then went to the D.I. hut. Maguire sat behind the desk and began writing on a stack of yellow papers. Midberry went to the sink. He ran water in the tin pot and set it on the single-burner hotplate.

"How about some coffee?"

"All right with me."

Midberry took his and Maguire's cup from the board shelf beneath the window. He spooned out the instant coffee.

"Looked to me like you was too soft on a couple of them," Maguire said. "Like Booth. Looked like he was half asleep, for Chrissakes."

Midberry didn't turn. He stared at the screened window, holding the spoon above the cup. Moths plunked their furred bodies against the screen. The hot plate's burner coil clicked.

He was watching the whole time, Midberry thought. Spying. And now he's not even trying to hide it. He doesn't give a damn who knows.

"I think you should've given him some pushups. Just as a warning."

The water began boiling. Midberry filled the two cups and brought one to Maguire. He opened the small icebox, took out some cream and poured a bit into his coffee. "I don't know," he said. "Booth just hadn't gotten the port position down pat yet. Now I think he's got it. I showed him how."

"Don't care why he did it. A maggot fucks up—you

34

got to lay it on him. That's the only way they'll ever learn."

"Maybe," Midberry said. He held down his anger. His first impulse had been to ask just what the hell did Maguire mean anyhow by spying on him as if he couldn't be trusted alone with the platoon for half an hour. Yet Maguire had been so open about his spying, Midberry would feel odd bringing it up. It would seem as if he were questioning some official procedure. If Maguire had slipped, letting out the fact of his spying, then trying to cover it up, it would have been different. Instead, he acted as if it were part of his job. And maybe it was. The senior D.I.'s job was to advise and instruct the junior D.I. Whether or not the process of instruction included spying was, Midberry supposed, strictly up to Maguire.

"Called headquarters," Maguire said. "About some more help here. They say they can't spare anybody right now. We maybe'll get another buck sergeant in a week or so. 'Maybe,' they said. Shit! Here we are with seventy maggots on our hands and only two of us to handle them, and they're telling us 'maybe.'"

Midberry nodded. The news unnerved him. He'd been hoping for at least one more J.D.I. so he wouldn't have to work alone with Maguire. He'd heard stories about Maguire. Whether they were true or not, he didn't know. No matter, he was let down and a bit frightened by the knowledge he'd be on his own with Maguire.

"Second battalion's running full strength. Four D.I.s a platoon. Even most of the mobs here in first got three. Shit."

"Well," Midberry said. "Isn't that always the way."

"Hm?"

"I mean with the brass. Always saying maybe, maybe; promising." He shook his head. That sounded good, he thought. "Damn brass."

"Shit," Maguire said. "Anyhow, that just means we got to crack down a little bit harder. Like what I was trying to tell you. I'm not trying to blow smoke up your ass or anything, just telling you for your own good. A platoon is like an animal and the D.I.'s its trainer. Either you make it afraid of you or you end up afraid of it. And with only two of us—well, we got to work twice as hard is all."

"It seems to me. . ." Midberry was saying when Maguire suddenly stood, coming around the corner of the desk. Midberry took a step back and cocked his right, but Maguire didn't notice. He had pulled off his D.I. cover and tossed it onto the cot. Face down, he thrust his head forward. His pale scalp showed through the stubble of closely-cut black hair. A thin white scar about four inches long ran from the top of his head back toward his neck.

"Souvenir from my first platoon." Maguire looked up. "When I was like you, trying to play nice guy."

"I'm not playing anything. I just. . ."

"So on the bayonet course, some goggle-eyed wop from Altoona, seventeen years old, one of the ones I never laid a hand on, he hauls off with an M-1 like it was a baseball bat and puts me into sick bay for a week." Maguire moved back behind the desk. "And lemme tell you this, I'm thankful to that kid. He taught me a lesson that maybe saved my ass from getting killed by one of these sweethearts. Only one thing a boot respects and that's fear."

"I don't know," Midberry said. He felt it was useless to argue. Maguire had experience on his side. All Midberry had were his feelings.

"I know you don't know. That's why I'm telling you. Trying to save you some stitches, that's all."

Maguire returned to the papers on the desk. Midberry sat on the cot, sipping his coffee.

"What happened to him?"

"Who?"

"The kid from Altoona?"

"Oh, I didn't run'm up or anything. I told sick bay I fell in the shower. When I got out I took that little wop into the head and give him a working over that'd last him through four hitches. Five weeks he was laid up."

"You should've reported him."

"Sure! And have'm kick his ass out."

"That's the regulations."

"I figure any maggot's got the guts to cold-cock his D.I. has got what it takes to make a damn good combat marine. That's my job, making marines. Regulations, hell. A D.I. has got only one rule: Do whatever you got to do to turn these nothings into marines. And they got to be good. You all the time got to ask yourself—'are they good enough I'd want one of them beside me in a foxhole?' "

"I don't know."

"You seen any combat?"

"No," Midberry said. He got up and took his cup to the sink, rinsing it under the tap. He was afraid Maguire would bring up combat. Now he wished he had kept his mouth shut. A brand new D.I., no combat record, what right did he have to question how Maguire trained recruits. He put his cup on the shelf. When he turned, Maguire was looking at him.

"Look," Maguire said. "The recruiting posters maybe don't say it, but a D.I. had better fucking know it. A marine is nothing but a trained killer. He kills whoever and whatever the brass tells him to kill and he don't ask any questions about it neither. I was in Korea. I seen it and I know. It's got to be that way. If it wasn't, you think we could've licked the Japs or held our own with the gooks? Shit, you'd be bowing to Hirohito or some other little slant-eyed sonuvabitch right now if it wasn't."

"You've been at it longer than I have," Midberry said. 'You oughtta know." Right now he would agree to anything. He was tired and had a headache coming on and all he wanted was to get back to his own quarters and to get some sleep.

"Not that I think you don't mean right by it. But this ain't no boy's military school where we teach them to be neat and clean and respect their elders. It's P.I. and we teach'm how to kill. You remember that."

Midberry put on his cover and went to the door. He waited for Maguire to say something that would make him feel free to leave.

"First of next week," Maguire said without looking up, "you'll start taking the platoon alone. Every other morning we'll be switching on and off with the duty. Shorthanded like this, nothing else we can do."

"Okay." What was this, Midberry wondered, a reward for giving in or just Maguire's way of smoothing things over; showing he trusted the J.D.I.? "Guess I'd better get some sleep."

"Yeah."

Maguire concentrated on his paperwork. Midberry hesitated, looking at Maguire's head, making out under the overhead light the beginning of the long, white scar. He saw then that Maguire was finished talking to him, and he left the hut, clicking the door shut behind him.

FOUR

It surprised Midberry he hadn't heard the house mouse's first call. Having looked forward all week to his first day alone with the platoon, he'd had a hard time getting to sleep the night before. Lying on the foldout cot, hearing the soft, even steps of the firewatch passing the hut regularly, he'd thought of all that could possibly go wrong.

Still he had expected to wake up on his own. Now, a sudden knocking and a high, thin voice—"Sir, the time on deck is zero four zero three"—snapped him awake. He propped himself onto his elbows.

"Sir, the time on. . ."

"Get in here," Midberry ordered.

The door opened and Cooper, the house mouse, the recruit who woke the D.I.s in the morning, ran errands and cleaned the hut, a small and skinny boy with small, scared eyes, stood in the hatch at attention. "Sir," he said in his squeaking voice, "Private Cooper requests permission to enter the drill instructor's quarters."

"I already told you to get in here, didn't I?" Midberry sat on the edge of the cot. "Empty the shitcan and the ashtrays."

"Yessir. I'll clean it up real good, sir."

Midberry stepped to the washbowl and ran it half full of hot water. He splashed his face, then sprayed some menthol shave cream onto his fingertips. "How many times you have to call me?"

"Sir," Cooper said, quickly putting down the wastebasket to stand at attention. "I called the drill instructor four times, sir."

Midberry turned, his face white with shaving cream. He motioned to Cooper with a razor blade. "Don't get to attention every time I talk to you, okay boy. You won't ever get done that way."

"Yessir. Sorry, sir, I didn't think."

"Get hot then."

"Yessir."

Cooper tried a smile. It looked weak and joyless, as if he had winced at a gas pain. Midberry turned back to the washbowl. He knew that Cooper was constantly afraid. He could see it in the boy's eyes or in his smile or just in the way he held his back during close-order drill. And when Maguire harrassed him, spitting questions out rapid-fire, the boy would start to stutter and make things worse for himself. His eyes would water then too, and Midberry hoped that if and when Cooper cracked, finally letting himself break down and bawl like a baby, it would come on one of Maguire's duty nights, not his.

In the round shaving mirror Midberry watched Cooper dusting the desk. The fear showed even in the way Cooper dusted, moving the rag quickly as if the desk too might shout at him.

Midberry stretched his neck, shaving down from his chin. He could not honestly say he liked the boy. He felt sorry for him, yet whatever pity he felt was mixed with he wasn't sure just what. He could not for the life of him understand why Cooper had enlisted. It was obvious the boy was not a marine, that he simply didn't pack the gear. Couldn't he see that for himself? What was he trying to prove?

Finished shaving, Midberry put on his starched, sharply-creased utilities. Both trousers and jacket were deeply faded. He might be new as a D.I., Midberry thought, but his faded utilities, compared to the dark new green of the recruits' uniforms, would show the platoon their J.D.I. had been around at least a little while.

He rubbed a scrap of nylon hose over the toes of his polished boots. From the wall locker, he took the brown D.I. cover, the coveted "Smokey the Bear" hat, and set it on his head, tilting it slightly forward so it half hid his eyes. He checked himself in the full-length mirror on the back of the door, then went to the desk. In the top drawer were two long, black, fifteen-cent cigars he'd gotten the day before at the PX. He took one and slid it into a pocket of his utility jacket.

"Cooper."

Cooper was wiping the shaving mirror. He dropped the wadded paper towel and went rigid. "Yessir."

"What'd I tell you, boy? Don't jump every damn time I open my mouth."

"Yessir."

"Keep on with what you're doing."

"Yessir." Cooper picked up the towel and returned to the mirror.

"Why'd you join the Corps, boy?"

Cooper started to stiffen, then kept working. But as he spoke, he twisted his neck to look back over his shoulder. "Sir, my father thought it would be good for me. That it would make a man out of me, sir."

"You think he was right?"

"Oh YESSIR," Cooper fairly shouted. He had finished cleaning the mirror and, taking up a rag, began scrubbing the washbowl.

"How come you're so jumpy?"

"Sir, I guess I'm just the nervous type."

"What about?"

"Sir?"

"What makes you nervous?"

"Well, I. . . sir, I don't know. I mean, you know how. . ." Cooper stopped, glancing at Midberry, his eyes widening. He looked quickly down at the washbowl. "Sir, I. . .I don't know."

Cooper had made the same mistake with Maguire only a few days before. Calling the drill instructor "you." Now Midberry watched Cooper concentrate on scrubbing the washbowl. He knew the boy was waiting, fearfully holding his breath, to see if he'd been caught. "Go on," Midberry said. "What is it gets you so nervous?"

The tension visibly eased from the boy's thin shoulders. "Sir," he said, turning, "it's just the way Sergeant Maguire . . . the way he acts, and then all the confusion and everything, sir. I guess I'm just not used to it." Cooper's

41

eyes had begun watering and his fingers wadded and re-wadded the wet rag he held. "When we first come in, I thought we'd just learn to be soldiers, like . . . I mean, marines. But I mean learn to march and take orders and all, but nothing like this. Sir, the books I got from the recruiter's office. . . And my father, sir, he didn't say anything about this, either. I mean, sir, if only Sergeant Maguire wouldn't act like he hated us and sometimes almost like he. . . well, like he was crazy-mad or something and like you don't know just what he might do to somebody. I mean, sir, there's only so much, like. . ."

"All right, all right," Midberry said. He held up a hand to halt Cooper's overflow of speech. Midberry hadn't expected such an outpouring. "Sergeant Maguire is just doing his job," he said. And he was pretty sure he spoke the truth, though there had been frequent small incidents when it seemed to Midberry that Maguire overstepped the duties of the D.I. Even so, what could he, Midberry, say. Maguire was the senior D.I. It was his show.

Midberry looked at his wristwatch. Four-eighteen. Suddenly, he was tired of having Cooper near him. It was as if he had been left alone too long visiting a cripple or someone dying. A taste of disgust began to outweigh any pity he felt. He was well and alive. He didn't have to be dragged down with the sick. Recognizing his change of feelings made Midberry feel guilty and still more uncomfortable, and he resented Cooper for it. Cooper's problems weren't his problems. He had enough to think about his first day handling the platoon by himself, without worrying about the house mouse's nervous condition.

"Okay," he said. "Get the shitcan on outta here and hustle back to the squad bay. I'll be out in two minutes to get the mob outta the sack."

"Yessir." Cooper picked up the wastebasket. "Sir, I mean I appreciate the drill instructor's. . . I mean, taking time. . ."

"Let's go, boy. Let's go. Git."

Cooper shouted "yessir" and ran from the room. Midberry sat on a corner of the desk. He took the long, black cigar from his pocket and peeled away the red paper band and cellophane wrapping. He slowly licked the end of the cigar, then lit it, drew in, and blew a ball of gray smoke at the ceiling.

That was the trouble with recruits. They took advantage of any kindness or slight loosening of discipline. Maguire said all a recruit was capable of respecting was fear. Midberry had disagreed at the time and, in principle, still did. But he could see now how Maguire had come to believe it. Midberry was sure Cooper wouldn't have opened up to Maguire as he had with him. Just like the "you" business. Maguire would have turned the recruit inside out. And Midberry wondered maybe if he should've called Cooper on it, rather than letting it slide by. If he had given Cooper a few pushups then, that would have cut it off nice and neat. Instead, he'd left himself open for the buddy-buddy routine. Sir, I appreciate. . . . Hell, he appreciates what? Midberry asked himself. He appreciates the J.D.I. not being as tough as Maguire, that's what.

He checked his watch again. It was twenty-three after and he had planned to wake the platoon at four-twenty sharp, ten minutes before reveille to be sure to get them outside on time. He didn't want anything to go wrong his first morning in charge and now he was already behind schedule.

"Damn!" He checked himself once more in the mirror, then with the cigar firmly between his teeth walked down the passageway and into the dark squad bay.

"Outta those racks, people! Hit it. Hit it." He flicked on the lights, and recruits, like cockroaches fleeing for the woodwork, scrambled from upper and lower racks to stand at attention.

Adamczyk sat up slowly, looking about him as if uncertain where he was. Midberry stepped quickly across the aisle, grabbed the boy's arm and jerked him from the rack. Adamczyk landed in the aisle on his hands and knees, then jumped to his feet at attention.

Midberry turned back to the platoon, shouting "count off!" He waited, chewing on the cigar, feeling a nervous anger mounting in him as each recruit called out his number. DeBasie, at the far end, called "seventy" and Midberry told the recruits to get dressed and be outside

43

standing tall in platoon formation with rifles, piss pots and cartridge belts in five minutes. Five minutes! Then he walked out the squad bay's front hatch to stand on the small iron stoop.

It was still dark. In the east the sky had lightened from black to gray, but as yet showed no sign of the sun. A chilly breeze blew in off the Atlantic. It had an indistinct smell to it—seaweed or fish, Midberry couldn't tell which. It was the same smell he'd known as a recruit on the island six years earlier. A different battalion and a different squad bay, but the same smell, the same parade ground, the same routine with its predawn bustling about, drilling and running, shouting and harrassment. Except now he was on the other end of the stick. Now he began to see the reasons behind some of the actions he'd questioned as a recruit. No wonder his D.I.s hadn't loosened up with the platoon—hadn't allowed any personal contact. They had known what all D.I.s knew or learned. Given an inch a recruit took a mile.

Midberry took a deep breath and held it. Goddam stupid people, he thought. They don't know when they've got it good. Somebody tries to treat them like men, they walk all over him. Whose fault was it D.I.s turned into Maguires?

He slowly released the deep breath through his nostrils, then took another, held it, let it slip away. Calming himself.

At the time it hadn't seemed important to call Cooper on his slip-up. Midberry was certain it hadn't been intentional. The boy was nervous and had made a natural mistake. That was all there was to it. Besides, Midberry could not see how it would help make Cooper a better man or better marine to badger him every single time he stepped out of line. The boy already had the look of a whipped dog. If he wasn't let up on once in a while, he'd crack.

He then remembered one of Maguire's homilies. "Shit, you want some of them to crack. P.T.'s like heaven, Sergeant Midberry. Ain't everybody can make it." But no matter what Maguire in all of his practical wisdom

44

said, Midberry knew his job was to make marines, not psychos.

Still, he had doubts that he had picked a good time to begin taking it easy. He was still unfamiliar to the platoon. The recruits would be sizing him up, maybe looking for a weak spot. What had Cooper thought of him? Had the boy thought his J.D.I. was simply slow and that the slip-up had gone over his head? Or that since he was a new D.I. he hadn't been sure what to do about it?

Recruits began running out of the hatch. Midberry pointed the first few men to the area where he wanted the ranks formed. Puffing on the cigar, he watched the ranks fill out, man by man, until the entire platoon stood below him at attention. In the graying light and pre-reveille hush, the silent platoon looked unreal to Midberry. For a moment it seemed to him that merely by pointing his finger and willing it, he had conjured the platoon from nothing.

Reveille sounded, the sharp notes of the bugle breaking in on Midberry's private phantasy. Lights came on in the barracks down the line.

"All right," Midberry said. "Port. . .harms."

The recruits brought their rifles to port. Midberry came down the iron ladder and walked along the ranks. In the third rank, he stopped at Adamczyk's position.

"Little sleepy this morning, hey?"

"Yessir."

Midberry drew in deeply on the cigar, then blew the smoke slowly and evenly into the recruit's face. Adamczyk blinked, but kept his stare locked above the drill instructor's eyes.

It struck Midberry that off the island, in a bar or maybe even with a regular infantry platoon, what he'd just done would have meant a fight. Either at the moment or some-time later off duty, he would have had to back up his action. Stripes wouldn't be enough to pull it off. But this was no infantry platoon. These were not yet marines. They were recruits and stared straight ahead no matter what. Like dummies dressed up to look like men, Midberry thought.

45

He realized then he'd been daydreaming, and felt he ought to say something to break the awkward silence. "All right," he said. He stopped, then said quickly and loudly, "That had best be the first and last goddam time I have to get you up, boy. You hear?"

"Yessir."

He saw nothing particularly wrong with the rifles' positions and so returned to the front of the platoon. "Listen up, people," he said. "Those aren't brooms, those are weapons. You hold them diagonal across your chest, four inches out, and you had best put some pride into it." He looked at Cooper. "House mouse!"

"Yessir."

"Didn't I just tell you that's a weapon you're holding?"

"Yessir."

"Then how come you're still holding it like some damned broom?"

"Sir, I didn't mean. . ."

"Don't start whining, boy. A marine never makes excuses, he just does. Now you wanna hold a broom, that's okay with me. Get inside and get one. On the double."

When Cooper ran back into ranks, he held a pushbroom at port arms.

"That's better," Midberry said. He called a "right, face" and moved to the head of the platoon's three files. Booth, the guidon bearer, held the guidon high in the air. The gold pennant, "B. Co., Plt. 197" stitched in scarlet, fluttered in the breeze. "Forward. . .harch."

The platoon moved out, Midberry striding beside it, the seventy sets of heels hitting the black-top in ragged unison. Chuck-chuck-chuck-chuck. Midberry called the cadence with a smooth, musical rhythm. "Uh-one, uh-reep, uh-reep for you lep. . . ." He felt it was a much better cadence than Maguire's unintelligible grunting. Midberry had copied the cadence from a gunny sergeant at Twenty-Nine Palms. When he'd first made platoon sergeant at LaJeune, he hadn't used it because some of his platoon had been with him at Twenty-Nine Palms. They would have known he'd copied the cadence and he'd have felt as if he were only playing at being a platoon sergeant.

46

"You lep, raht'll lep...." He practiced the cadence often, trying to get it to sound natural. He still felt somewhat uneasy with it, but thought that in time he would get used to it, as to everything else.

And he was certain no one else could tell how he felt. For all Maguire knew, he had been using the cadence for years. As for the recruits, he doubted if they had the slightest inkling he was nervous or at times a bit uncertain. To them he wasn't Wayne Midberry, someone with a home and parents and problems with women and with himself—someone who might at times wonder how others saw him. To them he was simply Sergeant Midberry, the J.D.I., nothing else.

FIVE

"A small favor," Adamczyk said. He wished Waite wouldn't make him beg. All he wanted was someone to go along with him. As a friend. If he had to argue about it, then it wasn't any good.

"I got to finish my boots first. Then my rifle. Then I just wanna take it easy for awhile, okay?"

Adamczyk tucked the tail of his clean utility jacket into his trousers. He sat beside Waite on the locker box. Waite alternately rubbed black polish and spit into the leather of his boots. Adamczyk began lacing his boots.

"You oughtta stay back yourself."

"You crazy?"

"Look at your boots."

"They'll wait." Finished with the laces, Adamczyk kept his head down, his elbows on his knees. "I have to go," he said. "I have to be able to just sit quiet for a bit, y'know what I mean? Be able to think without somebody screaming at you." He suddenly jerked up his head. "That's right. I forgot. Nothing ever gets to you, does it? Big John Wayne himself."

Adamczyk stood. He looked down at Waite and, furious with himself, asked again. "C'mon, Joe, will you? You think I like being the only one from third squad?"

Waite put down one boot, picked up its mate and resumed the same, slow, sure, circular polishing motion. "I'm not even Catholic."

"So what?"

Waite pulled his dogtags over the neck of his T shirt. He held one of the thin metal tags for Adamczyk to see. Beneath the stamped U.S.M.C., the space for the wearer's

48

religion was blank. "Maguire," Waite said, "might wonder about my sudden conversion."

"I'll bet he never even asks to see them."

"Maybe. Maybe not."

"Come on then."

"You go ahead. Maybe next time."

"Sure." Adamczyk took a toothbrush and tube of paste from his footlocker and walked down the passageway lined with recruits shining shoes, cleaning rifles or reading guidebooks.

"Hey Doubleshit! Hey, say a couple prayers for me too, okay?"

Adamczyk ignored Fillipone's shouting. Fillipone was a big Italian, the second squad leader and, Adamczyk thought bitterly, a filthy-mouthed bully and stupid wop. Next to Maguire, he hated Fillipone most. But he'd seen the Italian fight twice already and was afraid of him. He told himself though, as he ignored the remark and went into the head, that he was rising above Fillipone's level.

Waite capped the can of polish and began buffing his boots with nylon.

The squad bay doors swung open.

"TEN-HUT!"

"At ease, animals," Maguire said. "You maggots going to Devine Services be out on the hard stand in ten minutes. You will fall in with church details from the other platoons and march to the chapel in one big mob. They'll tell you there, Protestant, Catholic, whatever the brand, where to go. Now the rest of you pussies I want to get into your P.T. suits. This squad bay needs a field day and we won't have time for it Monday. Squad leaders, front and center."

Neal, Fillipone and Waite ran to Maguire.

"I want you to get your maggots hot on this dump, y'hear."

"Yessir."

"I want this deck white, windows spotless, and I want that head so sanitary and sparkling that my own grandmother, God rest her soul, would be proud to go in there and take a dump."

"Yessir."

"First squad, deck. Second, windows. Third, head."

"Yessir."

"Dismissed."

Neal and Fillipone took one step to the rear, did an about-face and returned to their racks.

"Sir, Private Waite requests permission to speak to the drill instructor."

"Speak."

"Sir, I had planned on going to church."

"You got somebody can handle your squad?"

"Yessir. Danielle, sir. I can tell'm what to do."

"Then you'd best step on it, sweetheart, before the rest of the saints fly off without your young ass. Git."

"Yessir."

"Church detail," Maguire said. "Eight minutes, out on the hard stand. And I had best not hear of any of you maggots getting out of line. You fuck up Divine Services and you'll need more than prayers when I get hold of you."

The red brick chapel was stifling. The metal fans flanking the altar only served with their droning motors to make even more unintelligible the chaplain's monotonous Latin mumbling.

Waite, chin on his chest, dozed in his seat. Adamczyk followed the mass in a small pocket missal. The chaplain completed the reading in Latin, bowed his head and went to a wooden lectern which substituted for a pulpit.

Waite's breathing deepened. Adamczyk nudged him.

"Hm?"

"You were asleep."

"How about that."

The chaplain cleared his throat. "The reading of the Epistle," he began, "is from the Second Letter of Paul to Timothy. Verses seven to fifteen. Brethren. 'For God did not give us a spirit of timidity but a spirit of power and love and self-control. Do not be ashamed then of testifying to our Lord. . . .'"

50

Waite glanced about at the base personnel who, with their wives and children, filled the main part of the chapel. Recruits occupied only the last five rows. A corporal assigned to the church detail stood in an aisle where he could oversee the recruit group.

The chaplain continued, raising his voice over the fans. " 'For this Gospel I was appointed a preacher and apostle and teacher, and therefore suffer as I do. But I am not ashamed, for I know whom I have believed. . . .' "

Waite's gaze wandered to the open window. High above the thick, flatbottomed white clouds hanging over the Atlantic, four jet fighters traced contrails against the blue sky. Waite watched the thin white lines swell and fade until his eyelids grew heavy. He let his head sag.

" '. . .in the faith and love which are in Christ Jesus; guard the truth that has been entrusted to you by the Holy Spirit who dwells within us.' Please stand for the Gospel."

Adamczyk poked Waite. "Gospel."

"Who?"

"Get up. Get up."

Waite got up and leaned against the seat in front of him as the chaplain read the Gospel. The chaplain finished and closed the heavy Bible.

"You may be seated."

The faithful rustled and sighed into their seats. Waite hoisted his feet over the unpadded kneeler to stretch out his legs. The chaplain blotted his forehead with a small white handkerchief.

" 'But I am not ashamed, for I know whom I have believed.' Words taken from today's Epistle." He paused. "I know it's not the easiest thing to do to harmonize a Christian way of life with a military career. In fact, it sometimes becomes very difficult. Sometimes we might feel that it is too difficult for us; that it's impossible. And yet aren't all things finally possible? No good marine would question that, would he?" The chaplain smiled at his congregation. "Well, no good Christian would question it either, for with God's help everything is possible.

"No matter what walk of life we have chosen, there are obstacles to living a life, as Saint Paul has said, 'in

51

faith and love.' But it is especially difficult, perhaps, in the military. And one of the major obstacles—I think perhaps even the single greatest obstacle—to a Christian life in our Nation's armed forces is the ridicule of one's fellow servicemen. And it's not just marines I'm talking about, but soldiers and sailors as well; not just enlisted men, but officers as well. We have all felt the embarrassment of having . . ."

Waite looked sideways at Adamczyk. The redhead leaned forward listening. His head was slightly bowed, his small, freckled hands between his knees. The palm of his left hand rubbed continuously against the knuckles of his right, and Waite noticed that his fingernails were bitten to the quick.

He takes it seriously, Waite thought. But then why shouldn't he? Adamczyk was a good six, seven years younger than himself. Still a kid really.

Adamczyk glanced back at him and Waite looked down at his boots. Alongside his, Adamczyk's boots looked even duller than they normally did.

Waite would make a point of it that Adamczyk shine his boots and shoes as soon as they returned to the squad bay. He'd check on his rifle too. He'd have to keep on Adamczyk all the time because Adamczyk was a dreamer. He wasted time worrying and praying and therefore couldn't get properly squared away. And if Adamczyk kept screwing up, Waite knew he would hear about it from Maguire. Like it or not he was Adamczyk's squad leader. And he didn't like it, he thought. Not one bit. Adamczyk was trouble, and Waite wished he had never met him.

"So," the chaplain said, "no matter what the odds; no matter how much abuse or ridicule we might take from our fellow servicemen, we must work—just as we work to be good officers and good enlisted men—to be good Christians. We must work to lead a good Christian life. It's our duty. As military personnel, we must obey commands. As Christians, too, we must obey commands. We must obey God's command to work toward our heavenly home, as well as Christ's command to love our neighbor. And no matter who or how many in their ignorance laugh at our religion, we must obey Saint Paul's command to Timothy: 'Take your share of suffering as a good soldier of Christ Jesus."

The chaplain crossed himself, "In the name of the Father and of the Son and of the Holy Spirit, Amen," and returned to the altar.

Waite's heavy breathing teetered on the edge of a snore. Adamczyk considered poking him again, but decided against it. He appreciated Waite's coming with him. It made him feel that he had at least one friend in the platoon. And now that Waite had finally opened up at least a little, Adamczyk was sure they would get to be buddies. So he let Waite sleep. It was his way of showing that their friendship worked both ways.

Mass ended and the recruits remained seated as the regular congregation crowded down the narrow aisle and out of the chapel. A server came onto the altar, genuflected, and began extinguishing the candles.

"Ten-hut."

The five rows of recruits sprang to attention.

"Face the aisle," the corporal said. "First two rows move out. First man in the next row steps out after the last man in the row ahead of him. Let's go, people. C'mon c'mon c'mon. Move out."

The recruits began filing into the aisle. Waite stood behind Adamczyk as they waited for their row to begin moving. Adamczyk twisted his head.

"Joe?"

"Yeh?"

"Thanks."

"For what?"

"You know, for coming along."

"Forget it."

The row ahead of them was moving now. Waite leaned forward.

"Hey, Red?"

"What?"

"What rank is a chaplain?"

SIX

"Run, goddamit, run maggots. Move out fat boy. Pick'm up, short stuff. You had best move your asses, herd!"

Shouting an unbroken litany of curses and commands, Maguire trotted across the parade ground. Before him, the recruit platoon ran in a disorganized pack, M-1 rifles carried at high port, silver-painted helmet liners jouncing wildly.

"There'd best be none of you maggots outside that hatch when I get there."

The recruits clattered up the iron stairway, scuffling with one another, trying to be first into the squad bay. Maguire approached the rear of the group and rifles clacked against helmet liners as the frenzied recruits pressed forward. A handful of men clogged at the hatch, then, as Maguire reached the walk in front of the barracks, they broke and one by one dove inside. Maguire sprinted up the steps and latched onto Cooper's belt. Gripping the belt and neckband of Cooper's utilities, he pulled Cooper off balance and kicked open the screen door, carrying the recruit at waist level.

Midberry stood near the rifle-cleaning table. Maguire stopped beside the Junior D.I.

"If these animals had minds, Sergeant Midberry, I'd say they had a mental block against marching. I've seen Chinese fire drills look better than this herd trying to do a column right."

Maguire suddenly let go of Cooper. The recruit dropped his rifle and fell to his hands and knees.

"Get up, thing."

Cooper stood. He picked up his rifle and held it at port, his thin fingers white against the dark-grained stock.

"Why'd you drop that weapon, maggot?"

"Sir, I . . . I don't know."

"Shit you don't know. You didn't wanna get your fingers smashed, right?"

"Yessir. I guess so, sir."

"You guess so. You guess so. How many fingers you got?"

"Sir, I have ten fingers."

"Eight, shitbird, and two thumbs. Right?"

"Yessir."

"How many rifles you got?"

"Sir, one."

"What?"

"Sir, I have one rifle."

"Well that is exactly right, maggot. So don't you ever let me see you drop that weapon again, understand."

"Yessir."

"I don't care how many fingers you mess up, you hold onto that weapon. Understand?"

"Yessir."

"You don't act much like a marine, you know that?"

"Yessir."

"You don't even look like a marine. You look like a goddam baby, that's what you look like."

Midberry and the platoon watched Maguire slowly pace a circle about Cooper, then stop to jab a finger into the recruit's belly. "You look like something somebody'd find on their doorstep, you know that?"

"Yessir."

"That's it," Maguire said, appearing suddenly enlightened. "Sure, that's how a maggot like this got in this man's Corps. One of them W.M.s got herself knocked up and had to ditch the kid on our doorstep. Ain't that right, Sergeant Midberry?"

Midberry put on a smile and nodded.

"Well," Maguire went on, "I suppose we oughtta keep him. What about the rest of you animals? You think we oughtta adopt this baby for our very own? Maybe keep him around as sort of a mascot?"

"Yessir."

"Course we'll have to feed'm. How about it, pig?"

"Sir?" Klein said.

"You think you can handle the feeding?"

"Sir, I don't know what the drill instructor means."

"Shit you don't know. You gotta bigger set of tits than most broads I seen. Don't you get any milk outta those lister bags?"

"No sir."

"Well, I don't know then. . . ." Maguire scratched his head, then called the first squad leader front and center.

Neal stepped quickly from his rack to halt, clicking his heels, in front of Maguire. "Sir, Private Neal reporting as ordered."

"Get into the hut and bring back the coffee cream from the ice box."

"Yessir."

"Can't let our mascot go hungry. The goddam humane society'd be on our ass. Isn't that right, herd?"

"Yessir."

Neal ran back into the squad bay carrying a small bottle half filled with cream.

"Put it on the table and get back to your rack."

Maguire took a transparent prophylactic from his wallet. "Gotta knife or something on you, Sergeant Midberry?"

Midberry tossed a key ring with a small penknife onto the table. Maguire opened the blade, pricked a hole in the tip of the prophylactic and stretched it over the improvised baby bottle.

"There y'go, herd. Now we'll be sure baby here gets its proper nourishment."

Some of the recruits, despite their efforts, laughed. Maguire ignored them. He loosened Cooper's belt buckle and slid the bottle beneath the web belt.

"Now whenever you get hungry, little one, you just suck on that. Maybe then you'll have enough fucking energy to get your ass through that goddam hatch next time I tell you to." Maguire looked at Cooper in disgust. "Get outta my sight. G'wan, git!"

"Yessir." Cooper ran to his rack, clutching his rifle, his cheeks red and the bottle wedged beneath his belt.

"Study time, girls." Maguire watched the recruits take out their guidebooks before he and Midberry left the squad bay.

Maguire gone, the recruits felt free to laugh. Openly, or out of shame hiding it, they all experienced a certain release in seeing another recruit punished. This was especially true of the platoon's attitude toward Cooper. He held the lowest rung on the survival ladder. Each recruit judged the security of his own position on the basis of how far removed he was from Cooper. Witnessing Cooper's punishment, therefore, gave the rest of the platoon a certain *esprit de corps*. Cooper was invaluable to the recruits' morale. Each of them took assurance from the fact that if Cooper lasted, it meant anyone might make it. Or, when and if Cooper broke, then that would be one down, and every recruit dropped cut down on the others' mathematical chances of being one of the ten percent; the wash-outs.

Even Adamczyk, who felt sorry for him, was grateful for Cooper's presence. Without Cooper, he might have been made house mouse. And the platoon joke as well, for the recruits were as tireless as Maguire in harrassing the odd-balls. House-Mouse, Weasel, Pig, Sister Mary, Garbage Mouth, Goggles, Scuz, Doubleshit—they were all objects of constant ridicule.

They never let up, Adamczyk thought. Especially Fillipone. Sitting on his locker box pretending to study his guidebook, Adamczyk watched Fillipone needling Weasel. The big Italian pushed his long, mean, hawk's face close to the Weasel's so he could not be ignored. His buddies, three other Italians from Fillipone's hometown, New Castle, Pennsylvania, leaned on racks nearby.

"Weasel, baby," Fillipone said. "I'm just trying to help. Ain't that right, Tony?"

"That's right," Castaldi said.

Weasel tried to keep his attention on his guidebook but Fillipone reached over as he talked and closed the book's cover.

"On the sheets, see, everybody can tell."

"Okay," Weasel said, trying to smile, to make himself part of the joking to take away the sting. "Okay. Okay."

The Weasel's real name was Logan, but his heavy, wet, loose lower lip had earned him his nickname. Beside his locker box was a dented metal bucket. Logan's name and serial number were neatly printed in green marking ink along the bucket's rim. The first week of training Maguire had claimed that the Weasel was so ugly he might scare the other recruits during drill. Whenever platoon 197 was on the parade field, therefore, Weasel wore the bucket on his head.

"Get me one of your socks," Fillipone told Weasel. When he had the white sweatsock, he rolled back the cuff and held the sock against his groin. "Like so," he grinned, his right hand moving quickly back and forth over the empty sock.

"C . . . c'mon," Weasel said. The wet lower lip trembled, a fat pink worm with a life of its own. He managed a smile, his cheeks flushing.

"Aw no, now I went and embarrassed the Weasel." Fillipone looked up in mock surprise. Castaldi and the others laughed.

Adamczyk bit at the inside of his cheek. The skin there was already shredded and he chewed now on one of the shreds. He glanced at Waite who was, no pretense to it, dutifully reading his guidebook. As usual, Waite seemed completely cut off from what went on around him.

"I was just trying to help him," Fillipone told his audience. "Tony noticed that Weasel keeps getting these funny yellow spots on his sheets."

"C'mon," Weasel said. "I . . . I . . . ccc'mon."

"Oh for God's sake," Adamczyk muttered. Even in his anger he was careful to keep his voice low enough so Fillipone wouldn't hear. Once before he'd made the mistake of interrupting Fillipone's harrassment. Yet instead of stopping it, he had simply deflected the banter from Cooper to himself. Fillipone had tried to push him into a fight and Adamczyk, hating himself and his rank fear, had let himself be the butt of the joke, the harmless fool, thereby escaping unbeaten. Later he had complained to Waite.

"You had it coming," Waite had said.

"What?"

"Keep your nose where it belongs."

"The way he was riding Cooper?"

"That's not your worry."

"The hell it isn't."

"That's up to you. But don't come crying to me afterwards. You stick your chin out and you're gonna get hurt. Me, I wanna leave here in one piece."

Remembering their talk, Adamczyk glanced again at Waite. He'll come out alive all right, Adamczyk thought. If anything was a sure thing, it was Waite's survival.

"In days of old," Fillipone started. He nodded for Castaldi and the others in the area to join in. They kept their voices low so the noise would not carry to the D.I. hut. ". . . when men were bold and rubbers weren't invented."

Fillipone poked Weasel. Weasel shook his head, but Fillipone gripped his arm tightly and Weasel took up the chant.

"They wr- . . . rrrapped a s . . . ss . . . sss . . ."

"Sock," Fillipone said.

"Around their c . . . cccock." Weasel's lip trembled violently, spittle dribbling onto his chin.

"And fucked away contented," Fillipone finished the chant. "See, Weasel, now you know what to do. When you're done you just roll the sock up and toss it into your laundry bag and nobody'll be able to tell a thing."

Fillipone stood. Weasel opened his guidebook and looked down at it. His cheeks were still flushed.

"Don't you even want to thank me?"

"Oh, th . . . thanks," Weasel said without looking up.

Fillipone returned to his own rack. Castaldi and the others followed.

Adamczyk hated Fillipone. The Italian was scum, and he hoped and prayed Fillipone would somehow fail to graduate. But he knew there was little or no chance of that. Fillipone was tough. He obviously had what it took to be one of Maguire's marines. In fact, Fillipone was a lot like Maguire. That was probably the reason he'd been made squad leader.

Adamczyk looked at Weasel who sat on his locker box hunched over his guidebook. Adamczyk could clearly see the pendulous, pink lip and the thick eyeglasses in their colorless plastic, military frames hanging halfway down the long nose. He wished he had done something to help Weasel. Realistically though, he questioned what he could have done. He wondered what Weasel was thinking. Or did he think? Maybe, Adamczyk thought, wanting to believe it to lighten his depression, Weasel didn't really care anyhow. Some people weren't bothered by a lot of kidding and maybe Weasel was that type. With a face like his he must always have had to take kidding. Maybe he'd gotten used to it. By now, Adamczyk thought, Weasel most likely barely noticed what people said about him.

Suddenly Adamczyk saw the slump in Weasel's shoulders not as a sign of dejection and loneliness, but as one of craft and endurance. Other recruits got angry or bitter, but no matter what happened Weasel just went into his slump and stuck it out. Probably nothing in the world could really touch him.

The Weasel, Adamczyk thought. He was another one nobody had to worry about. He'd take care of himself. Good old Weasel.

But later that night after the recruits had been to evening chow and were cleaning their rifles, Adamczyk's depression returned. Fillipone and Maguire, Weasel, House-Mouse, Pig, Waite, himself, they all jammed together in Adamczyk's mind, shouting and cursing, punching and crying until he felt that right then and there in front of everyone he might start screaming.

"I've had it," he hissed. "I've taken all I'm going to take. I'm through."

"Through?" Waite said. He laughed. "What're you gonna do, quit?"

"What am I supposed to do, put up with Maguire's . . . have to watch stuff like Cooper and his bottle?"

"That's right."

"You maybe. Not me."

"Cooper didn't get hurt."

60

"Oh Jesus!' Adamczyk said. He bit at his thumbnail and peeled back a thin half-moon. As he talked, he chewed on the strip of nail. "What about that guy from first squad? Johnson?"

"What about him?"

"Yesterday morning, he was gone. His sack was made up when reveille went. Nobody I talked to knows what happened to him."

"He was probably sick or something."

"Why doesn't Maguire tell us then?"

"Why don't you go ask him?"

"Sure, and have'm start on me."

"Then why talk about it? Besides, you didn't even know the guy."

Waite leaned across in front of Adamczyk, picked up the olive-drab can of bore cleaner, uncapped it and poured a little onto a cleaning rag.

"Johnson was the kid always picking his nose," Adamczyk said. "Weasel told me he heard him nights crying in his rack."

"All right. So he cracked up."

"So . . ." Adamczyk started. Yet he had no idea what they should actually do. He just knew that the whole situation was wrong and that it made him sick to even think about it. "It's like stories you hear about the Nazis. Or Communists."

"Come off it, Red. Johnson's probably on his way home right now."

"It makes me sick."

"Then don't think about it."

"It does."

"You gonna throw up? Or faint again?"

"Funny," Adamczyk said. "So we all let Maguire get away with it?"

"With what?"

"The way he treats us. We let'm get away with it?"

"That's right."

Adamczyk looked at Waite, hoping to shame him, but Waite looked neither shamed nor guilty. Even as Waite talked, he continued methodically cleaning his rifle. "Maguire's the drill instructor, so you do what he says.

If you could get that into your head and quit worrying so much about what you think you ought to do, maybe you'd start doing what you have to do. Then maybe you wouldn't fuck up so much." Through talking, Waite screwed a wire brush onto the tip of his cleaning rod and shoved it down the bore of his rifle, pulled it out, shoved it down again.

Adamczyk's stomach burned with anger at Waite's reminding him of what a misfit he was. No matter what Adamczyk said nobody would listen to him. He was one of the fuck-ups and a fuck-up knew nothing. Yet the others didn't understand at all why he didn't square away. They didn't suspect what Adamczyk knew. He was sure he could square away any time he chose, but he didn't simply because he refused to give in to Maguire. The others were too stupid or scared, or else like Waite they just didn't care to see past the surface. But what difference did it make, Adamczyk thought. He didn't need them. Not even, or maybe specially not, Waite. Adamczyk realized how stupid he had been to have thought even for an instant that he could make Waite his friend. It was impossible. He might just as well try to make friends with a robot or some kind of zombie.

Waite extracted the trigger housing group from his rifle. He began cleaning the tiny crevices behind the sear and springs with a pipe cleaner. Adamczyk watched him, his lips pressed together in hate and disgust.

He must have been blind not to see that Waite would always advise him to stick it out, ride with the punches, not fight back. Waite was his squad leader. If Adamczyk caused trouble it would mean trouble for his squad leader. And all Waite cared about was steering clear of trouble and saving his own skin.

Well, Adamczyk thought, he wouldn't make a fool of himself anymore. He was glad now that he hadn't told Waite of his plan. He almost had earlier. He'd wanted to tell someone to relieve himself of the weight of the secret. But he'd stopped in time. Now he would keep it strictly to himself. He knew what he was going to do, and tomorrow, first chance he got, he would do it.

SEVEN

Adamczyk had done what he'd planned. Maguire had accused him of merely trying to escape the morning P.T. session, had ridiculed him as a psalm-singer, and finally, all else failing, had backed him against the wall and vowed to beat him black and blue if he caused any trouble for the platoon.

Despite his fear, Adamczyk had weathered Maguire's attack and in the end got permission to see the 1st Battalion's Catholic chaplain. At the time Adamczyk had thought he'd won a victory and that he was on the brink of solving his problems. But since that morning's session with the chaplain, his thoughts and emotions had gotten hopelessly tangled. No matter how hard he had tried, he had not been able to clear his mind, and his distraction had cost him frequent mistakes during close-order drill. He was lucky, he knew, that it was Midberry drilling the platoon. As it was, his only punishment was the first two hour shift of the nightly firewatch, and Adamczyk was actually glad to have it. He could not have slept anyhow and felt less tense up and moving.

He paced the long, dark passageway between the double row of double bunks. He concentrated on listening, on making out in the dark the shapes of bunks, on putting one foot quietly and regularly in front of the other. His mind avoided thought. He'd wasted the whole day thinking and was now as confused as he had been that morning.

A whimpering caught his attention. Adamczyk flicked on his flashlight, aiming the beam at the ceiling. In the light's indirect glow, he could see a form twisting and kicking in a nearby bunk. It was Weasel. His face was screwed tight as if in pain and his teeth gnawed at the loose lower lip. Adamczyk leaned down and shook Weasel's shoulder. Weasel jerked, not waking, then went silent, his muscles relaxing.

Who doesn't have bad dreams here? Adamczyk thought. He remembered the one he'd had two nights before. Sinking in quicksand, yet the whole platoon and the D.I.s stood at the pool's rim watching and ignoring his yells for help.

Remembering it, not only the dream seemed dreamlike. Waite at attention in the morning seemed no more real than Waite watching him sink into quicksand. The same with Maguire and the others. The entire platoon and the island seemed one bad dream to Adamczyk. He was no longer sure what was real and what wasn't. He wished now that he could pinch himself and be back home in the world he knew for sure was real—a world where normal people agreed on what things mattered and on just what a man should and shouldn't do.

The flashlight beam still spread out against the white ceiling. Adamczyk looked at the rack where Weasel in the lower and Carruthers in the upper bunk slept. Both blankets, like all the blankets in the squad bay, were drab green with the letters U.S.M.C. printed in black across the middle. On the front corners of the metal rack frame hung two drab green cartridge belts, each with a bayonet and scabbard hooked onto the left, a first-aid packet at center-rear. A silver-painted helmet liner sat atop each cartridge belt. Below, on the cross bar of the lower bunk, hung two drab green haversacks. The sets of straps on the haversacks were neatly rolled, loose ends tucked in at the buckles. A green wooden locker box with its black-faced, chromium-cased combination lock sat beneath the haversacks. At the rear of the rack was a second box. Beneath the rack was a double line of footgear; black boots, the uppers braced with rolled newspaper, white tennis shoes, spit-shined dress shoes. All the footgear was laced to the top, the lace ends tucked inside the shoe.

The rack's upper and lower bunks were arranged identically. The gear too was identical. And, Adamczyk knew, picturing it clearly in his mind, though staring down the dark pasageway he could only make out the dim outlines of racks and lockers, each of the thirty-five double bunks looked exactly the same. The position of the racks—the alignment was periodically checked by means of a chalk line—and the gear, the sleeping recruits themselves, everything was identical.

Adamczyk clicked off the flashlight. Cool night air blew in softly through the screened windows behind the racks. Adamczyk waited, listening, uncertain of what it was he felt he wanted to do. Surrounding him was the sibilance of relaxed breathing, a soft, even sigh ruptured by snores or abrupt coughing. In the dark Adamczyk felt he was listening not to the breathing of some sixty individual recruits, but rather to one huge body. He felt there were only two living things in the squad bay, two distinct presences, himself and the platoon whose hiss of breathing surrounded him. Himself. The platoon. The idea shook him. He felt starkly small and alone and he tried at once to discount the notion.

It was only the dark and his fatigue which depressed him, he decided. Cutting short his circuit of the squad bay, he pushed open the swinging doors and went into the dimly-lit passageway between the squad bay and the hut. He looked into the head, seeing no one, then stopped beside the door to the hut. He held his breath, listening, and over the plunk-plunking drip of a shower, he could detect a slight snoring.

He felt easier knowing Midberry was asleep. He'd heard stories from other recruits about the habit D.I.s had of sneaking up on the firewatch, and he'd been afraid Midberry might do it to him as part of his punishment.

Adamczyk turned back to the squad bay. Beneath the ceiling light, a single sixty-watt bulb enclosed in a wire cage shaped like an overturned bowl, the passageway widened to form a large open area used mostly for exercise. It was here the understrength recruits performed the nightly exercises prescribed by Maguire to help them measure up. In one corner rested a set of black-iron barbells, the extra plates stacked beside the loaded bar, and a tangle of bright, coiled-steel springs with red wooden grips. A long iron pipe used as a pull-up bar ran the length of the near wall. The other wall was taken up by three full-length mirrors and, to the left of the mirrors, a life-size picture of a dress-uniformed marine. The picture was accompanied by printed instructions, arrows connecting the instructions to particular body areas, explaining proper military dress.

Adamczyk stood looking at the locked outside doors. All he had to do to escape was to unlock the heavy wooden doors, then the screen doors, and walk out. He wished it were really that easy: just walk out and close the doors behind him on Maguire and the Corps. But he could not swim well. He wouldn't try it if he could because of the sharks reported near the island. The only other way to the mainland, the causeway, was heavily guarded. He had no choice. He had to stick it out. Last night there had been hope, but the morning had erased it. Not erased, Adamczyk thought, correcting himself, because it was never actually there. It was as though what he hadn't been able to recognize the night before had become obvious with daylight. Morning had revealed that his one possibility existed only in his mind.

Adamczyk went to the outside doors, unlocked and swung them open. The cool ocean breeze touched his forehead. The air was calm and good, peaceful, and he leaned against the hooked screen doors, looking out across the parade ground. Headlights blinked and flashed along the hardtop road the other side of the high, steel, barbed wire-topped fence.

Watching the tiny lights moving freely in the dark, Adamczyk cursed the complacency of the drivers and their passengers. He was sure they had no idea how lucky they were. They took it all for granted. Lord, he thought, how wonderful to be beyond the fence going anywhere you wanted. Outside the fence. On his own. Free. Driving along, he'd roll down his side window to let the wind stream in on him, battering his ear, and he'd turn the radio up as high as it would go. Hearing the blast of music, the dark car lit dimly by dashlights, Adamczyk held the ridge of the steering wheel in the easy curl of his fingers. The right hand on the wheel, the left arm crooked over the door. Or the left hand on the wheel and his right maybe holding a girl close to his side; his fingertips maybe brushing the soft warm curve of her breast. His girl. His car. His own time. To go when and where he wanted; driving, feeling the spinning tires regularly thumping over the concrete road's tarred patching strips. Each thump taking him further from the island and Maguire.

Adamczyk's right foot ached and he shifted his weight. The headlights on the road disappeared momentarily in their steady sweep from one darkness to another. He knew what hid the lights; the monument. He hated it. He'd hated it since the first week on the island. The exaggerated twenty-foot figures looming over the drilling recruits as if taunting them "Here's what a real marine is, boy. Measure up. Measure up."

The worst thing about it was it was a lie. Adamczyk had read somewhere once, *Reader's Digest*, he thought, that the Mount Surabachi flag raising wasn't an actual combat photograph. It had been posed for after the battle. He hadn't believed that article then. Now he knew it must have been true, for he'd found that the whole island, the whole Corps, was a pose. Why didn't they make the statue life-size? Or better yet tear it down and put one up of the celebrated Staff Sergeant Maguire whipping a recruit with a belt. The same with the recruiting posters. Take down all the ones with the blond farm boy and the blue-eyed W.M. in church together and replace it with one of Maguire putting rubbers on milk bottles. Adamczyk felt that the statue, the posters, the John Wayne movies, the T.V. shows had all conspired to cheat him. He'd swallowed the lie hook, line and sinker; had enlisted to wear dress blues, become a man and be called a marine. Instead he wore drab utilities and got called Doubleshit or, at best, maggot. And worst of all he had been forced to recognize he was a coward.

Adamczyk's mind was again filling with the confused welter of thoughts he'd tried the whole day to suppress. He recalled the chaplain's office and how the picture on the wall, the standard metal-framed glossy of the Sura-bachi flag raising, had been the first thing he'd noticed and how his hopes had right then gone dead inside him and he'd known he was a fool and was wasting his time.

"Sir," he said, "Private Adamczyk requests permission. . . ."

"No need for that here," the chaplain said. He smiled to relax Adamczyk. "Have a seat, private."

Adamczyk sat facing the olive-drab metal desk. On the desk top was a casing from a 105 howitzer shell. It had been cut down to serve as a letter holder. A large wooden cross with a gilt Christ figure hung on the wall directly behind the desk.

The chaplain swiveled his chair about. He leaned his elbows on the desk and said, his voice sounding slightly too deep for his narrow chest, "Go right ahead, private. What's the problem? Here, you can feel free to say whatever you want."

"Well . . . sir, father, I . . . I'm sort of confused, sir."

"Father is fine."

"Father. You see . . ." Adamczyk began. He went on, trying to organize into logical statements his thoughts about Maguire and the training and what he felt was basically wrong. He failed, and finished his speech knowing he'd succeeded only in proving he was right in the first place. He was sort of confused.

Later, riding back to the squad bay in a jeep driven by a silent corporal relentlessly chewing gum, Adamczyk thought out his failure and had blamed it on his surprise. Or, more accurately, the chaplain's lack of surprise. In planning his speech, he had expected to shock his listener into indignation. Yet at the actual meeting the chaplain had never broken from his unruffled fatherly attitude and that had thrown Adamczyk off balance. He had told how Maguire mistreated Cooper and Weasel and the others, of Johnson's being taken away during the night, of Maguire's remarks about religion, of his language in general. The chaplain then had launched into a long speech about Adamczyk's double duty to God and Country, but Adamczyk had heard only the first few phrases. He sat staring at the desk until the chaplain finished, then apologized for taking up so much time and said that he thought now he understood his duty and that yessir, he'd try harder and yessir he'd keep up his prayers to be given strength to succeed in whatever trials might come his way.

The chaplain was a goddamned fool, Adamczyk thought. Maybe himself too. What had he expected anyhow? That's what Waite would say if he knew what had happened. "What the hell'd you think, that he was gonna tell you to pack up and go home? Shit, Red, the man's a Navy officer." It angered Adamczyk to imagine Waite's smugness. Nothing ever bothered Waite. He stood back from everything, just out of reach, and looked right through the top layer everybody else saw to what he called the "actual facts." What angered Adamczyk most was that no matter how wrong Waite's attitude seemed, the actual facts had so far proved him right.

His elbows on the screen door's cross piece, Adamczyk chewed at the loose strips of skin beside his bitten fingernails. He stared at the tiny wire squares of screen inches from his eyes.

Why shouldn't he have expected something different? He'd been brought up differently from Waite. He had close family ties. He had his religion. What did Waite know? What could someone know who didn't care about anyone or anything else but himself?

Adamczyk wished he could talk to Father Matuzak. He'd have liked especially to take the chaplain with him and to watch his old, stern pastor set the chaplain straight about religious duties. There was no doubt Father Matuzak could and would do it. He was an impossible man to argue with. When he spoke his mind, none of the doubts the average person felt about right or wrong showed in his voice. It was precisely his complete certainty that made his parishoners, perhaps Adamczyk especially, follow him with no questions asked.

Oh Lord, Adamszyk thought, how he wished he could somehow talk things over with Father Matuzak right away. A letter wouldn't do. It wasn't so much what the old priest said as the way he said it, his just being there, his look and tone of voice, that cleared up one's confusion.

EIGHT

Adamczyk dragged himself through the rest of that week and the next full week in an apparent trance. Though the platoon seemed locked within a single, specific day which drearily, endlessly repeated itself, Adamczyk had won a certain peace. He went through the repetitive motions of training, his mind numb. Though his harrassments increased with his mistakes, punishment only increased his numbness.

Nights, he lay awake in his rack. He felt the lumpy pad beneath him. His hands crossed behind his head, he felt the hard metal rack frame against his knuckles. He felt the certainty in Waite's breathing and the fear in the firewatch's slow, soft steps. His senses touched everything around him, yet his mind organized nothing, formed no conclusions. As if from some high vantage point, his mind seemed to be watching his body's ordeal. It would watch, but that was all. It had come to understand that there was nothing it could do to help. Beaten back into the corners of his mind, Adamczyk no longer identified with his body. His feelings went no further than a detached sympathy for the poor hounded flesh of the recruit called Doubleshit. His body would have to solve its own problems. Adamczyk had given up. And for the first time on the island, he felt secure. No matter what Maguire did to Doubleshit, he could no longer touch Adamczyk. No one could touch him.

During evening free time, Waite had tried to penetrate Adamczyk's daze. He coaxed him with reminders of his family's pride in him, shamed him with his inability to measure up, frightened him with the simple facts of survival. At least Waite tried coaxing, shaming and frightening Adamczyk. But nothing worked.

And talking to, or at, Adamczyk, Waite often found himself having to consciously control his temper. There was something in Adamczyk's animal passivity which infuriated Waite and he fought down sudden urges to grab the tall, thin redhead and shake the stubbornness out of him once and for all. His reaction, especially its intensity, surprised and frightened Waite. It was a new experience for him and one he wanted to avoid. His anger rising, he'd break off speaking, swearing to himself that he would waste no more time on Adamczyk.

The only reason he'd tried snapping Adamczyk out of it in the first place, Waite told himself, was because Adamczyk was in his squad and keeping the squad alert was Waite's job if he wanted to stay clear of trouble. Well, he had tried. If Adamczyk washed out no one could say Waite hadn't tried.

Nothing got through to Adamczyk. Waite ignored him, Midberry lectured him, Maguire harrassed him, one sweating eighteen-hour training day regularly replaced another, day by day, and Adamczyk through it all remained aloof. And in the end it wasn't his, but another's, punishment that snapped his daze. Klein, the fat boy Maguire called Pig, did not pass the fifth week strength test. He was the only one in the platoon to fail.

In gym shorts, T shirts and tennis shoes, their shirts sweat-drenched, the recruits double timed in platoon formation from the athletic field to the squad bay. Maguire jogged beside the formation, frequently grunting the cadence to correct the beginnings of a confused shuffle.

Recruits close to Klein sneaked glances at him. They wanted to know how he was taking it. Each of them uncertain of his own reaction in the same situation, the recruits studied Klein's behavior under the pressure of certain, yet threateningly indefinite, punishment. Klein's round face, however, the slight double chin set quivering by the jogging, hid whatever fears he might be feeling.

"Justice is swift," Maguire announced. "And me, I'm always one step ahead of justice."

The recruits, still wearing their P.T. suits, stood at attention before their racks.

"You maggots remember that."

"Yessir."

"You think you can remember that, Pig?"

"Yessir," Klein said.

"How come you're sweating?"

"Sir, from . . ."

"Now here's the Pig sweating like a double-cunted cow pissing on a flat rock," Maguire said to the platoon. "And for no reason whatever that I can see. That right, Pig? Or is your drill instructor wrong? You put out today?"

"Sir, I did my best."

"That wasn't good enough though, was it?"

"Nosir."

"That means you can't cut it, right? You can't measure up?"

"Sir, I . . . I guess so."

"Whaddya mean, you guess so? You pass that fucking strength test or not?"

"Nosir."

"Then what's the guessing about? You just don't pack the gear, Pig. Now ain't that the simple truth?"

"Yessir."

"Yessir what?"

"Sir, I just don't pack the gear."

"You can't make the grade, right?"

"Yessir."

"Yessir what?"

"Sir, I can't make the grade."

"You can't shape up, right?"

"Sir, I can't shape up."

Maguire turned to the platoon. "Any of you maggots here remember me saying that the rule here was to shape up or ship out?"

"YESSIR," the platoon shouted.

"And if a maggot don't shape up, what's left?"

"Sir, ship out."

"Y'hear that, Pig?"

"Yessir."

Maguire lightly punched Klein's belly. "You're soft, maggot. Only thing I can see is for you to go to S.T.U. You know what that is, Pig?"

"Nosir."

"Special Training Unit." Maguire punched Klein again, slightly harder and higher, his fist landing against the recruit's solar plexus. "Fat boys' platoon. Sissies, pusguts, mama's boys, pussies platoon. That's where they try to make you over into something half-ass normal enough you can pass a strength test which any ten-year-old who's not hunchbacked or blind or lame oughtta pass!" Maguire continued slowly and regularly hitting Klein in the solar plexus. "Course, that means you'll spend another two or three weeks extra on the island. Maybe more. All depends how long it takes S.T.U. to work you up to normal. Some maggots spend six weeks there."

Maguire watched the recruit closely. Klein, his flushed cheeks bright against his pale face, stared straight ahead. His nasal breathing was sharp and quick.

"Then too you won't graduate with this mob. You'll be stuck into a new herd to take up wherever you left off here. But that don't bother you, does it, Pig? You don't give a shit about this platoon anyway, do you?"

"Yessir," Klein said. "I . . ." Maguire's fist landed again. Klein's breath snagged.

"Don't hand me that bullshit! If you cared anything about sticking with this mob, you would've worked out more nights."

"Sir, I did . . ." Klein's voice was high in his throat. He stopped as Maguire's fist landed, tried to snatch a quick breath. "Tried . . . t'work out . . . every night."

"How come you flunked the test then?"

"Sir, I don't . . ."

"I'll tell you why," Maguire said, hitting Klein and making him grunt involuntarily. "You just do not give a shit. Like the time you thought things were so funny over at the barbershop, right? You got the idea this man's Corps is one big joke, don't you?"

"Nosir."

73

Maguire punched harder. Klein bent forward, then straightened.

"That right?"

Maguire waited. Klein didn't answer. Maguire saw that he had started to smile. Shocked, he stared for a moment at the recruit, then Klein began laughing and Maguire grabbed his T shirt, jerking him forward. "You think it's funny, Pig? Huh? You goddam clown!"

Then Klein was crying. His mouth twisted downwards and tears ran down his cheeks and his soft body suddenly sagged. Maguire freed Klein's shirt-front and the fat boy crumpled to the deck, openly bawling.

Later, Maguire had told the platoon that Klein would be all right. He had been taken to sick bay and the corpsman there said he'd be fine with a couple of days' rest. And it was Maguire's brief speech that had crystallized Adamczyk's resolve. The Klein incident had only jolted Adamczyk back into his immediate surroundings. Maguire had shown Adamczyk a real possibility of changing those surroundings.

For Adamszyk knew Maguire was lying. It was certain that Klein was not all right. Klein probably would not be all right for the rest of his life. Maguire had driven Klein crazy. It was that simple. That's why Maguire had to lie. He was afraid of an investigation. If the brass uncovered his treatment of recruits, Maguire would find out once and for all that he wasn't God, that he had to toe the line like everyone else. Yes, the truth about Klein could finish Maguire as a D.I. It could set free the platoon. All that was needed was someone with enough guts to talk. Whoever had the guts to talk held Maguire's career in the palm of his hand. Even Doubleshit could do it, Adamczyk thought, and then in a rush of pride and determination he swore that Doubleshit would.

His spirits were lifted by his decision. Adamczyk was glad for the chance to break Maguire's power. Then, remembering Klein, he felt ashamed of his optimism. Thinking it over, though, he decided his reaction was no more than natural considering the circumstances. Besides, and this point encouraged him still more, his exposure

74

of Maguire's brutality would not just be a way of relieving pressure on himself, it would even things up for Klein too. The more Adamczyk thought about it, the more he recognized that as his basic purpose. He was out to avenge poor crazy Klein.

He saw from the first, however, that the real problem would be lining up other witnesses. Recruits would pretend to believe Maguire's lie, for coiled in the gut of each was the fear that what had happened to Klein would happen to anyone crossing Maguire. Even so, Adamczyk thought he'd have to have someone to back up his story. He'd never be believed on his own. He was one of the ten percent.

Returning from evening chow, Adamczyk approached Weasel, Garbagemouth, Sister Mary, Scuz and a half dozen other recruits. None of them would hear him out. They all advised him to forget it and to keep his mouth shut. A couple of them laughed, and a big blond Nebraskan named Hammarburg threatened to break Adamczyk's polak neck if he tried to stir up trouble.

All else failing, Adamczyk went to Waite. "Are you serious?" Waite asked him. Waite went on to point out that it did not pay to worry about fine points of behavior in a place like Parris Island. You did what you had to do in order to get by. The rules were made by the D.I. They were not like those on the outside. Trying to live by your old rules would only buy you trouble. Waite explained that anyhow it was basically a waste of time to fight back because it made absolutely no difference what one man did or even two or three. To have any chance at all, you'd have to line up a majority of the recruits. And that was impossible. And, Waite reminded Adamczyk as his final point, the most important thing at the moment to each and every recruit was graduation. It was something Adamczyk should think about, because if he talked and lost the case, he wouldn't graduate. All the trouble he'd managed to endure until then, and the beating he would take when Maguire found out he'd talked, would be wasted. He wouldn't have a thing to show for it.

"But somebody's got to do it," Adamczyk protested.

"I know what you're thinking," Waite said. "You think

75

you'll be some kind of hero going it alone. Don't kid yourself. Nobody's gonna be telling you 'Oh what a noble thing!' and all that crap. Uh-uh. You'll be just another wash-out. Couldn't make the grade and so had to be shit-canned, that's all."

Adamczyk had expected Waite to refuse. He'd known before talking to Waite that his plan was a failure. No one was going to back him and he himself, Adamczyk admitted, tasting self-hatred like bile in his throat, hadn't the nerve to go it alone.

That night during free time Adamczyk sat hunched forward on his locker box. His chin resting on his clenched fists, he stared through and beyond the rack opposite him. The jungle of confusing ideas and emotions he had suppressed earlier, had returned. He bit a fingernail. He could see Klein being hauled from the squad bay, laughing and crying, almost howling, his fat cheeks reddened and wet, and Maguire yelling for him to shuttup and act like a goddamed man.

Adamczyk was totally ashamed of himself. His heroic plan had failed not because the others refused to help but because of his own weakness. It was more than his physical weakness, though that had much to do with his fear of Maguire; no, it was his weakness of purpose. That's why he'd had nothing to say when Waite downgraded his plan. Waite's offhand arguments had made Adamczyk doubt his own carefully thought out, morally proper plan of action. Moreover, he'd been forced to realize that he was so weak he could be made to doubt everything he believed in by someone like Waite who believed in nothing.

Adamczyk wished that just once he could be absolutely certain he was doing what was right. Then, no matter what the punishment, he knew he would be capable of sticking to it. But he was always so confused and unsure of where he stood. He was always having to ask others how to make up his own mind. And he never failed to get a dozen different answers, confusing him further.

Waite seemed sure of himself. Maguire obviously had no self-doubts. The same with Midberry. The chaplain, even though he was wrong, seemed confident enough.

And Father Matuzak, actually in the right, was always fully aware of his position, making his choices and decisions with never a second thought.

Back home as an altar boy, Adamczyk had thought he'd found what he needed. He had even considered for a long time the possibility of becoming a priest. Then for some reason—to spite his father? to prove to his uncle that he was a man? to prove it to himself?—he had joined the marines. Now, at Parris Island, completely cut off from the cool, quiet, high-domed church of Saint Stephen, Adamczyk was no longer sure of anything. Faced every day with Maguire, what had once seemed obvious and permanent began to look more and more doubtful. Adamczyk felt he'd been betrayed somehow. He'd been counting on a support that had collapsed under the first stress. His mind was left with no defense and the questions, the questions, the questions kept coming at him, confusing him.

NINE

Waite sat on his locker box at the rear of the rack. He did not want to sit with Adamczyk. He could see at the front of the rack the thin shoulders hunched and the carrot-haired head erect and unmoving, and he knew Adamczyk was as usual staring into space like a cow awaiting the slaughterhouse hammer. What in hell, Waite thought, did the kid enlist for anyhow? Had he spent his weekly allowance on John Wayne and Richard Widmark movies? Signed up then so he could be a hero too?

Waite had no use for Adamczyk or anyone else who lived in his own dream world and came crying when the real world wouldn't play along. He himself had had no illusions about enlisting. He hadn't been blinded by the glory of the Corps or by someone waving the stars and stripes. He had wanted to get away from home and be lost among strangers, that was all.

"Waite!"

He jumped to his feet. "Yessir."

Midberry stood in the opened passageway hatch. He told Waite to report to the hut. The double doors swung shut.

What now? Waite wondered. He ran a quick check on the day's happenings, but could think of nothing he'd done wrong. Then it would have to be about one of the others in the squad. Probably Adamczyk.

Waite tucked his T shirt into his trousers, hurriedly laced his boots, and ran from the squad bay to stand before the D.I. hut. He pounded his fist three times on the door jamb. "Sir!" he shouted, "Private Waite requests permission to enter the drill instructor's quarters!"

'Granted."

Waite took two forward steps, his arms at his sides, did a left face and stepped across the sill. He clicked his heels and stood at attention. "Sir," he said. "Private Waite reporting as ordered."

Midberry glanced at Waite without speaking. He walked to the desk, took up a half-full cup of coffee and sipped it, studying Waite's stolid expression from the side.

He liked the way Waite had entered the hut precisely by guidebook procedure. He'd at first questioned his idea of talking privately with any of the recruits, afraid that whoever he chose might try to take advantage of the situation. But he had watched Waite carefully and now was sure his choice had been right. Waite was neither a whiner nor a worrier. He would not be one to start trouble.

"You and Adamczyk rack together, right."

"Yessir."

"Who racks across from you?"

"Sir, Logan."

"Klein used to rack with him, didn't he?"

"Yessir."

Midberry poured the luke-warm coffee into the sink and rinsed the cup under the tap. He felt foolish, as if he were mimicking a television lawyer, yet he wasn't sure how to start. He didn't want it to seem too open, like a challenge, or too devious, like a plot. He wanted it seemingly offhand and accidental.

"How'd Adamczyk take Klein's cracking-up?"

"Sir, all right."

"He talk about it with you?'

"Yessir, a little."

"What'd he say?"

"Sir, he was worried about Klein. But I think it scared him too. He seems to be trying to shape up a little harder now."

"Good. Did it surprise you? Klein, I mean."

"Nosir."

"You expected him to crack?"

"Nosir."

"You said you weren't surprised."

"Sir, I hadn't thought much about it either way."

79

"He did seem the type that'd crack, though, didn't he? I mean without much pressure."

"Sir, I couldn't say."

"You're a squad leader. You're supposed to be able to tell whether or not a man can take it."

"Sir, Klein wasn't in my squad."

Midberry went to the desk and sat in the swivel chair. Waite's eyes stared at the wall behind Midberry's head.

"Like last night. I'm sure Sergeant Maguire didn't torture him or anything. Yet I hear Klein started crying. What caused that?"

"Sir, it's probably like the drill instructor said. Klein couldn't take it."

Midberry played with a lead pencil, doodling neat, heavy-lined squares on the back of an envelope. "Was it just his flunking the strength test? Was that what he couldn't take?"

"Yessir. That and the training."

"I mean just last night. After the strength test. What made him crack then?"

"Sir, I'm not sure."

"Sergeant Maguire didn't beat him, did he?"

"Nosir. I wouldn't say that."

"Well what would you say?"

"Sir, not much."

"Did Sergeant Maguire hit Klein?"

Waite hesitated. Midberry was careful to keep his eyes on the envelope.

"Yessir," Waite said.

"Where?"

"Sir, in the stomach."

"More than once?"

"Yessir."

"Hard?"

"Nosir. Not at first."

Midberry drew small squares interlocking the larger ones. He laid the pencil on the desk and looked up. "Well anyhow," he said, "let's not get side-tracked on Klein. What's happened, happened. It's Adamczyk I wanted to talk about. You say he's doing all right?"

"Sir, he's not doing too bad. Considering."

"You think he'll make it?"

"Sir, I'm not sure. He acts sometimes like he's dreaming."

"Then you keep on him and snap him out of it, okay."

"Yessir."

"You're his squad leader. It's your job to see he shapes up."

"Yessir."

Midberry looked back down at the desk. "Dismissed."

Waite took a step backward. His heels clicked together. He shouted "Aye aye sir," turned sharply and left the hut.

Midberry went to the hot plate. He switched on the burner and put water on for coffee. He was glad he had called in Waite. He'd gotten enough if not all the details he'd wanted. He supposed it would have been easier to have gone right to Maguire and asked him. He doubted that Maguire would have lied about Klein. He might even have bragged about it. But Midberry would have felt as if he were prying. And this way he knew without Maguire knowing that he knew. He could make up his mind about what had happened without having Maguire eye-balling him to see just how he was going to react.

Watching the tiny bubbles beginning to hiss and pop in the small tin pan, it struck Midberry that perhaps he was being excessively, even foolishly, cautious. After all Maguire was his partner. D.I.s were to work as a team. A fire-team, a squad, a platoon, any team was based on trust. *Esprit de Corps.*

The water boiled. Midberry took up the pan using his handkerchief to wrap the hot handle.

Team or no team, he thought, it would not be a good idea to trust Maguire too far.

TEN

"You could have given him another chance. That's your prerogative, isn't it?"

Midberry sat across from Maguire at one of the small square tables covered with red-checked oilcloth which filled the noncommissioned officers' section of the mess hall. He stirred his coffee, watching Maguire scrape the last hunks of syrupy apple and a single fragment of browned crust onto his fork. Maguire chewed unhurriedly, then took a swallow of coffee. He picked a fleck of crust from the corner of his mouth. Holding it on the tip of a stubby forefinger, he looked at it, then thumbed it off into an ashtray.

"I mean it was up to you, wasn't it?"

"You don't gotta explain it to me," Maguire said. His cheeks puffing, he soundlessly belched. "I know what the word means."

"What?"

"What you said the first time. Prerogative. Don't always be thinking I'm as dumb as I look."

Midberry had noticed before Maguire's knack of turning an argument around to gain the offensive. But Midberry did not apologize or excuse himself. He waited for his answer. The sweephand of his wristwatch crawled slowly around the face of the dial. A full minute passed.

"Sure it was up to me," Maguire said abruptly. "Chrissakes, you think I don't know that by now?"

"How come you didn't give him another chance?"

"I was going to. I was. What d'you think, I was thumping him just for kicks? If I was gonna set him back, then I wouldn't have wasted my time on him. I thumped him cause I was gonna keep him. Pure and simple. He had to get something for flunking the strength test, didn't he?"

Maguire filled both their cups from the table's coffee pitcher.

"You don't think you overdid it?"

"Hell, no! How'd I know he'd crack on me? Anyhow, that's the way it is. Some just can't cut it. What d'you want, everybody comes in to make it?"

"Just asking."

"Look, I know you don't like it, the way I operate. But it's part of the job. Still, I'm not telling you y'have to beat heads. You wanna try kindness on the herd, that's okay by me. It's your neck."

"Thanks."

"Just don't go too far.'

"How far's that?"

"Well, I wouldn't want you should start siding with them against me. I got enough to worry about now."

"Sure," Midberry said. There were circles under Maguire's eyes and the popped eyes were bloodshot. Working at half strength, doing the work of four men, maybe it was only the extra tension that made Maguire thump Klein. Or maybe it was like he said, it was part of the job. Who was Midberry to say?

"But if that's the way you wanna run it, then go ahead and treat'm easy. I crack down and you ease up. Some guys, D.I.s, work it that way all the time; have one of them act the nice guy. Good guy and bad guy routine. That way the animals always got somebody they figure they can come to with their troubles. And that way a D.I. always knows just who's ready to cry to the brass."

Midberry looked down at the white styrofoam cup. He stirred his coffee with a plastic spoon. He'd tried this time to keep the offensive, but the discussion had as usual been turned back onto him. Now Maguire was offering to make allowances for his weaknesses. How was it Maguire could always make him feel second class; that he didn't quite have what it took to make a good D.I.?

"You're still pretty new at this," Maguire said. "Later maybe you'll come around to my way of thinking. Maybe not, who knows? Right now, though, we'll play it this way. Good guy and bad guy. All right with you?"

"I guess so."

Maguire stood. "I got to be getting the animals back out. You take over at twenty-two hundred."

"Right."

Midberry watched Maguire leave by the front door, then he walked out the back to where his car was parked in the noncoms' lot. He wanted to be by himself for awhile and so he drove to the beach.

Lying on his back on a white beach towel, Midberry closed his eyes and felt the hot afternoon sun warm his body. Sweat beads popped onto his forehead and chest. He felt a trickle of sweat run down into his navel.

Maybe, he thought, he basically wasn't a good marine. If he and Maguire were so different, and Maguire—and the record seemed to prove it—was the perfect marine, then what was he, Midberry?

He'd had the same doubts before, and had come close to walking out of the captain's office the day he was to sign his re-enlistment papers. Since then he sometimes felt certain he had picked the wrong career. Not because he questioned the Corps, but because he questioned his own abilities as a marine. He knew, for all its failings and excesses, that the Corps and the military in general was necessary. That was the point he'd often argued with Bill, his brother-in-law, a Methodist minister, against the whole idea of the military. When he'd been home on leave at Thanksgiving, Midberry recalled, he and Bill had spent the entire day on the subject.

"How in the world can you square your job with your religion?" Bill had started. "You teach people how to kill, don't you?"

Midberry and Bill sat at the diningroom table finishing their coffee. Midberry's sister, Phyllis, helped his mother clear away the dishes.

"How to defend themselves, that's what a D.I. teaches recruits. Maybe I'm not a very good Christian then, I don't know. I think we oughtta love our neighbor and all that, but I know that if somebody broke in here trying to hurt Mom or Phyl, then I'd go for'm rather than pray. But not you, huh? He's going to stab Phyl and you'd tell him 'Thou shalt not kill,' right?"

"I might try to talk to him."

"Oh c'mon."

"Or maybe I'd grab one of Earl's shotguns and blow his head off. How can I tell what I'd do till it happens?"

"Blowing somebody's head off doesn't seem too Christian to me." Midberry smiled.

"Okay, I'm human. Is that your point?"

Midberry only shrugged.

"But your example isn't fair, Wayne. I mean, you're talking about a sudden, immediate threat. Then anyone might fight back. Saint Peter, remember?"

"Don't start preaching, okay."

"I'm not."

"Sure you are. Every time we go round on this and you get your back to the wall, you preach. Saint Peter and all."

"All right, leave Peter out. All I'm saying is that it's altogether different fighting back on the spur of the moment than spending all your time training how to kill."

"But suppose somebody does break in, two or three of them maybe. You're the only one between them and your family. Then what?"

"I already told you. Maybe I'd fight. I don't know."

"And you think you could handle all three? What if they've got knives or a gun? Oh no! Not if you haven't been trained right, you can't."

Phyllis came back from the kitchen carrying two pies, pumpkin and mincemeat, to the table. Big in a green maternity dress, she bent over the pumpkin pie, tracing with a wet table knife the outlines of equal wedges. "Wayne?" she said. "Bill?"

"Pumpkin," Midberry said.

"The same," Bill said, then to Midberry. "Okay, but is it worth it? I mean you spend your whole life learning how to kill, doesn't it change you somehow? In a way, aren't you already dead?"

"Oh, come off it!"

"Your soul, I mean."

"Here he goes again. The preacher."

"More coffee?" Midberry's mother asked them. She refilled the cups without waiting for an answer. Phyllis dished out the pie and sat down. "Earl!" Midberry's mother called toward a storage room off the kitchen. "C'mon now."

"A minute."

"The pie's ready. We're all waiting."

"Where's that new duck call. I want Wayne to see it."

"Hey, Dad. I can see it later."

"And what if there isn't any war," Bill said. "Then you've trained a pack of killers, changed them into killers, for what? Nothing."

"Are you kidding? There'll always be a Cuba or something. You'll always need . . ."

"When you start talking foreign policy, then you're really on shaky ground."

"Oh, politics!" the mother said. "Not at the table. Earl!"

Midberry's father came into the dining room. He was a short, dumpy man with thinning brown hair. He grinned and blew a loud squawk on the duck call. Midberry's mother started.

"Will you come and sit down and stop playing around!"

His father sat at the head of the table and Phyllis passed him a slice of mincemeat pie.

"Ducks and politics," his mother said. "You'd think they couldn't keep till dinner's over."

Later that day Phyllis and Bill, as a late birthday gift, gave Midberry a thin, silver-plated, key ring knife. His name, W. E. Midberry, was engraved on one side.

"I ought to make one stipulation," Bill said. "I don't consider that an offensive weapon."

"Okay."

Phyllis and Bill laughed and Midberry, pretending, laughed with them. "Okay," he said again, shaking his head, the miniature clasp knife cradled in his cupped palm. "Okay."

Midberry sat up on the towel and dabbed sun tan lotion onto his nose. He rubbed some on his legs and lay back down.

He was glad Bill knew nothing of Maguire. It would be all the more difficult then for him to defend the Corps and his job against his brother-in-law's criticisms. For Maguire, Midberry realized, had made him question for the first time whether or not the Corps was right.

Yet what the hell was a marine supposed to be anyhow? You put on a uniform—was that supposed to automatically cut off your emotions and your questions? Because he actually listened to Bill when they argued, or because he sometimes questioned his own actions or choices, or because he wondered how the recruits took the training or how Maguire's harrassment might affect them—did that make him less of a marine? And did it make him less of a man?

Midberry remembered how he had once believed that when he made sergeant he would feel more self-confident. Just what he had expected he wasn't sure. Were three stripes supposed to transform him, make him as cocksure and untouchable as his sergeants had seemed to him when he was a Pfc?

He told himself it was crazy. He had never really believed rank could do all that. Stuck in his mind as solidly as his serial number was the discomforting knowledge that he would stay basically the same no matter how much he changed outside. Private, sergeant, staff sergeant, maybe some day even sergeant-major, no matter; Wayne Midberry would stay Wayne Midberry.

Still, he couldn't avoid the fact that he had worked hard to make sergeant and that when he had made, or become, sergeant E-5, W. E. Midberry, 1892500, U.S.M.C., he'd discovered he was disappointed. Some part of him had expected more.

And yet maybe he had become what he'd wanted after all. Maybe he just wasn't aware of it. Situations always looked different inside-out than out-side-in. His sergeants had probably squirmed under the same doubts he had, but had kept them hidden. In fact, the recruits of platoon 197, Midberry thought, most likely saw him now the way he'd seen his D.I.s—all marine through and through. He was sure there was nothing he'd done to make them think otherwise. He tried his best to set a good example for them; to give them someone they could respect. His tropicals and utilities were always starched and pressed, the military creases knife-edged, and there weren't many nights he didn't spit-polish his dress shoes and boots. He did calisthenics every day and played handball twice a week. He kept his weight at an even one-sixty and could match anything the recruits had to do in their P.T. drills. He studied the regulations and, what was more, followed them. He realized his handling of close-order drill could be better, but this was his first platoon and he felt that with practice he would improve. Most important, he could not recall at any time letting the recruits get the best of him.

It seemed logical to him then that the feeling he sometimes had that he was only playing a role, acting out his idea of a marine sergeant and a D.I., was simply because he was new at the job. Come September he'd have put in a full five years in the Corps. But he'd been a sergeant only a year, a D.I. little more than six weeks. And five years in the Corps was nothing compared to most D.I.s. Maguire was going on fourteen. By the time he had been in that long, Midberry thought, the Corps' way of acting and talking would have become second-nature to him.

He turned onto his stomach. He crossed his arms and laid his chin on them.

It was stupid for him to waste time worrying whether or not he measured up. He had the stripes to prove it. Besides, everybody in the Corps knew only the most squared-away noncoms got tapped for D.I. duty. And as for questioning whether the Corps was good or bad, right or wrong, useful or worthless—that too was a waste of time. Whatever he might decide, he couldn't do anything about it. Right or wrong, the Corps was. All he had to do then was to keep his mind on his job and leave the philosophizing to people like Bill who got paid to do it.

Midberry rolled over and jack-knifed to a sitting position. The beach was nearly empty. The lifeguard in the near tower held a leather-cased transistor radio to his ear. Down the beach, two couples splashed in the water with a red beachball.

Midberry decided that whatever Maguire thought of him was not important. Maguire did his job as he saw it, Midberry would do his as he saw it. Who was to say which of them was the better marine?

"Hell," Midberry said, getting up and stretching, "he's probably on edge is all. Worried I'll try to put him down somehow, so he gets to me first."

Saying it, he wished he believed it, then he broke off thinking and ran down the beach to the water. Lifting his feet high he ran splashing into the water until it reached his thighs. Then, a whitecap rolling in toward him, he gulped a breath and threw himself at the Atlantic.

ELEVEN

Wearing only utility trousers, his scapular and dogtags swinging back and forth across his narrow, hairless chest, Adamczyk sat on his locker box working on a letter to his parents. He used for the first time the U.S.M.C. stationery he'd gotten on the platoon's last trip to the P.X. The white, eight by ten sheets had a faint, pale-blue silhouette of the Mount Surabachi flag raising in the center of the page, and a gold eagle, anchor and globe imprinted at the top.

He wrote hurriedly of his passing the History and Tradition test that morning and of placing third highest out of sixty-six recruits. He told his parents too about Midberry taking the platoon that night to the base theatre to see "The D.I." It had been the platoon's reward for everyone passing the test. He started to write how much better things would be if Midberry ran the platoon rather than Maguire, then stopped and scribbled over the phrase. He was afraid Maguire might read the outgoing mail. He explained instead that it was almost sack time and that he had to quit writing. He signed his letter, "Love, Tom."

Adamczyk stripped off his utility trousers, pulled his dogtags and scapular over his head and lay them on his bunk. A white towel about his waist, he trotted into the steamy, gray-concrete shower room, hung up his towel and pushed a way through the tangle of naked, wet bodies to a showerhead being used by only two recruits. Someone in the room mooed loudly and the recruits laughed. Standing on the showerhead's free side, Adamczyk waited his turn, ducked in, wet himself, ducked back out. He soaped his body thoroughly, again waited his chance, then stepped under the needling spray to rinse. Another recruit moved into the spot Adamczyk had left open. Adamczyk elbowed his way back out of the shower room and began drying himself. Behind him, the mooing sounded again. There was a brief scuffling and then a cry, "Gang bang! Gang bang! Cooper dropped the soap." Adamczyk finished drying, knotted the damp towel about his waist and returned to his rack.

Dry and clean and in white skivvie shorts, Adamczyk felt nearly cheerful. He had enjoyed going to the movie. Like mass on Sundays, it gave him a chance to escape at least momentarily the squad bay and Maguire. Sitting in the theatre cut off by the dark from those around him, Adamczyk had felt as if he'd escaped the island altogether.

Even the sudden real flash of lights, the glittering screen gone dark, the platoon's return to the confining, well-lit squad bay had not succeeded in deflating Adam-czyk's near cheerfulness. He felt a bit more confident since his performance on the morning's test. The movie too with its story of a confused recruit who eventually squared away had encouraged Adamczyk.

After Midberry had ordered them into their sacks, Adamczyk reviewed the plot of the movie. Despite his mistakes, the odd-ball recruit had finally graduated with the rest of the platoon. At the film's end there he was, not just marching with the others, but stepping out in front as guidon bearer, the platoon pennant flapping above him, a brass band playing the Marine Corps Hymn, spectators applauding. Jack Webb, the D.I. everyone had thought was so brutal, ended up a good guy after all. It turned out the only reason he was hard on recruits was he wanted them trained well enough they wouldn't get killed in combat. All along, he was really pulling for the recruits to make it. When he went marching off with his platoon at the end of the film, Adamczyk had not been able to keep his eyes from watering. He'd had to hide it from the others when the lights came on.

"Hey," Adamczyk whispered. "Joe?"

"Yeh?"

"How'd you like the show?"

91

"I slept."

"C'mon, really."

"C'mon, hell. I was beat.'

"I thought it was pretty good myself."

Waite flopped heavily onto his side. His sudden move trembled the metal rack frame. "Red, that Jack Webb's so full of crap it's coming out his ears."

"Y'know what it made me think of? I mean the kid who was always screwing-up? He was just like me. Really."

"Go to sleep."

Adamczyk sat up in his bunk, twisting his head to one side to look up at Waite. "But I think I've squared away more now, don't you?"

"Sure."

"Like today on the test."

"You want me to whistle 'The Star Spangled Banner, or can we get some sleep?"

Adamczyk lay back down. "Night."

"Sure."

Adamczyk had begun to doze when he heard Waite's voice.

"It's not really such a big thing, Red."

"Whaddaya mean?" He waited, but Waite didn't answer.

A guy like that, Adamczyk thought, you can't figure him out. Nothing he says ever makes sense.

Adamczyk took the rosary from a pocket of his cartridge belt and crossed himself with the metal crucifix. He offered the rosary as thanks for the day as well as for the intention he wouldn't fail rifle qualification at the range the next week. His lips silently began 'I believe in God the Father Almighty, creator of heaven and earth,' while his mind planned how, by offering a rosary each night and by paying strict attention to the range instructors, he might manage to qualify.

Waite was awake when Adamczyk began to snore. He lay on his back looking at the white ceiling. He was not his usually calm self. He felt a vague uneasiness which he brushed off as fatigue. Yet he didn't seem to be able to sleep.

He had gotten a letter that evening from Carolyn. She'd written that there were no hard feelings on her part and that she wished him much luck in recruit training. Earlier in the week his mother had written to tell him that she heard Carolyn was dating "a very nice young man that Mrs. Macklin says is the assistant manager of the big Sears store downtown."

So, Waite thought, that was that. After all his worrying about how to get free, it had turned out to be surprisingly easy.

He and Carolyn had never been really engaged. They had been what his mother and Carolyn's parents considered "unofficially engaged," which meant that they had dated regularly for more than two years and that neither family could see any reason why they shouldn't eventually marry.

Waite had been introduced to Carolyn by a cousin at a New Year's eve party and since he had found her neither unattractive nor ignorant they had begun dating. She enjoyed swimming and movies and they went to the movies, as Waite did not care for swimming, at least twice a week. If nothing good was playing downtown, they went to a drive-in where Waite, after the main feature, would go as far as Carolyn allowed—which was, he remembered, precisely to the leg bands of her white cotton panties. Although that memory was particularly sharp to him now, at the time he had not felt terribly frustrated. Carolyn's holding back had given Waite a feeling of security. He wanted their relationship defined and limited.

Adamczyk moaned in his sleep. Waite listened for a few moments as Adamczyk quieted and fell back into an even breathing.

Carolyn could cook and she had a secretary's job that paid well enough. If she worked when they were married and saved her money, in a year they would have the down payment on a home of their own. All in all, Carolyn seemed such a logical choice for a wife that even Waite could not deny it would be common sense to marry her. Moreover, their families and friends had accepted the idea of their marriage so easily that Waite went along without much question.

93

Yet, although he had not rejected outright the possibility of marrying Carolyn, neither had Waite let himself actually think about it. Marriage, he had reasoned throughout the unofficial engagement, was something which happened to most everyone and which would most likely happen to him in turn. But it would happen later, not in the near future, not on any specific date. Like death, marriage was a vague and distant threat which seemed less real the less a person thought about it.

And now, no matter how he tried to reason it away, telling himself that Carolyn would not have been happy with him anyhow and that the assistant manager was a much better prospect, he felt guilty. He had let her plan her future around him, when, if he had let himself face it, he knew all the time that he didn't want to get married. He'd gone along with the idea of the unofficial engagement because it seemed to please his mother and Carolyn and Carolyn's parents, and because it was easier than refusing. He seemed by nature incapable of saying *no*. *Maybe* was so much easier all the way around. Or so it had seemed.

It was in the same way that he'd stuck to the family dry cleaning shop. Although with his brother Jerry and his mother the business was the center of their lives (with his father, too, before his heart had finally given out because he'd ignored his doctor's advice and had worked too hard and worried too much), with Waite it had simply been a job, better than other jobs because it saved him the trouble of clipping want ads and enduring interviews. Besides, his clerking at the store gave his mother hope that he would someday develop an interest in the family business. Waite had seen no reason to tell her different. As long as it pleased her, he let her believe what he knew to be foolish.

She had always had such high hopes for him. Twenty-four years old, still living at home, working half-heartedly in the family business, reluctant to set a marriage date—anyone else could have seen that Waite hadn't the slightest interest in anything worthwhile; that if it weren't for the family he'd be a bum. His brother saw that. But not his mother. Waite remembered eavesdropping more than once when his mother and Jerry argued over him.

"You be patient a little longer," she would tell Jerry. This was always her advice when the older brother complained that without him the store would fold. "Joe gets married, things will change. Right now, what's he got to worry about? He's got his room here and I fix his meals. He puts in his time at the store, that's all. And I don't need you or anyone else to tell me that if I didn't keep after him, he wouldn't even do that much. But married, then he's got himself a wife, children maybe, a home of his own, something to work for. He'll learn then how important the store is."

"And what if he and Carolyn don't get married? Then what?"

"What do you mean, they don't get married? Didn't you get married?"

"I'm not Joe."

"So why shouldn't Joe? It's not like there's something wrong with him. We can thank the Good Lord he's not like poor Mrs. Hendrix's boy. The whole neighborhood knows about him, and him teaching at an all-boy's school. No, Joe will get married when it comes his turn just like you did when it came yours."

"He and Carolyn could have an argument, couldn't they?"

"He'll get married," Waite's mother said. "And you wait and see if it doesn't make a world of difference. I know my Joe. He's exactly like his father was. You had to start a fire under that man to get him to move, but once he got going he did just fine for himself."

But he hadn't gotten married. Carolyn had pressured him constantly in her half-kidding way to let her set the date. Evading her questions as long as he could, Waite finally offered to buy her an engagement ring. They went downtown, picked out a moderate diamond, and he put down twenty dollars deposit.

He faked being cheerful that evening, but he was scared. The ring was concrete, inescapable. He realized as they were leaving the store that she would no longer have to ask him 'When?' or 'How much longer?' as the ring on her finger would do that for her.

After dropping Carolyn at home, he drove around trying to think, stopping finally at a neighborhood tavern. Drinking beer at the bar, he'd met a friend he'd not seen since high school. The friend told Waite he was quitting his job and joining the marines.

"How come?"

"Where am I getting at Chevvie? I took the test twice for foreman. Flunked both times. Eight hours a day goddam spray-painting chassis. The way that dust gets into your lungs, you tell me how long I can keep that up."

"You already signed up?"

"Uh-uh. Gonna go down in the morning."

"Maybe," Waite said, "I'll go with you."

"Why?"

"Why not?"

One week later a train carried Waite to Yemasee, South Carolina, to a bus which carried him to Parris Island, South Carolina, to a truck which carried him to Processing and to staff sergeant Maguire.

Anyhow, Waite thought, sitting up on the side of his bunk, his legs dangling over the edge, that was all over now. Carolyn had written she had no hard feelings. His brother was no doubt happy to have him out of the way. And his mother would in time get over it. Maybe she even believed the slogan that the marines made men, and would come then to see his enlistment as still another hopeful sign.

Waite dropped to the deck and went into the head to urinate. Coming back to his rack, he looked in on Adamczyk.

The redhead had one arm thrown into the aisle. The other was bent onto his stomach where his hand held the black-beaded rosary. Waite untangled the string of beads, then slowly and gently pulled them free of Adamczyk's hand. Adamczyk sighed, but did not wake up. Waite balled up the rosary and, having heard each night the unsnapping of a belt pocket, stuck the rosary into Adamczyk's cartridge belt and climbed back into his bunk.

Twice before, Waite had found Adamczyk asleep with

96

the rosary in his hand. He supposed he could have simply left it there for someone else to find. Fillipone would have gotten a laugh out of it. Instead, Waite had put it away. Why he'd done so, he had no idea. He didn't owe Adamczyk anything. Beyond keeping him halfway squared-away as a member of the third squad, Waite took no responsibility for what Adamczyk did or what happened to him.

And he could just picture what would happen if Adamczyk woke up and found him taking his rosary. He'd probably accuse Waite of stealing it. As if that wasn't a joke, Waite thought, that he'd ever want some cheap string of beads.

He could picture, too, the look on Adamczyk's face if he tried to explain about the rosary. Waite was sure Adamczyk would never believe he had meant to help him. Because he didn't have the same saintly ideals or high-blown emotions as Adamczyk, that made him a bum incapable of doing anything worthwhile.

So what? Waite turned onto his side, burrowing his head against the pillow. So who the hell was Adamczyk anyhow? A kid was all. A young dumb kid. A mama's boy. A holy joe. A shitbird so worried about his own precious problems, he couldn't understand that other people might have problems of their own.

TWELVE

"Night prayers, people," Midberry said. "Loud and clear. This is my rifle. . . ."

Standing at attention before their racks and holding their rifles at present arms, the recruits took up the prayer. "This is my rifle. There are many like it, but this one is mine. My rifle is my best friend. It is my life."

"Can't hear you people."

"My rifle without me is useless. Without my rifle, I am useless."

And it is an equal partnership, maggots, Waite thought, recalling Maguire's words. Well, maybe it was at that.

"I must fire my rifle true. I must shoot straighter than my enemy who is trying to kill me. I must shoot him before he shoots me. I will!"

The nightly prayer seemed extra long to Waite tonight. He thought how stupid they all must look, many of them grown men, holding their rifles directly out in front of them so that each recruit could shout at his assigned weapon just how much he needed and respected it. Like chimpanzees trained to perform on command. All the trainer needed was the magic words: right face, port arms, about face, forward march. Waite glanced to the side. Adamczyk, his thin face set dead ahead, nearly screamed the words. This stuff and the church business, Waite thought. Dead serious about it all.

"You're slacking off, people!" Midberry yelled. "Waite, quit dreaming. Can't hear you, Moore. Foley, suck that gut in."

Midberry had noticed a big change in the platoon since the first few weeks. Now when the platoon marched, heels hit together; when it sang out, it seemed like one voice. All seventy . . . no, not that many anymore, Midberry remembered. There'd been Johnson and Klein, Tillits and Quinn shit-canned and that made sixty-six. Sixty-six men acting in perfect unison. That's what it took to make good marines. And whatever Midberry might think of him personally, Maguire did seem to train good marines.

"My rifle is human. . . ."

"Too quiet, girls! Let's hear it again."

"My rifle is human," the recruits shouted, bodies and weapons rigid, "even as I, because it is my life."

And so what? Waite thought. If it was an equal partnership like Maguire said, so what? He'd have to be an idiot to start worrying about things like that now. Who cared anyhow? Not him. Not anyone else either as far as he could see.

"I will learn it as a brother. I will learn its weaknesses, its strengths. . . ."

"Louder."

"We will become part of each other."

"Keep it up. Keep it up."

"Before God I swear this creed. My rifle and myself are the defenders of my country. We are the masters of our enemy. We are the saviours of my life."

"That's enough, people. That's enough. Put your weapons away and get by your racks."

The recruits hung their rifles at the rear of their racks and stepped to their racks.

"Prepare to mount. . . ." Midberry reviewed the recruits and the squad bay. Everything was in order. "Mount!"

Recruits leaped into bunks Midberry waited for the springs to stop squeaking.

"Tomorrow morning, people, we go to the rifle range. We will be there three full weeks. During that time you will learn everything you need to know about your weapon in order to pass marksmanship qualification. Now there is no such thing as a marine who can't shoot. You either qualify or you ship out. You remember that the next couple weeks."

"Yessir."

"Get some sleep." Midberry flicked off the lights and left the squad bay. There was a light on in the hut. Opening the door, Midberry found Maguire heating water on the hot plate.

"Thought you were going home?" Midberry said. What was Maguire up to now? Spying again? Didn't he trust his J.D.I. to handle the platoon yet?

"Got ourselves a problem." Maguire nodded toward the corner where a recruit named Wood stood at attention.

Damn, Midberry thought. How could he have missed Wood? He'd thought they were all in the rack. All of them, he'd been sure. He wondered were any of the others missing? What was this anyhow, one of Maguire's tricks? His way of keeping the J.D.I. in place? Midberry was tired and wished to hell Maguire would ease off once in a while so he could too. Why didn't Maguire go home when he was supposed to instead of always prowling around? Was his wife that ugly that he'd rather stick around the squad bay? What was he, queer for recruits?

"Glad you caught up with him," Midberry said in what he thought was a casual manner. "I was just gonna report him over the hill." He watched Maguire closely as he spoke but detected nothing in Maguire's look that suggested suspicion.

"Oh, he ain't trying to go nowhere. He come in here just as I was leaving. When you went out to put the maggots to bed."

"What for?"

"Somebody in our little family has got light fingers. How much you say was missing, boy?"

"Sir, fourteen dollars. I'm sure it was in my locker box. I remember I looked right after we. . . "

"All right, all right. We'll find it."

The water began boiling and Maguire took the pan from the burner. "How about some coffee?"

"Uh-uh. Who took your money, Wood? Any idea?"

"Nosir. I had it right in my locker box, sir. I don't know. . . ."

"Better have some of this," Maguire said to Midberry. He dumped two teaspoons of instant coffee into his cup. "Could be a long night."

"What are you going to do?"

"Find out who took it."

"How?"

"I'll find'm. I mean to tell you there ain't nothing except a coward I hate worse than a thief." As he talked, Maguire jabbed the teaspoon at Midberry for emphasis. Midberry noticed Maguire's face beginning to flush. "A marine has always got to be able to trust his buddy. If a man don't trust the next one to back him up, then you get a platoon into combat and it'll fall apart. I seen it happen and I know." Maguire took a cup from the shelf and filled it with water. He mixed in a spoonful of coffee and handed the cup to Midberry.

"You report it yet?"

"I figure a maggot that can't be trusted to back up his buddy," Maguire was saying, "then he ain't fit to be a marine. We shit can'm."

"You call the provost marshall's yet?"

"I can handle it." Maguire looked at Midberry. "We can. You and me." Midberry sat on the edge of the desk. He was not going to let Maguire run this thing all his own way. D.I.s had rules like everyone else. If Maguire wouldn't call for an official investigator, then Midberry would do it himself. What would Maguire do then? Try to stop him?

"Drink your coffee."

"I think we ought to make it official." Looking at the deck, Midberry spoke slowly as if trying to objectively consider the situation as he was speaking. "The provost marshall's got people trained for this sort of thing."

"Yeah and they got bigger things to do than help us find fourteen bucks."

Midberry twisted about on the desk and put down his cup. "Still, I can give'm a call and see what they say." He pulled the telephone to him and picked up the receiver. "Won't hurt to see what they say, right."

"Wood," Maguire said abruptly, "get back to your rack. Don't talk to nobody, just get into the sack. We'll be out in a couple minutes."

"Yessir." Wood ducked between the two D.I.s and ran from the hut.

"I don't want you calling anybody, Sergeant Midberry. I want you to put the phone back so we can get down to business."

Midberry lay the receiver on the desk to have both hands free. He felt his heart pumping. But he knew he wasn't afraid. He was younger and in better shape than Maguire and he was sick and tired of being ordered about as if he were just another recruit. It was high time to set things straight. "This is our business," he said. "The way I see it any marine's business is to do his job and to follow the rules. And the rules say investigations are handled by the provost marshall."

"I'm the senior D.I. here and . . ."

"Dammit, senior or junior, same rules!"

"Fuck the rules! The brass can take the rules as far . . ."

"Listen. Listen to me, will you. What've you got against doing it by the book? We let a regular investigator handle it and we keep our noses clean. We can even get a good night's sleep. Hell, we can both use a good night's sleep, right? Look, I'll call and see."

Midberry reached for the receiver and Maguire grabbed his wrist. He tried to yank his arm away, but could not break Maguire's grip.

"All right, sea lawyer," Maguire said. "All right, now you listen to me. I got two damn good reasons for not calling any brass in on this. One, we ain't got the time. You get an official investigation going and we're not gonna make it to the rifle range tomorrow. You wanna set the whole platoon back a couple days? Maybe more? Not just that either, but you call for help and maybe you get one of these hot-shot second lewies in here that's hungry for rank. He starts asking the wrong questions and next thing you know we're in hot water."

Midberry glared back at the bulged eyes, hating them, the pig face, the voice, the cigarette-stinking, stale breath, everything about Maguire. He hated Maguire. He was not Maguire's buddy. They were no team. "I got nothing to hide," Midberry said. "Far as I'm concerned they can ask all the questions they want."

Maguire loosened his grip slightly and Midberry pulled his wrist free. He walked to the window and back again, rubbing the wrist, breathing hard. "You don't mean us, jack, you mean you! Somebody asks the wrong questions and you are in hot water. Not me. You."

Maguire was not going to get off easy this time, Midberry thought bitterly. He was going to find out just who he couldn't push around. Before this was over Maguire would wish to hell he'd left well enough alone.

"Shit" was all Maguire said.

"I told you all along I didn't like it, right? That I didn't go for beating heads."

"And who else?"

"What d'you mean?"

"Who else you tell?"

"Look, I got something to say I'll say it to your face, not go running behind your back."

"So you didn't tell anybody?"

"That's right."

Maguire laughed.

"But I'm telling you now," Midberry said. "You hear me?"

Maguire shook his head. "And you got nothing to lose, huh? Shit! They'll run us both up. What can you tell'm? You didn't know what was going on? Hell no, you knew all right and that makes you every goddam bit as guilty as me."

"I don't think so."

"Yeah, but what you think ain't gonna count."

"I don't think a court martial board would think so either."

"Even if they didn't, you sure these maggots won't say you hit'm?"

"I never touched them."

"Don't matter. You're a D.I. That's enough. Boots ain't known to have much love for a D.I. no matter who he is. If they think they can get back at you, you can bet they will."

"For what?" Midberry asked.

"I told you. For being their D.I. Private Midberry and Private Maguire. You want it that way? Not me, buster.

I worked a long time for these stripes. I'm gonna keep them."

Midberry went back to the window. He looked out at the dark night sky. He knew he shouldn't let himself think; just pick up the phone and call. Even if Maguire was right, were the stripes that important? He banged his fist on the window sill. He wished Maguire would shut his mouth.

"And you think you got nothing to lose? How long you been in the Corps anyhow?"

"You know goddam well how long I been in so don't ask, okay? And don't start in telling me how green I am, okay? I'm sick of hearing it!"

"Look," Maguire said. "Look, siddown a minute, will you?"

Midberry stayed standing. "You got something to say, say it."

"All right. Look, I'm not trying to put you down. Being new on the job, you do all right for yourself. You got a lot of high ideas though, about how the Corps oughtta be run. That I don't mind. That's good, y'see? I like that. You're a good man, good marine. But you gotta know too that everybody don't agree with you. What the brass puts down on paper, that's one thing. What they do, now that's another thing. Every D.I. on the island knows the rules say we ain't to touch a recruit. Yet I'll bet ninety percent beat heads. You know why? There ain't no other way. It's that simple. Over in third battalion they thought they'd try it different, follow the book right to a tee. Not one of their maggots had a hand laid on'm, there was none of the usual harrassment, the squad bays were new, air-conditioned yet! An experiment they called it. Well, I'll tell you what they turned out—garbage! The maggots from third couldn't shoot, couldn't run, couldn't march. You should've seen them at final field. Jesus-fucking-Christ. they looked like a pack of Mexican bandits. You think somebody did them a favor? Sure, P.I. was a ball. They all laughed about it. And they get into combat someday they'll get slaughtered. The brass might just as well marched the whole damned battalion out the first day and had those maggots shot one by one. Leastways, it would've been quicker."

"C'mon, who. . ."

"Lemme finish. You know what happens then? After final field? The brass comes down hard with both heels on the third's D.I.s for not doing their job right and turning out good platoons. So this is what I'm trying to get into your head. You think the brass don't know we're running thump calls, knocking heads when we have to? Shit. The only way to make a maggot shape up is to kick his ass. And everybody here knows it.

"It's like this," Maguire said. "The brass tells us we gotta do a good job training boots. We gotta come up to the standards they set. Now to do that, we have t'lay on hard and they know it. But there's two sets of rules in this man's corps; the written and the unwritten. That's something you got to learn yet. The brass knows damn well we're breaking the written rules, but as long as they don't see it and nobody squawks too loud, it's all right—that's one of the unwritten rules.

"Once it gets into the open, though, about D.I.s kicking ass," Maguire drew a finger across his throat, "then they got no choice. They run us up. Then they can brag in all the papers how the Corps won't tolerate brutality and how they plan to make an example out of ex-sergeant so and so's case. It's a game, don't you see? A joke. And it'd be funny too except it's always the D.I. gets the shitty end of the stick."

Maguire went to the desk and replaced the telephone receiver on its cradle. Midberry stood with his back against the window, arms across his chest, eyes on the deck.

He knew he wouldn't make the phone call now. He should never have waited. He was doing fine until Maguire grabbed his arm. The power of the grip surprised him; that and the wild look in Maguire's eyes. Despite his own anger, Midberry had suddenly felt a spasm of fear. He felt trapped in the small hut. He had no idea what Maguire might try once he got himself worked up. If he forced a showdown with Maguire, it would be one with no holds barred. So he had sat and listened. And the longer he sat and the more he heard, the less determined he was to make his call. Maguire scared him, then confused him. Drinking his coffee and avoiding Maguire's eyes, Midberry waited for Maguire's next move.

"I don't get no particular joy outta kicking ass on these maggots," Maguire said. "But like I say, it's part of the job."

Midberry finished his coffee. He held the empty cup in his hands, feeling it slowly begin to lose its heat.

"More?"

Midberry shook his head.

"We got the same job," Maguire said, "and we got to work together. I figure there's enough brass laying for us without we start going for each other's throats. Whaddya say?"

"What?"

"I mean, no sense in us losing our stripes over some little thing like this. Not when we can handle it ourselves. Hell, with the two of us working as a team, the provost marshall himself couldn't do any better anyhow." Maguire opened the door. "C'mon, you check the seabags and I'll get locker boxes."

"What else you plan to do?"

"Nothing. We find the one we want, we'll line up witnesses and put him in for an undesirable."

Midberry set his cup on the shelf and followed Maguire into the passageway.

"What if it doesn't turn up?"

"It'll turn up."

"Not if he already ditched it."

"Where could he go? Uh-uh, it's gotta be someplace in the squad bay."

"Maybe at chow. He could've shit-canned it."

"A maggot goes out of his way to lift something, he's not gonna toss it away."

"If he got scared, he might."

"Uh-huh," Maguire said. "It'll be around."

Midberry stepped ahead of Maguire to block the squad bay hatch. "The money's not marked. How we gonna tell if it's Wood's?"

"They all got that thirty bucks partial payment, right? We had one PX call since then and every maggot here

106

spent something. Now we find one of'm with thirty bucks or more, we figure he's the one."

"What if he won't admit it?"

"He's got the money, don't he? Where'd he get it—selling papers?"

"Cards maybe. Or craps."

"We told'm no gambling, right? If we got a big winner here, that's his worry, not ours."

Maguire moved for the hatch. Midberry side-stepped to face him.

"Wait a minute. Suppose we just can't find it. Then how do you find your man?"

"We're wasting time," Maguire said. He pushed past Midberry and swung open the squad bay hatch. Leaving the lights off, he shouted, "Hit the deck, maggots! Let's go! I mean everybody. Hit it. Hit it."

Adamczyk, jolted awake, was startled to see it was still dark and to hear recruits jumping from their racks and Maguire shouting. Fighting his nausea, he sat up, then realized he was holding his rosary. He stuck the rosary beneath his pillow and jumped to the deck.

Were they at war, he wondered, his mind racing. Maybe they'd been invaded or were being bombed. Oh God, he thought, now it would happen. He'd have to fight now. He was scared. He wished he'd paid more attention to the combat lectures. He wished they'd been to the range first. He didn't know how to shoot yet. They could've waited until after the range. It wasn't fair.

"First thing," Maguire said, "is get blankets over the windows. Each maggot's responsible for the window behind his rack. You animals on the end, cover the hatches. Hurry up. And make'm good. I'll be around to check'm."

Adamczyk worked quickly and quietly beside Waite fixing a blanket over their window. He thought it must be an air raid. But who in the world would raid them? What enemy? Russians? Chinese? Did Castro even have any planes? Adamczyk told himself it must just be a drill. They weren't at war. He was letting himself act foolish again. A drill was nothing to panic about.

Except, he thought, when Maguire was running it. And if it was a drill, where were all the sirens? No, Maguire was up to something. He'd gone crazy or was drunk and had come back to get the platoon during the night. There was a war all right, Adamczyk thought, and it was between Maguire and the recruits. Maguire was the enemy and he had control and the anger in his voice in the dark seemed to Adamczyk reason enough for fear.

Maguire went into the hut and returned with a flashlight to go from rack to rack checking the blankets. When he'd been to each rack, he told Midberry to turn on the lights.

"All right, maggots," Maguire said, the recruits blinking in the sudden flood of light, "get your seabags in front of the rack and open up the locker boxes. Move! You, Neal, get your ass away from that window. I don't want nobody going near those windows, understand?"

The recruits scurried about, obeying their orders. Maguire told Wood to wait in the hut. When the recruits had their gear in front of their racks and were back at attention, Maguire continued: "Somebody here's got fourteen bucks don't belong to him. Sergeant Midberry and I intend to find it. I don't care how long it takes or what we got to do, we'll find it. So whoever it was took it, you could sure as hell save yourself and the platoon a lot of trouble by speaking up now." Maguire waited. "It'd go easier on you if you speak up now. And we'll find you, you can bet on it." He waited again. "All right, suit yourself. Sergeant Midberry."

Midberry stepped to Maguire's side.

"Let's get started," Maguire said.

THIRTEEN

With the recruits at attention, their impassive faces hiding questions or complaints, Maguire and Midberry searched the platoon's gear. They began by checking wallets but, as Maguire had predicted, found nothing. Next they checked bunks. They ripped off sheets, pulled covers from pillows, ordered recruits to strip the covers from their mattress pads. Maguire found a crinkled photograph of a teenaged blonde cupping her small, bared breasts toward the camera, and he uncovered Adamczyk's rosary. The picture he kept. The rosary he looped over Adamczyk's head so it hung like a beaded necklace atop his scapular and dogtags.

"There you go, Doubleshit. Looks real becoming on you."

Adamczyk stared above Maguire's head. His teeth were clenched tight and the color rose in his cheeks.

"A holy roller wouldn't lift another maggot's money, would he?"

"Nosir."

"Maybe though you know who did?"

"Nosir," Adamczyk said. The idea came to him to say it was Fillipone or maybe Waite. He could lie and turn the tables on the ones making it tough on him. Show them how it felt for a change. But he kept silent. He'd have to have proof. If he didn't, he'd only get himself in trouble.

"Well, maggot, you had best start praying for yourself and the rest of this herd that we find the one who done it. You do know how to use those beads, don't you?"

Adamczyk did not answer. His body clenched and lips pressed tightly in an expression of disgust, he kept his eyes locked above and beyond Maguire. The stupid pig, he thought.

Maguire pinched Adamczyk's cheek. He pulled the recruit's face to him. Adamczyk's mouth was stretched open and his head forced down at an angle.

"You deaf as well as dumb, Doubleshit? Huh?" Maguire pinched the cheek harder. "Well?"

"Nosir," Adamczyk managed to say.

"You gonna pray like I told you to?"

"Yessir."

"You sure now?"

"Yessir."

Maguire pulled until his nose brushed Adamczyk's. "Don't," he said in a hoarse whisper, "play tin Jesus with me, maggot. Don't even think about trying it."

"Yessir."

"You get your young ass on a high horse and I'll kick it off for you, understand? Every fucking time, understand?"

"Yessir." Adamczyk, his mouth working like a carp's at a hook, tried to swallow the saliva pooling behind his lower teeth. Some of it ran down his chin.

"You are nothing, understand?"

"Yessir."

"A shitbird."

"Yessir."

"A maggot."

"Yessir."

Maguire suddenly thrust his arm forward, his knuckles digging into Adamczyk's cheek and forcing the recruit's head against the metal struts of the rack frame. Then Maguire released his hold.

"You make me sick with your pissing and moaning, you know that?"

"Yessir."

"You had any balls at all you'd know what we're doing's for your own good."

"Yessir."

"You'd shape up rather than fucking off all the time."

"Yessir."

110

"You get in combat, there won't be no time for those beads. Nothing but your weapon to keep you alive. That and what you learned here. Then, Doubleshit, you are going to thank your lucky stars you had that old bad-ass Sergeant Maguire to make you into a fighting marine."

"Yessir," Adamczyk said.

Maguire moved to the next rack and Adamczyk stood with his cheek throbbing and the rosary hanging about his neck. He wished the rosary were a coil of wire he could use to strangle Maguire, to cut off his stinking breath and his stinking talk once and for all. Or maybe he could sneak a cartridge back from the rifle range. Then he could even things up. He imagined with pleasure the shocked look on the pig's face when Maguire saw the loaded weapon aimed dead center between the bugged eyes. Then Maguire would change his tune. He wouldn't be so ready to call anyone Doubleshit then. It'd be the other way around. He'd do whatever he was told; apologize, kneel down and beg, anything.

Adamczyk's back and legs ached. His stomach would not quiet down and he was afraid he'd vomit or faint before Maguire found the money. He eased his back against the rack frame. He had to stay on his feet. If he fainted the others would all laugh at him again. And what would Maguire do? Fear rushed back over Adamczyk, washing away his hatred. He was a fool to dream about revenge. If he had a loaded weapon it would jam or he'd miss or Maguire would take the bullet and keep on coming. Adamczyk knew he would never try smuggling a cartridge into the squad bay. He'd been kidding himself even to think about it. If he really wanted to and had the nerve to take on Maguire, there was a bayonet hanging from his rack. All he had to do was turn around and take it from the scabbard. He could put it right between Maguire's shoulder blades. He didn't have the nerve. Maguire would hear him. He could never be a match for Maguire. No one could. Maguire like the Surabachi monument was hard and untouchable. You could hate him or fear him, Adamczyk thought, but you couldn't beat him. All you could do was stay out of his way the best way you knew how.

111

Finished with bunks, Maguire and Midberry began searching seabags and locker boxes. Midberry went from rack to rack, kneeling by each locker box and carefully going through its contents. "Check the mail too," Maguire called to him. Midberry returned to the first rack and ordered the recruits to hand over their mail. He opened and took out the letters from parents and girl friends, unfolding them in case the money was hidden between the sheets of stationery.

Further down the line Maguire checked seabags. He hoisted each bag onto his shoulder to empty it onto the deck. Then, squatting, he ran his hand into socks, overcoat linings, trouser and jacket pockets, opened razor cases and band-aid boxes, all the time scattering the searched objects about him. His progress was marked by a path of debris in the center aisle.

Three hours after the start of the search, after bunks had been stripped, seabags and locker boxes emptied, recruits were beginning to waver on their feet, some furtively cocking a knee or leaning on a rack. Maguire stopped for a smoke. Midberry sat beside him on the rifle-cleaning table.

"Some of these people are out on their feet," Midberry said, keeping his voice low so the recruits couldn't hear him. "Let's let'm sit a while."

Maguire shook his head.

"Having them keel over isn't gonna find us the money, is it?"

"Sure it is." Maguire took a deep drag on his cigarette. "Whoever the maggot is, he gets tired of standing, he'll talk."

"What about the rest?"

"What about'm?"

"Not their fault that somebody. . ."

"So what d'you wanna do, let half the herd sit it out and hope light-fingers is in the other half?" Maguire stubbed out the cigarette. "Uh-uh. Till we find the right one, everybody's guilty." He pushed himself from the table. "We can keep at it all night, maggots. You're gonna stand right there until somebody comes up with that money. How about it?" He began pacing the double line

112

of recruits. "I sure wouldn't wanna be in light-fingers' shoes when the herd finds out who it was kept'm up all night. Especially with tomorrow being the first day at the range."

Maguire suddenly turned and grabbed the T shirt of the recruit to his rear. "I heard you, maggot. Whining like some goddamned dog."

"Sir," the recruit said, "my leg cramped."

"And still whining! Giddown. G'wan, down on all fours."

The recruit dropped to his hands and knees.

"Whine."

The recruit began whining high in his throat.

"Good. Good dog. Now you crawl into the head and back out like that. Keep up your whining. I want everybody to be able to hear it. Git." Maguire watched the recruit crawl away from him, then he turned to the platoon. "The rest of you maggots strip. Yeah, yeah, don't stand there catching flies, just get outta your skivvies. Move!" He watched the recruits pulling off their shirts and shorts. "Your shirt too, Cooper, you stupid shit."

"What're you gonna do?" Midberry asked.

"Don't look so worried. I'm all right. Got a wife and kids to prove it, don't I?"

Midberry didn't answer. He no longer felt there was anything he could do to make Maguire stop. Earlier, he could have called the provost marshal. He'd had his chance then. Maybe he would have been lucky and bluffed his way through. Now he could only stand by and watch. He could, he supposed, openly refuse to help Maguire harrass the recruits. But that would help nobody but himself, his own conscience.

The recruits stood naked. Adamczyk's body was stark white, his arms, neck and face burnt a dark red. Under the bright overhead lights, his hair showed almost orange. Tall and thin, standing stiffly at attention, Adamczyk kept his blue eyes staring straight ahead. The triple necklace of rosary, scapular and dogtags against his hairless chest gave him the appearance of a strange tribesman lost in new territory.

What was Maguire going to do now? Adamczyk wondered. His nakedness scared him. It made him feel totally defenseless. There was nothing between him and Maguire. There was nothing Maguire couldn't do to him. Adamczyk wondered why someone didn't stop Maguire. Midberry should stop him. Or the officers. Adamczyk's eyes flicked to the other naked recruits. Why didn't any of them speak up? There were recruits as strong as Maguire. Mister Clean or Fillipone, they didn't have to stand for this. Recruits were to be trained, not tortured. Someone should make an official complaint. When the captain came in for inspection, maybe someone could complain without Maguire noticing.

At Adamczyk's side, Waite, shorter, stockier, darker, stood waiting for Maguire to begin. His body ached, but he forced his mind to remain as blank as his stare. Imagining what might happen could only make things worse. Waite's key to surviving Maguire was to meet things as they came, never to think ahead.

The dog recruit crawled into the squad bay. At his rack Maguire ordered him to strip. Then Maguire made him resume his crawling. Adamczyk and Waite watched the recruit crawl from the squad bay into the head. His bare cheeks caught the light and his testicles hung swinging.

Adamczyk felt he was going to be sick. He tried to regulate his breathing to calm his nerves.

"All right, herd," Maguire said. "Two steps forward, harch. About . . . hace. Spread your legs shoulder-width. Lean forward and grab your ankles. Good." Maguire looked at the double line of naked asses and laughed. "Too bad Klein's not here, hey. The Pig would be grinning from ear to ear."

Midberry ignored Maguire's joke. "Wood could be lying," he said, "He's sitting this out and maybe he's just covering up for losing the money himself."

Maguire's grin faded. His eyes were bloodshot and had bluish circles beneath them. There was a grayish patch on his lip from his cigarettes.

When the hell does he sleep? Midberry wondered. He's always here. Always on duty. "I mean, there's no sense keeping this up if Wood's lying."

"Right."

"Why don't you get some sleep," Midberry said, pushing his advantage. "I'll have'm square away their gear and hit the sack. In the morning. . ."

"Uh-uh." Maguire tapped a cigarette from the near-empty pack and lit it.

"You just said. . ."

"That you had a point. Wood could be lying. Go tell'm to get in here."

"We don't know he's lying. Anymore than we know the money was stolen. Maybe he lost it and thinks it's stolen."

The whining recruit crawled past them.

Maguire whistled and the recruit stopped. "Get into the hut and tell Wood I want'm in here on the double, y'hear. I tell you to get up? Then giddown and git going. Go boy! Fetch!"

The recruit crawled toward the squad bay hatch. Midberry noticed tiny blood smears on the deck and realized the concrete in the head was shredding the recruit's knees. He looked at Maguire. He thought there must be some way short of shooting Maguire to stop him.

"Don't go looking holes in me, sergeant. I know what I'm doing."

"Sure." Midberry turned and went to the front of the squad bay. He tried to avoid looking at the recruits bent forward in their humiliating positions. He wondered why they didn't say something. That would make it easier for him to oppose Maguire if the recruits complained. No one then would be able to claim he'd acted only from personal motives.

He reached the front hatch. He'd meant to look out the window but had forgotten about the blackout blankets. He didn't dare pull back a corner of blanket unless he wanted to chance bringing the duty officer down on them. Though that might stop Maguire. Glancing over his shoulder, he saw Maguire watching him. No, Midberry thought, when he went up against Maguire he wanted it face to face. Doing it on the sly, even if it did stop the harrassment, wasn't what he wanted. Nothing would be proved that way. Except maybe that he was clever and a sneak.

Midberry pulled a locker box to the hatch. He dropped the lid and sat. The entire length of the squad bay was filled with recruits facing their racks, rumps outward.

Lot of testicles showing, Midberry thought, but no balls. The recruits were supposed to become marines, combat troops, yet they couldn't even begin to act like men. What man would stand for the treatment they were getting? Midberry wondered what kept them from turning on Maguire. Could graduation be that important? Were they scared of the brig? Didn't they have the sense to realize that if they caused an investigation it would hurt Maguire more than it would them? Was it just fear then? Each one of them afraid of Maguire and afraid no one else would back him up if he tried to fight back on his own? It was ridiculous. Sixty-six so-called men afraid of one beer-bellied staff sergeant. Like circus lions being bullied by a chair and a whip into jumping through hoops. Midberry knew that if he tried to stop Maguire he wouldn't be able to count on the recruits' help. He'd have to go it alone.

The whining recruit was headed toward the back end of the squad bay. Wood had reported to Maguire.

"How much you missing?"

"Sir, fourteen dollars."

"Sure about that?"

"Yessir. It was in my locker box."

"And it come up missing when?"

"Sir, I looked for it after chow and it was gone."

Maguire glanced down the passageway at Midberry sitting on the locker box. Then he turned back to Wood. "You gamble?"

"Nosir."

"You don't think maybe you lost it somewhere?"

"Nosir. It was in my locker box. I'm almost positive that. . ."

"All right, all right. If you're sure."

"Yessir."

"In Korea we'd capture gooks sometimes. Sneaky little bastards they was too. I mean, you had to search'm everywhere. If they had any papers on'm when they was caught, they'd stuff'm in their mouth or even between the cheeks of their ass."

116

Wood's eyes wandered to the rows of naked recruits.

"Now I already checked their mouths," Maguire said.

"Sir?"

"You finish up. Start down at that end."

"Sir?"

"Asshole inspection, maggot! You're in charge. Get hot."

"But sir, I. . ."

"You wanna find your money, don't you? Don't tell me me and sergeant Midberry have been breaking our balls for nothing."

"Nosir . . . I. . ."

"You had best move then, shitbird. Before I lose my temper. Move!"

Wood came reluctantly to the end of the squad bay near Midberry. He hesitated, then faced the bare, upraised ass of the first man, stepped to the second and third and was moving to the fourth when Maguire stopped him.

"Hold up. Hold up." Maguire walked slowly to Wood. "You can't tell nothing that way. Use your hands, for chrissakes. Y'gotta pull those cheeks apart if you're gonna find anything."

"Sir," Wood said. He stopped, then glanced at Midberry.

Maguire grabbed Wood's ear, pulling him back around. "You telling me you refuse to follow orders?"

"Nosir. But I don't think. . ."

"Good! Good, you just do what I told you. Now."

Wood turned from Maguire and reached for the recruit nearest him.

"From the beginning of the line," Maguire said.

Wood went back to the first man in line. He stopped behind him, then hesitatingly touched the white cheeks with his fingertips, spread them, and stepped to the next man.

"Jesus!" Midberry hissed. He looked down at the white, fine-grained planking of the deck. He'd thought for a moment Wood was going to ask him for help. If he had, Midberry knew he would have helped. All he wanted was a sign from the recruits.

Wood made his way along the length of the first line, Maguire continually coaching him: "Spread'm open, Wider. That's it. Take a good look, dammit, it's the other end that bites. Get in there. See anything? All right then, let's go. Next one. That's it."

Adamczyk heard Maguire's voice coming closer. His stomach churned and he felt cold sweat breaking out on his forehead. He knew he was going to be sick and he felt helpless and scared, wanting to disappear or run away. His stomach began heaving. He tried to hold it back by tightening his stomach muscles and clamping shut his mouth. The heaves grew stronger. Maguire and Wood had reached Waite when Adamczyk gagged. His mouth dropped open and the vomit sprayed onto his rack and the deck, splashing onto his and Waite's bare feet.

"Damn!" Waite started, jerking up his head and jumping back. Maguire slapped the back of Waite's head. Almost in the same motion, he kicked Adamczyk hard in the ass. "Stay put, maggot," he said to Waite. "You too, Doubleshit!"

Waite returned to his stance. The yellowish-green vomit wet the soles of his feet. A piece of chewed corn stuck to the arch of his right foot.

"You are a real prize, Doubleshit," Maguire said. "You really fucking are!"

Adamczyk kept his head down, vomit and spittle dripping from his mouth and nose. His right cheek where Maguire'd kicked him hurt badly. It throbbed, and Adamczyk wondered if he had something broken. Oh wouldn't that be a fine platoon joke, he thought bitterly, Adamczyk shit-canned with a broken ass bone. How he hated Maguire! How he hated the platoon! "Sir," he managed, "Private Adamczyk requests permission . . ."

"Shuttup. You just shuttup. You just stay right there and shut your scuzzy mouth, understand?"

"Yessir."

"Oh, but you are a prize. Check'm, Wood."

Adamczyk felt Wood's chill fingertips push against his cheeks. Then they were gone and Maguire and Wood had moved to the next man.

His eyes began flooding with tears and Adamczyk bit his tongue to fight against openly bawling as Klein had done. He felt he could take no more. He'd reached his limit. Nothing about it was fair or right. Whatever happened, happened to him. There was someone always riding him, Maguire or the recruits. What chance did he have? They wouldn't leave him alone. They picked on him. No wonder he screwed up.

Adamczyk couldn't suppress his frustration any better than he'd held down his supper and he began sobbing softly, gasping for breath with his mouth hanging open. "Jesus," he whispered. "Jesus, Jesus . . ."

"They stick me with you," Waite hissed. "Why the hell didn't you stay home? Goddam cry-baby, shuttup will you. Shuttup. Will you shuttup!"

When Wood had checked each man in the platoon—Maguire even stopping for inspection the whining recruit whose knees left long bloody streaks on the deck—Maguire again addressed the platoon.

"Still nobody ready to talk? All right." He unbuckled his web belt and pulled it through the trouser loops. Prying loose the clamp and removing the brass buckle, he handed the belt to Wood. "Like this," he said. showing the recruit how to wrap the length of belt about his hand for a solid grip. "Start with the first squad."

"Sir?"

Midberry left the locker box and came quickly down the passageway. He had been up and walking toward Maguire before he'd given himself a chance to plan his action. Once started, however, he would be damned if he wouldn't see it through this time. This time he was not going to back down. Yet at the same time, he'd have to leave Maguire some way out. And he couldn't do that if he called him in front of the platoon. He turned abruptly toward the squad bay hatch.

"Sergeant Midberry?"

"Gotta make a phone call." Midberry pushed through the hatch and half ran to the hut. Inside, he went to the window corner and took a walnut M.P. stick from behind the radiator. He turned to wait for Maguire.

119

Maguire banged open the hatch. He looked at the desk and then, surprised, saw Midberry at the window. His eyes went to the nightstick and back up to meet Midberry's.

"We've been at it four hours," Midberry said. "We're getting nowhere and I think that's cause there's no money for us to find."

"Sooner or later. . ."

"And I don't think Wood's lying either."

"Shit."

"No sense in him pushing it this far if he was. I think he probably lost it and has got it into his head somebody took it."

Maguire took out a cigarette and crumpled the empty pack and tossed it into the wastebasket. He lit the cigarette. "So?"

"It's time to quit. We can keep our ears open and maybe later we'll find out something."

"You making the decisions here?"

"I went along with you earlier. As long as I thought we could turn up something, I said okay. But there's no sense in keeping it up any longer. I'm asking you to listen to me for a change."

Maguire yawned.

"We're a team, right? That works both ways then, doesn't it?"

"All right," Maguire said. "All right, fair enough. We'll try it your way this time."

"Thanks," Midberry said and immediately wished he hadn't.

Maguire pointed to the nightstick. "That wouldn't have done you any good."

Midberry shrugged.

"I'm just too beat to argue," Maguire said. "You put'm to bed, all right. I'm going home."

Maguire gone, Midberry stood in the empty hut looking at the hatch. He tapped the weighted walnut stick against the palm of his left hand. Outside he heard a car start. At the window, he watched Maguire's yellow convertible head down the short drive. Tires squealed and the convertible's red taillights moved off down the main road. Midberry put the nightstick back behind the radiator.

120

He felt the excitement spreading in him. He had actually won. Maguire had recognized his determination and had given in. Even the mistake of saying "Thanks" and Maguire's pretending he was leaving only because he was tired didn't ruin it. The all-marine hero had backed down. Now, Midberry thought, who was the one who was yellow?

He went into the squad bay. "Okay, people," he called out, "get dressed, put your gear away and hit the sack. Let's go. You can still get about an hour's sleep if you hurry."

While the recruits repacked their gear into seabags and locker boxes, Midberry sat cross-legged on the rifle-cleaning table explaining rifle range rules and procedures, even telling a few jokes. The recruits laughed at the jokes, yet kept busy and seemed respectful, and Midberry felt for the first time completely in command of the platoon.

FOURTEEN

At sick bay the records clerk told Midberry that Detar's knees were infected and that the recruit would be laid up for at least two weeks. Midberry walked down the long cool hallway to the end ward, the heels of his civilian shoes clicking against the white-tiled floor. He stood back at an angle from the open doorway and looked in. Detar, the whining recruit, was propped up in a hospital bed dressed in a clean white gown. He lay atop the white sheets, his legs bare and his knees wrapped in white gauze. He was reading the comics section of the Sunday paper.

Midberry had planned on saying something to Detar to make the setback easier for him. Now he was hesitant. He was wearing a sportcoat, tie and summer slacks and he felt ill at ease. He did not like the idea of visiting a recruit when he wasn't in uniform. Detar might even fail to recognize him without his sergeant's stripes. Besides, seeing Detar in the hospital bed made Midberry realize there was no longer anything he could say to the recruit. He had stood by while Detar had been made to crawl like a dog. Now Detar would miss two weeks' training and would have to be set back to another platoon. There wasn't a reason in the world, Midberry thought, why Detar should want to see Platoon 197's Junior D.I.

Leaving the sick bay and heading his car toward the far side of the base, Midberry wished he had turned down Maguire's dinner invitation. Maguire had surprised him by asking him and he'd surprised himself even more by not refusing.

"My wife's idea," Maguire had said. "Says she feels sorry for you having to eat all the time in the mess hall."

"Oh, that's okay."

"She can cook, all right. That's where I got this pot. Besides, with the herd at the range, you got nothing but time, right? How about Sunday?"

"Well. . ."

Maguire had written directions and the address on a scrap of paper and had handed the paper to Midberry. "Bout thirteen hundred, all right?"

And he had taken the paper. "Sunday?"

Driving toward Maguire's Midberry knew he should have refused. Getting buddy-buddy with Maguire could only complicate the situation further. Should he say anything about Detar? he wondered. How much did Maguire tell his wife?

"Detar's knees are infected," Midberry imagined himself saying as Maguire's faceless wife passed him a bowl of mashed potatoes. "Swollen bad and full of pus. He'll be laid up a couple weeks."

"That's a shame," she said. "What happened?"

Midberry spooned the creamy potatoes onto his plate. He passed the dish to Maguire, meeting the pale blue eyes. "Detar had to crawl around. As a punishment. That concrete sure chewed up his knees."

"That's terrible." She was looking now at Maguire. "Why was he being punished? What for?"

"Well," Maguire started.

"Whined," Midberry said.

"What?"

"Whined. He'd been standing at attention for three hours straight and one of his legs cramped and he sort of whined. It's a dirty shame about his knees. Still, these kids have to learn some discipline." He looked at Maguire who was avoiding his wife's stare. "One way or another, right sarge?"

Maguire would kill him, Midberry thought. Or maybe not. It could be Maguire's wife wouldn't even notice, just smile and go on passing the food. Maybe she's already heard from Maguire what he'd done to Detar. Maybe she was the type enjoyed hearing it. After all, she had married Maguire.

123

Midberry took the directions from beside him on the seat. He checked the number of the turn-off road and put the paper back onto the seat.

He should have said no. Either that or he shouldn't have gone to see Detar. What was he supposed to do now, go to Maguire's and enjoy the meal, chatting and laughing while Detar was laid up in sick bay? Detar stuck in Midberry's mind. He hadn't personally done anything to the recruit, still Midberry felt guilty for not doing more to help him.

He flicked the radio on, punching the buttons from static to talk to some banjo picking, then turned off the radio.

Well hell! What about Detar? If it hadn't been for him, Midberry told himself, Detar would have had a lot worse trouble than skinned knees. Midberry felt it was only his efforts had stopped Maguire from inflicting more serious injuries on the recruits. He felt sorry for Detar, sure. But there was no sense blowing up the incident out of all proportion. The infection wasn't fatal or crippling. In a week or so Detar would join another platoon where he'd be free of Maguire. Looking at it strictly from the recruit's viewpoint, Midberry thought, the infection had actually been a stroke of luck.

At five to one, Midberry drove into the trailer court's gravel drive. He cruised along a line of the two-bedroom aluminum trailers the base provided for noncoms with families. Air conditioning units jutted from a front or side window on most of the trailers. A few trailers had awnings. Near the end of the first row Midberry spotted a metal mailbox with "J. Maguire" painted in black on its side. The letters were hand-painted and uneven and the final "e" had been squeezed in at a slight angle. Maguire's yellow Mercury convertible was parked beside the trailer, and Midberry eased his car into the space between the Mercury and the neighboring trailer. Getting out, careful not to bang his door against Maguire's, he noticed the black tape patching the Mercury's top. The plastic rear window was scratched and cracking.

"Over here." Maguire stood in the trailer's door. Midberry came from between the cars and crossed the small scrubby lawn. Maguire told him, calling him "Wayne,"

124

to come in and take a load off his feet. Midberry held up a moment before the single concrete-block step, wondering how it would sound if he called Maguire "Jimmy." That's what the company gunny called Maguire. Why shouldn't Midberry? They were both sergeants, staff or not.

"C'mon," Maguire said. He took Midberry's arm and led him inside. He wore tan slacks and a blue knit shirt which plainly revealed the paunch his pressed tropicals and starched utilities usually helped conceal. He motioned to an armchair and Midberry sat.

"Couple minutes yet," Maguire said. "Wanna beer or coffee or something?"

"Beer sounds good."

"Coming right up."

Maguire gathered up the Sunday paper scattered on the couch, stooped to get the comics from the floor and left the room.

Midberry wished he hadn't worn a tie. The white shirt would've been more than enough. He could hear Maguire in the kitchen talking to his wife. Midberry pulled his tie loose and folded it into his sport-jacket pocket.

The living room was small and clean. In the far corner a portable television with a black plastic cabinet sat on a metal rollaway stand. A *TV Guide* lay on the stand's single shelf. On the wall above the couch—hung high, middle and low in a diagonal line—were three small white-framed pictures of flowers: roses, violets and lilies.

Midberry settled back into an armchair. On the footstool beside the chair were a half-dozen children's books. Midberry picked up the topmost one, *Rackety Boom*. He opened the small yellow cover. "Rackety Boom," he read to himself, "is an old, blue truck. The kind of truck that might get stuck. . . ." The pictures and text had been scrawled over with red and orange crayon. Midberry smiled, not at the book, but at his idea of Maguire as a monster. What had he expected, lampshades made from recruits' hides? "He lives on a farm with farmer Brown, and carries the chickens into town." There was so much tension and hustle in the squad bay it was easy to see only one side of things. But being in the trailer's small living room, seeing the pictures and holding the book

125

helped Midberry establish a realistic perspective. "He's a nice old truck."

"You can take that along with you if you wanna finish it."

"Oh." Midberry tossed the book on the footstool. He laughed, shrugging his shoulders. "Sure," he said, waited, but could think of nothing clever to say.

Maguire handed Midberry a bottle and glass and sat on the couch. Midberry poured the beer into his glass until the foam teetered on the rim.

"You got two girls, right?"

"Right," Maguire said. "Still trying for a boy. And I do my best, y'know." He laughed. "Right now, Dotty tells me, we've got one in the oven. Odds are this time it's a boy."

"Well, good luck."

"Jim," Maguire's wife called from the kitchen. "Will you turn on the TV and get some cartoons. The girls are done. They can come in there while we eat."

"All right," Maguire said. He went to the television set and squatted to twist the channel selector knob.

Getting fat, Midberry thought, watching Maguire. What is he, close to or just past forty? Forty, two kids, another on the way, a pot belly, a wife who tells him to turn on the TV, transfers coming up to who knows where, an understaffed platoon, promotions he might or might not get. . .

Maguire straightened in front of the television. He looked down over his belly at Popeye gulping a can of spinach. Olive Oil screamed in the clutches of a burly, black-bearded villain.

A girl of about three with dull brown hair and milk on her upper lip came running from the kitchen. She looked at Midberry and swerved widely away from him, half stumbling, to run into Maguire. She wrapped her skinny arms about one of Maguire's legs. "Pye Pye!" she shrieked, seeing the cartoon.

"You can come out now," the voice from the kitchen called.

"C'mon," Maguire said "Let's eat."

126

Midberry drove along the ocean road, taking the long way back to his own quarters. A red setting sun bloodied the horizon and the landward breeze had begun to take on its evening coolness.

So what, Midberry thought, if Maguire was a D.I., a marine staff sergeant? He did his job, that was all. Like any other guy doing his job except Maguire wore a khaki shirt instead of a white or blue one. Just another middle-aged family man working to bring home the bacon. Midberry felt sorry for Maguire as well as relieved. Maguire was no threat to him. That had only existed in his own mind, an idea stemming no doubt from his own insecurity. He'd been so touchy worrying whether or not he could handle the D.I. job, he'd taken everything Maguire said in the wrong way. What he should do, he reminded himself, was to keep his mind on the job he had to do and do it the best he could and not waste time asking himself and others useless questions.

Midberry passed the road leading to the barracks where he and other single noncoms were quartered. He kept driving. He wanted time alone to think.

They would pick up the platoon the next week at the rifle range. Three weeks later, the recruits would graduate and he and Maguire would get another seventy miscellaneous people to process into a marine platoon.

Three more weeks of training. The roughest part was over for both the recruits and himself. By now Midberry felt he knew Maguire fairly well. Maguire could be dangerous, but he was also a human being and could be controlled. Midberry had proven that the night of the search. He felt, too, that Maguire respected him more since that night. That would make controlling him all the easier.

What still bothered Midberry was the knowledge that to control Maguire he would have to wait for just the right moment to step in and take over. Waiting for that moment meant standing aside while Maguire beat heads. In his own way then he would be agreeing to the beatings. He'd be as guilty as if he'd done it himself. Wasn't that, he asked himself, what really had stopped him from facing Detar? Maguire had said a court martial would consider both of them guilty. And Midberry wondered if his brother-in-law might not feel he, Midberry, was even guiltier than Maguire.

So what was he supposed to do, turn Maguire in? He'd considered it—had at one time been almost convinced he should do it. Now he was less confident than ever that it was the right thing to do. The brass would only break Maguire and that wouldn't change anything. There were plenty of other D.I.s on the island beating heads. Could he get all of them broken too? Even if he could, and he knew damned well he couldn't, should he? The others were mostly men like Maguire, men with families doing their job the best way they knew how. Besides, if the brass really wanted the beatings stopped they could stop them without any help from him, Midberry was sure of that.

What choice did he have except to go along and do the best he possibly could? Quit, Bill would say. An easy answer. But then Bill made his living giving out easy answers. Quit? What would that accomplish? It would only leave Maguire a free hand with the recruits. Quitting would only be escape for himself, and Midberry would not do that. He was no quitter.

Midberry tried to push all thought from his mind and he focused his attention on the passing scenery. Street entrances were lined with white-washed stones. The lawns in front of the red brick headquarters buildings were cut close and kept free of litter. Along the roadside, palm trees stood neat and tall, regularly spaced like recruits lined at attention.

Memories of Maguire twisting Cooper's arm, strangling Adamczyk, punching Klein's soft belly flashed through Midberry's mind. He saw Detar in the white sheets with the white gauze about his knees. If Maguire wasn't a monster and was just doing his job, and wasn't responsible therefore for Detar, then who or what was? The job itself? The brass, because it was the brass that set the rules for the job? Maybe the Corps itself because without it there wouldn't be any brass or any D.I.s or any job or maybe any monsters?

He laughed, saying aloud over the wind streaming in the opened windows "I, Wayne E. Midberry, from Lima, Ohio, twenty-six years old, a sergeant E-5 with nearly six full years of service behind me, say the whole thing is wrong. The whole Corps is out of step except me. And it had best pick up the step right now because I say so." He laughed again.

That's what it boiled down to—one buck sergeant against the Corps—over a hundred-and-eight years of history and tradition. Midberry admitted he was no genius, but he wasn't dumb enough to think he knew more than all the commandants and generals and those on down the line who'd been running the Corps for almost two hundred years.

The sun set and the sky darkened quickly. Midberry turned on his headlights. He pulled onto the gravel shoulder of the road, made a "u" turn and drove back along the road the way he had come, returning to his quarters.

FIFTEEN

Cradling the weapon in the crook of his arm, Adamczyk carefully turned the M-1's small, grooved windage adjustment knob. The rear peep sight clicked sideways. He turned the knob on the opposite side of the weapon's receiver and the peep sight lowered. Sights set back on mechanical zero, Adamczyk checked his notes in the green spiral rangebook lying open beside him on the locker box. He lowered an ear to the receiver and slowly and carefully moved the sights three clicks right, two clicks up, the true zero setting for his weapon. He swung the M-1 up and pulled it into his shoulder. His right cheekbone pressed against the stock. Through the peepsight's aperture he saw Fillipone's back. The peep sight encircled Fillipone's broad, bare shoulders; the front sight blade midway between them.

"Bang."

Adamczyk lowered the weapon and looked at Waite.

"Get'm?" Waite asked.

"I was resetting my sights."

"Again?"

"Just wanted to have them right."

Waite took a can of bore cleaner and some cleaning patches from the jumble of cleaning gear on Adamczyk's locker box. "Your's clean already?"

"Not yet."

"Better get hot."

"I will. Don't worry about it."

"Who's worrying?" Waite said. "Not me. Not after today."

Adamczyk nodded. He had shown them all that morning what he could do firing for record. The big test at the end of rifle range training. Qualification day and he had made sharpshooter, missing expert by only three points. Seventh highest in the entire platoon. Way ahead of Fillipone. And Waite had barely qualified.

"You know what you are?" Waite said. "You're a natural with that thing. Really."

Adamczyk shrugged and Waite returned to his own locker box.

A natural. That could be, Adamczyk thought. Maybe that was why he'd done so well. The range instructor said he'd a lot rather start with a recruit that knew nothing at all about shooting. Starting from scratch he said was easier than starting with recruits who had to unlearn all the bad shooting habits they'd picked up plinking at cans.

Well they had certainly started from scratch with him. The first afternoon of live firing at the range, he had been terrified. He knew positively he would not be able to hit anything and he was afraid, too, of the rifle's kick. On the first round he fired, he flinched. The range instructor had stood above him suddenly then, screaming that the weapon was not going to kick him half as hard as he'd get kicked if he so much as batted an eyelash the next time. After that, Adamczyk had held the rifle as still as he could, his cheek tight against the stock which sweated linseed oil in the sun's heat. When he had finished his first clip of eight rounds, he'd been surprised to find his fears gone. The M-1's kick wasn't as bad as he'd expected. And he was astounded that he had actually hit his two hundred yard target twice.

Later the platoon moved back to the five hundred yard line to fire from the prone position. Squinting through his fogging glasses, Adamczyk could barely make out the target's head and shoulder silhouette. He pulled his weapon hard against his rifle jacket's shoulder pad and tightened the sling twisted about his left tricep and forearm until his arm nearly went numb. Holding the M-1 rigid with the hazy target balancing atop the center blade of the winged front sight. Adamczyk breathlessly squeezed off round after round, enjoying the quick solid jerk of the metal buttplate against his padded shoulder. Then, watching over the long stretch of grass reaching five hundred yards down-range to the sandbagged butts, he waited for the round markers to appear; white for a bull's eye, red for a four and on down to "maggie's drawers," a red flag waved for a clean miss. Adamczyk watched the white disc come up over the butts, then rise and fall a full eight times, followed by a red disc bobbing twice. The range instructor patted his shoulder and Adamczyk, loosening the sling and standing, experienced a surge of strength. Knowing he could hit whatever he aimed at, even at a distance of five hundred yards, gave him a feeling of confidence he had never before known.

Adamczyk fitted a white cotton patch onto the tip of his cleaning rod and ran the rod through his rifle's bore. The patch came out black and he got up and laid the rifle across his locker box.

"Where you going?" Waite called to him.

"Need a bore brush."

"Get me one too, okay."

"Sure." Adamczyk went to the rifle cleaning table, stepping over and around the clutter of disassembled rifle parts, cleaning rods, patches, rags, cans of oil and bore cleaner.

Like the other recruits in the hot squad bay, Adamczyk was shirtless. Except for his dogtags and chain, his chest was bare. He no longer wore the brown-stringed scapular of the Blessed Virgin and the Sacred Heart. He had lost it at the range. Most likely, Adamczyk figured, it had been torn loose by the rifle strap cutting across his chest in the prone position.

He passed Fillipone's rack, walking with a slight swagger. His utility trousers hung low on his slim hips. Dogtags and a c-ration can opener jangled from the metal-beaded chain about his neck. At the rifle range, the platoon had lunched on c-rations trucked into the field. A thin metal opener with a single, folding cutter edge was packed with each of the canned meals. Adamczyk, like the other recruits, had strung one of the openers onto his dogtag chain. He liked the feel of the added weight as the tags bounced and swung against his chest. And the opener was a souvenir of the range. It showed he was no longer a raw recruit.

At the rifle table, Foley, the recruit the others called "Mister Clean," was looking through the olive drab locker box which held the platoon's cleaning gear. With his shaven head, broad chest and shoulders and knotty biceps, Foley deserved his nickname. Standing beside him made Adamczyk acutely conscious of his own skinny body. He covertly flexed a bicep, then discouraged, looked back at Foley and waited for him to finish.

"Mothafuckin chamber tools're gone," Foley said, looking up, his thick, black brows knit in an unbroken line above his dark eyes. "Mothafuckers! You got one?"

"Not me," Adamczyk said quickly. "I need a bore brush."

"Here." Foley thrust a bore brush at Adamczyk. Its bristles were badly crushed and it was black with oil and dirt, but Adamczyk took it. "Thanks," he said. "Anymore in there, y'think? I could use another one."

"Uh-uh." Foley turned his broad, white back to Adamczyk and rummaged through the locker box gear with his huge hands. Adamczyk waited a moment, then returned to his rack.

"Find any?" Waite asked.

Adamczyk held out the bore brush.

"Only one left," Adamczyk said. "I had t'dig to find this one. You want it or not?"

"You go ahead. I'll finish up my trigger housing first."

"Suit yourself." Adamczyk went to his locker box and sat. He unscrewed the tip from his cleaning rod and screwed on the bore brush. "You won't do any better later," he said over his shoulder. "This is the only one left."

What the hell, Adamczyk thought. He stuck the bore brush into the muzzle of his rifle. The bristles were worn so thin that the brush slid easily through the bore and fell into the chamber. Adamczyk knew he would never get his rifle clean using the worn-out brush. That bastard Mister Clean, he thought. And then Waite acting like he didn't believe there was only one brush left. Why didn't Waite go see for himself? He should've gone in the first place.

Adamczyk bet Waite wouldn't have done any better, either. He would've taken the brush too and would've kept his mouth shut. With Mister Clean, you'd have to be a fool not to.

When he was sixteen, Adamczyk remembered, he had sent for the Joe Bonomo Speed Strength Course. He had waited for the mail each day that summer until the brown envelope came and he had taken the book and hid it beneath his underwear in the top drawer of his dresser. He wanted to keep it a secret until his parents and the kids at school began to notice his new muscles.

It was a six-week course with a cover picture of Joe Bonomo breaking chains across his chest. Each day's exercises were illustrated with photographs of muscled young men in scanty black or leopard-skin trunks, smiling as they performed a particular exercise. After each week there was a brief pep talk written and signed by Joe Bonomo himself. At the beginning, at the end of the third week, and at the end of the course, there were progress charts to be filled out. Adamczyk recalled his discouragement when he marked down his measurements on the first chart—six feet, one-hundred-forty pounds, biceps ten inches, chest thirty inches, chest expanded thirty-one inches. Yet he was encouraged by the section following the chart. No matter how skinny or how flabby he was, the pep talk told him, simply by following the directions in the book and by believing in his own potential he could make himself into a new man. All he needed was belief and will power. Joe Bonomo strongly advocated warming up before each day's exercises by taking ten deep breaths and saying with the exhalation of each breath, "I'm winning! I'm winning!" The secret to success was the will to succeed.

He had the will, Adamczyk had told himself. Mornings when he'd come home from serving mass, his parents still sleeping, he would take the book from beneath his clean, folded underwear and in jockey shorts would perform the day's exercises. "I'm winning," he would whisper so as not to wake his parents in the next room. The exercises he found impossible to do he checked with a red pencil as a reminder to do them later when he'd gotten stronger.

Adamczyk ran the cleaning rod down the bore of his rifle. He pulled it back up with little resistance, then let it slide down again. His arm following its slowly repetitive motion, the phrase began repeating itself in his mind "I'm winning. I'm winning. I'm winning."

And he was. He was sure of it. So he'd never finished the speed strength course. He'd quit after the third week not because he didn't have the will—he'd wanted muscles, all right—but because he was making no progress. The exercises checked in red outnumbered the ones he was able to do. His problem then was that he didn't have enough strength to get strong. It was different now. He was no Mister Clean nor Joe Bonomo and he knew he never would be. But he had gained weight and could make the two mile morning run without gasping for air and in general felt healthier. That was at least something. Besides, Mister Clean was not only stupid but hadn't been able to qualify record day at the range. With all his muscles then, he had a slim chance of making it through. Yet he himself, Adamczyk thought, he had done well on the I.Q. tests, had placed third on the Marine Corps History and Tradition test and now, as seventh highest man, had proven himself at the rifle range. Maybe Maguire and Midberry, Waite and Fillipone hadn't seen it yet, but it seemed certain to Adamczyk he was making progress.

That night after lights-out, Adamczyk lay in his bunk, exhausted. His right shoulder ached from the M-1's recoil and his entire body felt spent. Yet, showered and in clean skivvies, the fear of qualification behind him, his new self-confidence continued undiminished. He took out his rosary. No matter how tired he'd been, he had offered a rosary each night at the range for the intention that he would qualify. Now he made his offering one of gratitude.

Finishing the first decade, he caught himself dozing. He concentrated on forming the words—"Hail Mary, full of grace"—then realized suddenly that he wished he hadn't prayed at the range. If he hadn't prayed he could be sure he had qualified completely on his own—that he actually was, as Waite had put it, a natural. He tried brushing off the questions as stupid. Of course he had done it on his own. What else could it have been—a miracle? The miracle of the rifle range? Adamczyk smiled in the dark. The prayers had just helped him to do it on his own. In what way they had helped, he had no idea. But he was certain of one thing—he had qualified on his own.

He curled the rosary into a ball and slipped it back into the cartridge belt. Breathing deeply, he let his body's aches drain from him, felt the pleasant pain of his fatigue seeping into the mattress pad. He began to float and did not resist, gave himself to the slow spinning and slept.

SIXTEEN

They had spent two days on the bayonet range. The first morning they had been shown and made to practice the basic fighting movements—the slash, vertical butt stroke, horizontal slash, horizontal butt stroke and jab, all the while screaming and growling at the imagined enemy in the clear hot air before them. In the afternoon, bayonets fixed, but for safety covered with the green metal scabbards, the recruits had tried their tactics on ropehung dummies.

"Attack!" shrieked the baby-faced, pink-skinned staff sergeant in charge of the bayonet course. The ten recruits facing the dummies screamed, their teeth bared. Each recruit lunged forward on command to thrust and slash with the covered bayonet, to drive the M-1's metal-plated butt thudding against the stuffed canvas bag.

"Keep on'm," the staff sergeant yelled. "He's still kicking. Keep on'm. Get'm."

Maguire stood beside the bayonet instructor. "Get the goddam lead out," he shouted. "Show some spirit. Get in there and slash. Recover. Move."

The instructor blew a sharp blast on the silver whistle hanging from his neck by a braided rawhide thong. "Next bunch," he said, and the ten recruits stepped aside to be replaced by ten more from the orderly lines formed behind the bags. In olive-drab utilities the ten stood frozen at the ready position, their weapons thrust forward at the swaying, olive-drab dummies.

The second day the platoon was split into two groups. One recruit from each group was called to the center of the field where the bayonet instructor outfitted them with boxing gloves, football helmets, face-guards, and the tin-cupped jock-straps called "armored bikinis" which were tied on over the recruits' trousers. The instructor handed each recruit a pugil stick—a five foot pole, the handle wrapped with tape, the ends padded.

"You got to be aggressive as a combat marine," the instructor said. He stood between the two armed recruits as if he were a fight announcer presenting the main event. "A marine has always got to be coming forward, keep his enemy off balance. Now I'm going to bring two people at a time out here and see what you've learned. Remember to keep your weapon moving at all times. Don't ever let up. Not for one second. A marine lets up and he's dead. You remember that." The instructor stepped back. "Ready position."

The instructor blew a short, sharp blast on his whistle and the two recruits hurled themselves forward, screaming, punching and thrusting with the pugil sticks. The black-helmeted figure side-stepped and landed a solid blow to the side of the white helmet. The white-helmeted recruit skidded forward on the grass on his belly.

"Don't let up now," the instructor shouted. "Stick'm."

One pair of recruits after another fought with the pugil sticks in the grassy space between the two long lines of the split platoon. Adamczyk's line moved slowly forward. His hands were sweating. He counted the men before him in his line, then the spaces in the opposite line and his spirits lifted. He'd be going up against Cooper. He'd been worried he would find himself matched with someone like Fillipone or Mister Clean.

When his turn came he stood with his knees and elbows slightly bent. He held the pugil stick diagonally before his chest.

He wasn't quite sure how he should go about it. He wasn't good at fighting. Yet he thought, or hoped, this might be different. He would just try to follow instructions, lunging and slashing, remembering to yell and sound aggressive. And with all of the equipment, he assured himself there was no way anyone could get hurt.

At the whistle he let out a yell and jumped forward. Cooper jabbed the pole at his head and danced to one side,

138

ducking Adamczyk's half-hearted rush. Cooper's face was pale and behind the clear plastic face-guard his lips were pressed tightly together.

"Gotta be aggressive," the instructor said. "Don't ever back up. Get in there and mix it up."

"You maggots had best show some spirit!" Adamczyk heard Maguire shout from somewhere behind him. Then he lost the voice in the rising chatter of the watching recruits. A high shrill voice gave out a chicken call "buc buc buc b'buc ba-awk." The spectators laughed.

Adamczyk's ears burned. Sweat trickled into his left eye. As he moved forward he saw Cooper dance away, poking his stick out in front of him as if he were warding off a barking dog.

It was his fault, Adamczyk thought. He was trying to do his part, but Cooper refused to stand and fight. Even so, he knew Maguire would as soon beat him for not getting to Cooper as he would Cooper for running away. Rotten chicken-shit, Adamaczyk hissed, glaring at Cooper from beneath the fierce, rubber-lined brow of his black helmet. Gutless little chicken-shit too yellow to fight. Have to run. Have to mess it up for everyone.

Adamczyk came steadily forward, jabbing and slashing, the end of his stick thumping against Cooper's. Cooper back-pedaled, circling to his right, seemingly deafened by the white helmet to Maguire's threats and the recruits' jeering. Adamczyk lunged suddenly, faked a butt stroke and, as Cooper hopped left, brought his stick down over Cooper's guard solidly against his shoulder. Cooper staggered, "Hi-ya!" Adamczyk shouted. His opponent backing, he landed a hard right against the ribs, another on the groin cup, then jabbed the stick into the face mask. Cooper flailed back, his strokes missing or glancing off Adamczyk's stick.

Adamczyk heard the surge in the crowd noise about him. "Keep on'm," Maguire was shouting again and again amid the other voices calling for him to "Hit'm. Hit'm. Kill the yellow bastard!" And he kept on Cooper, forcing him back, grunting as he put his weight into the butt strokes and slashes. Cooper fell to one knee. Adamczyk banged two lefts onto the white helmet as Cooper, like a

139

panicked crab scrabbled sideways, then pushed himself up in a stooped, half-stumbling run. Adamczyk abandoned his strategic footwork and ran after Cooper. In the center of the open space Cooper turned, his stick starting up in defense, but Adamczyk was on him. He swung, shoulder and hip behind the blow, and landed hard and flush on Cooper's forehead. Cooper went down and Adamczyk raised his stick, then he heard the whistle and trotted back to his line.

Other recruits helped him pull off the helmet and gloves. "Hey killer," someone said. Adamczyk fumbled at the ties of the armored bikini. Maguire came to him, squatting to untie one side of the bikini as Adamczyk worked on the other.

"You get a man running backwards, maggot," Maguire said, "you got his ass."

"Yessir."

"Once you stop a man's forward progress, he's as good as dead." Maguire got the tie loose and stood. "Understand?"

"Yessir," Adamczyk said. He was having a hard time untying the last knot and sweat streamed down his flushed cheeks. Maguire's presence made him nervous. He was afraid he would make a mistake that would anger Maguire. Finally, he got the knot loose and tossed the bikini to the recruits outfitting the next combatant.

"Course House-Mouse wasn't much competition."

"Nosir."

The whistle blew, followed immediately by snarls and screaming and the thud of pugil sticks.

"But you done all right," Maguire said. "Get on back to the end of the line."

"Yessir." Beaming, Adamczyk ran down the line to wait for his next turn at mock combat. Maguire had actually complimented him! Adamczyk felt for sure now he had what it took to be a marine. He'd proved it on the tests, on the rifle range and now here. He hoped next time up he got someone a bit tougher—not too tough, but someone who would make it more of a challenge. Someone to make it a victory he could be more proud of.

He fell in line behind Waite. It seemed to him it would

140

be Waite's duty as squad leader to congratulate him on winning, and he was disappointed by the silence.

"Our guys are doing okay for themselves, hey."

"Yeah," Waite said. "We're real bad asses. Like Maguire says, trained killers."

Adamczyk dug the toe of his boot through the grass into the sandy soil. He used to think Waite was the perfect marine, close to being another Maguire; that there was nothing in the world could bother him. Now it seemed everything bothered him. At least, everything Adamczyk said or did.

"Don't you care how the squad does?"

"Sure," Waite said. He kept his back to Adamczyk as he spoke.

"What's eating you anyhow?"

Waite didn't answer. It made Adamczyk angry to have Waite ignore him, acting as if he wasn't good enough to talk to. Why all of a sudden was Waite acting so serious? He was the one who'd said it was all just one big joke in the first place, and that the best thing anyone could do was to play along. And now every time Adamczyk tried squaring away, Waite acted like some priest in the confessional, long-faced and solemn, pious.

"Shit," Adamczyk said. "It's not like anybody's about to get hurt. How could you get hurt with all that padding? The helmet and all? Cooper's okay. All it is is a game, don't you see."

"Sure."

Maybe Waite wasn't being serious, Adamczyk thought. Just scared maybe. That was possible. He'd acted tough the first weeks of training, but it could have been only an act. Maguire had said that the first weeks were easy, but that later the platoon would have the rifle range and the judo and bayonet fighting and that then he'd find out who the weak ones were. Waite could be cracking.

Adamczyk felt sorry for Waite. He knew though there was nothing he could do for him. Everybody in the corps had to pull his own load. He had tried to tell him, just as he himself had been told, that there was nothing to worry about as long as one played along. But that was all he could do. The rest was up to Waite.

141

Adamczyk turned to watch the helmeted recruits ducking and swinging in the center of the field. He hoped his second and third times out he'd do as well as his first.

The white-helmeted recruit staggered his opponent and the watching platoon cheered him on.

"Hoo!" Adamczyk yelled, wiping the sweat from his forehead, "stick'm. Keep on'm."

Judo was taught in a huge, hangar-like quonset hut. Wearing utilities, their feet bare, the recruits crowded in a semi-circle about the judo instructor.

The man they listened to was small and lean with darkly tanned skin and a head shaven nearly bald. He stood with his bare feet spread wide, knees bent, wearing a baggy white outfit tied at the waist with a black belt. His right hand gripped Mister Clean's utility jacket at the right shoulder, his left the recruit's left sleeve at the forearm.

"Hope Mister Clean don't hurt him too bad," someone behind Adamczyk whispered. Adamczyk hid his smile. The instructor did look terribly small and frail alongside Foley.

"With the hip throw," the instructor said, "you step in quickly with your right foot." He slapped his foot on the mat between the recruit's spread feet. "There. Then you pivot on your left, bend your knees to get beneath the enemy's center of gravity, thrust your right hip into his groin to break his balance, and using his own weight and momentum throw him over your hip, keeping your left arm tight to your body."

He slowly illustrated the action, stopping when he had hoisted Mister Clean from the deck. He lowered the recruit, still maintaining the two-handed grip.

"Everyone think they understand?"

"Yessir," the platoon shouted, their shout and its echo filling the quonset hut.

"In hand-to-hand combat, of course. . . ." The instructor suddenly pivoted and Mister Clean came flying over the cocked hip, bare feet kicking at air. The instructor dropped to one knee, his right hand on the recruit's throat. He held the recruit's left arm bent backwards over his raised knee. He dropped the arm and jumped lightly to his feet, hands

142

on his hips. "In actual hand-to-hand combat your moves are much quicker."

Mister Clean rolled onto his side, holding his throat.

"Christ," Adamczyk whispered. "Foley's all muscle and he got thrown like a sack of flour."

"You move quick enough and it won't matter how big and how strong the enemy is. Once you break a man's balance, he's yours. That's the most important thing, to get the enemy off balance and keep him off. Get him off balance, he's yours. That's the most important thing, to get Everybody got that?"

"Yessir."

The instructor went on to discuss the variations of the basic hip throw. As the enemy landed, he explained to the platoon, again illustrating the moves in slow motion, you broke his left elbow by snapping it backwards over your left knee. At the same time, he said, you could do one of three things with your free right hand. Using the downward force of the throwing action, you could: one, jam the web of your open hand against the enemy's Adam's apple, cutting off his wind; two, with the heel of your palm strike the point of the enemy's nose, thereby driving the bone up into the brain and killing him; three, with the index and middle fingers spread, drive them into the enemy's eyes. Any of the three moves would achieve the primary objective of incapacitating the enemy as quickly and thoroughly as possible. For number three to have its maximum effect, however, the instructor said, the fingers had to be strengthened. This could be done by practicing jamming the spread fingers into a bucket of gravel, starting with sand and working up to rough stones. Another good exercise was to practice poking out the eyes of cats.

"Some of you people here maybe think I'm joking," the instructor said. "But I mean it. You get hold of a stray cat sometime and find out what you are capable of doing and just how it feels to do it. One of the most important things to a marine in hand-to-hand combat is knowing he can kill when he has to. You can't stop to wonder whether or not you can stomach driving a man's nose bone into his brain or popping out his eyeballs. You do that and you're dead. Just like gun-slingers in the west. The pro's, they came primed to kill. They knew they could do it and that gave them the edge. Somebody else, some farmer or store-keeper who stopped to think about it, even only for a split second, he ended up dead."

That would be him, Adamczyk thought. Stopping to worry and ask questions and then ending up dead. He remembered in disgust the few fights he had had back home. He could never make himself hit first, even though he knew that with his build it was often his only chance to win. He would wait as if he were paralyzed, pushing back at the other's chest or shoulder, until he had gotten hit hard in the face or the other began swarming over him. Then he'd fight back and lose.

Although he would deny it if anyone else said it, he knew he froze simply because he was afraid. He felt if he did hit back right away it wouldn't do any good anyhow. His hands were so small and girlish and his arms so miser-ably skinny, how could he hurt anyone? He'd often had dreams in which he'd be in a fight and his hardest punches would only bounce off the face and belly of his laughing opponent. Even when he had gotten his hands on a gun the cartridges would fail to fire or, if they did fire, the bullets would always fall short. It was as if his fear created an invisible wall protecting his opponent. Adamczyk couldn't imagine himself winning a fight no matter what he tried, so he didn't try. He figured his best chance to escape a beat-ing was not to antagonize whoever was picking on him; to back down as much as he could. And his strategy often worked. It took all the challenge from a fight and the other, unless he was a hardened bully, would get disgusted or feel he had proven who was tougher and would therefore leave Adamczyk alone.

Adamczyk hoped judo would become second-nature to him. He imagined going home and showing up the high school tough guys. How surprised they'd be to throw a punch and end up flat on their back, having to beg before he would let them back up. It was hard for him to believe he could ever actually do that, but he reminded himself that this time his plan was not simply a pipe dream such as the Bonomo speed strength course. This time, as on the rifle range and the bayonet course, the instructors were right beside you and ready and willing to help you learn. Adamczyk figured if he paid attention and worked at it, there was no reason he couldn't learn judo as well as anyone else.

"But the very first thing," the instructor was saying, "is to learn how to fall. Before you begin learning the simplest throw, you have to be able to fall correctly. The object of making a properly-executed fall is to keep from getting the wind knocked out of you, keep from getting an arm broken, keep your balls from getting crushed. . . . In short, to maintain your combat effectiveness. To take what the enemy can give and get back up and incapacitate him. However, falling properly is not something a man knows naturally. You have to be taught to fall."

And the recruits spent the entire first morning learning how to fall. Spaced ten feet apart they began by sitting, then rolled back on command and slapped the left hand flat against the mat. Later they worked from a crouch. At the instructor's command, sixty-six right arms would swing down to knock from under the bodies sixty-six right legs, simulating a throw. Then the sixty-six bodies rolled back, the left hands slapping to break the fall. The instructor patrolled the ranks correcting positions, frequently calling the platoon to a halt so he could demonstrate again the correct falling procedure.

After a ten minute, mid-morning break, the recruits began falling from a standing position. The huge hut echoed the recruits' shouts and the thumps of their bodies striking the mat.

"Only way to learn is to practice," the instructor called to them over the shuffle of bare feet as the recruits rose after a fall. "Keep at it long enough, it becomes part of you. Ready . . . hit it!"

Waite swept his arm down against his leg and fell. He lay on his back until he heard the command to rise, then with the others jumping up on either side of him he got slowly to his feet and took up his position.

He wasn't physically tired, just irritated by the seemingly endless repetition of a single, simple action. But this was what he had wanted, he told himself. This was why he had enlisted. Orders, not decisions. Nice and simple.

"Hit it."

He rolled back and landed, waited and got up,

"Hit it."

then did it again,

"Hit it."

and again.

"Put some spirit into it, boy," the instructor was saying, facing Waite.

Waite caught and held his sharp reply. "Yessir," he said.

"Hit it."

The instructor stood watching him and Waite made his fall a good one, sharp and clean, then recovered quickly on the call to rise. The instructor grunted and moved down the line.

He had come unsettlingly close to telling the instructor just where he could put his "spirit." That, Waite thought, would have been real smart. Blow the whole thing with some wise remark.

The routine of training was making him edgy. The falls, the marching, the days themselves, like repeated strokes of sandpaper, had worn thin his surface calm. He realized he would have to make a conscious effort to control his emotions during the final weeks of training.

The falling practice lasted until noon. After chow, the platoon was marched back to the quonset hut. The recruits took off their boots and formed ranks in a semi-circle.

A new instructor came forward to face the platoon. Short and lean, in a white pajama-like outfit and black belt, he looked much the same as the morning instructor, except his hair was a lighter brown and his skin was not so darkly tanned.

"At ease. Seats."

The recruits dropped into cross-legged positions on the mat.

"What platoon is this?" the instructor asked, his gravelly voice nearly a growl.

"Sir, platoon one ninety-seven."

"What?"

"Sir!" the recruits screamed. "Plah-toon wan nine-tee seven!"

"Third battalion, right?"

146

"Nosir! First battalion, sir!"

"You say second battalion?"

"Sir, FIRST battalion!"

"You people sound like you're proud of that? That right, you proud of being in the First?"

"Yessir!"

"Good. My name is Sergeant Landon." He turned to the easel which stood beside him holding a six-foot diagram of the human body. The diagram looked as if the body's skin had been carefully stripped off and the flesh sliced away to reveal tiny black lines, red rivers and blue streams spreading in every direction. At various points in the tangle of black, red and blue lines were dark red circles.

"This is Charlie," the instructor said, tapping the diagram with a wooden pointer. "Charlie here's what you might call a field-stripped model of the standard-type human carcass, M2436A-X7250Y."

The recruits laughed. Waite didn't laugh. The platoon had run across other instructors who liked to play comedian and Waite disliked the pack of them.

The instructor touched the pointer to one of the red circles. "This," he said, "is a pressure point." He slid the tip of the pointer down the figure to the groin. "Let's start with one you all know about."

The recruits laughed again. Waite hunched his shoulders and sighed.

"You all know," the instructor growled, "that it hurts like hell when you get a size twelve planted smack in the family jewels, right?"

"Yessir."

"That's just the purpose of striking a pressure point. You wanna hurt the enemy bad enough that he's taken out of action, temporarily or maybe permanently." He tapped the pointer about the figure at the various circles. "You put pressure on any one of these points, you got the enemy in trouble. You can paralyze his arm," tap, "cut off his breathing," tap, "cripple'm for life," tap, "blind'm," tap, "in general disable him," tap, tap, tap.

The skinned figure on the chart angered Waite and he looked down at his folded legs. On his knees and at his

147

groin he imagined small red circles. In the distance he could faintly hear the pointer's tap-tapping and the instructor's growl.

The figure "Charlie" reminded Waite of the charts in Hygienics. There'd been charts for the muscular system, the circulatory system, the nervous system, every system. He remembered sneaking glances at them as he had waited for his pre-training medical check, standing stripped and at attention in a long line of naked recruits. A corpsman had come down the line checking the list of names. He drew a number in red crayon on each recruit's bare chest. When he had finished, he had come by a second time to make sure the numbers and names matched. He had been very systematic in everything, checking the recruits' numbers and names, keeping their lines in order, herding them into the various cubicles where their eyes, ears, nose, teeth, lungs, reflexes, blood pressure, testicles and rectum were thoroughly inspected.

"You throw a man," the instructor said, "You want to make sure he stays down. You can do that using the pressure points. You don't have to try to remember them all, just the main ones. That'll be enough. Memorize the main points." Tap, tap, tap.

Waite remembered a recruit at Hygienics mooing loudly. His D.I. had caught him and had written down his name. Waite wondered what happened to him. He doubted that the recruit was still on the island.

"All right, people, we'll start with the basic hip throw."

And let's put some spirit into it, people, Waite said to himself. Oh yes.

"On your feet."

The platoon, as one man, rose.

"I want you people to take the positions you had this morning, then pair off with whoever is next to you. And I had best not see anybody running around trying to latch onto somebody easy to throw."

The recruits followed their orders. Waite found himself teamed with Adamczyk. At least, he thought, he wouldn't have much to lift.

The instructor demonstrated the hip throw. "Now you people facing left assume the defensive position. That's

148

well. You others stick your right arm out like you just threw a punch."

Adamczyk put out his arm. His face had a serious and attentive look to it.

"I'll take it easy on you," Waite grinned.

"You better," Adamczyk said. "My turn's coming."

"When I call "Hi!" you people on defense step in and throw. Ready?"

"Yessir."

"Hi!"

There was a scuffling followed by the thuds of thirty-three bodies hitting the mat.

"Up."

Adamczyk got to his feet.

"Hi!" the instructor yelled.

Waite stepped forward, took hold of Adamczyk's utility jacket and, pivoting, threw Adamczyk over his out-thrust hip. Adamczyk, slapping the palm of his hand on the mat, yelling "tie!" to force the air from his lungs, landed on his back, his legs spread, knees bent. Waite dropped to one knee beside him and lay his palm on the redhead's nose.

"Up and switch. Ready . . . hi!"

Adamczyk shot his foot between Waite's feet, grabbed at the utility jacket and turned, trying to haul the heavier recruit over the bend of his hip. He'd not gotten the thrust right and Waite's body rolled off to one side.

"You," the instructor called. "Hey, carrot-top. You stick that bony goddam hip in there and pick'm up with your legs, not your arms. Try it again. Everyone."

They took their positions. Adamczyk tensed. On command, he got his hip low into the pivot and popped Waite onto his back, then bent, throwing the body over and down. Waite hit the mat and Adamczyk was on him, his hand jammed against Waite's throat.

"That's well," the instructor called.

The hand pressed hard on his neck and Waite grabbed Adamczyk's wrist. "Ease off," he said, looking up into Adamczyk's bright blue eyes. The hold on his neck relaxed.

"Sure." Adamczyk got up. "Sorry."

Waite moved into attack position. "Don't be so gung-ho. It's just practice."

"I said I was sorry."

"Hi!"

Waite put no snap into the pull, but let Adamczyk's own weight land him on the mat. He went to one knee and lay his hand on Adamczyk's neck.

Trained killers. That's what Maguire had promised. Well, they were getting their training. Crush the Adam's apple or pop out the eyes. Practice on cats until you get the feel of it.

He looked down at the thin, sunburned neck he held in his hand. He could feel beneath his fingers the blood pulsing in Adamczyk's neck.

What a hell of a way, he thought, to make a living.

SEVENTEEN

"Take'm off," Maguire said. "Everything but your skivvies. Fold your jacket and trousers and lay'm on top your boots so nobody loses anything."

In platoon formation in a broad aisle of the Clothing Issue Section, the recruits began shedding their utilities. On the wall before them a series of paintings illustrated the various uniforms of marines from the Corps' beginning to the present. A Revolutionary War marine in knee breeches and a blue coat with broad white belts crisscrossing his chest, stood holding a musket, his free hand braced on his hip.

Cocky looking, Waite thought. The same with the picture of the World War I marine, the leatherneck. But a marine was supposed to look cocky; looking tough and hard was half the battle.

"You can put the bucket down too," Maguire told Weasel. Logan reached up and lifted the bucket from his head. Sweat streaked his face and he squinted against the light. His pink tongue licked the spittle from his thick, loose, lower lip. He sat the bucket atop his folded utilities.

"Remember, Weasel," Maguire said. "It goes back on soon's we're done here."

"Yessir," Weasel shouted. At the rifle range he'd not had to wear the bucket. When the platoon returned from the range, however, a bright new aluminum bucket was on his bunk. "A present," Maguire had said. "More shine to this one. All the better to spot you by, my dear."

Utilities folded at their feet, the recruits returned to attention. The tailor got up from behind an olive-drab, metal desk. He was a thin, long-legged giant in a wrinkled white shirt and gray summer wash slacks. The baggy slacks were cinched tightly by a narrow pink belt.

Adamczyk regarded the tailor with distaste. The man's long black hair shined greasily and was curled up at the neck. The tailor moved in a slouch and his shoulders sagged badly. Adamczyk was glad he didn't look like the tailor, and he congratulated himself again on his gaining weight. He was twelve pounds heavier and felt stronger and healthier than he ever had before.

"Ah'd lahk y'all," the tailor said, "t'listen t'me careful as y'all can."

The tailor stood before the solid ranks of crewcut, sun-tanned recruits, his long, sallow face dotted with white-headed pimples. Adamczyk glanced at Maguire. The D.I. sat cross-legged on the tailor's desk, watching. A corner of his mouth curled slightly.

Attuned to Maguire, the recruits sensed his attitude. The tailor was no marine. He was only a civilian. He was nothing more than hired help. The tailor's presence made the recruits feel closer to each other and to Maguire, and they kept their positions of attention perfectly rigid and silent.

The tailor absently squeezed a pimple on his neck. He told the recruits that after he checked their sizes, he wanted them to go single file down the line of clothing bins and pick out one khaki shirt, one tropical shirt and a pair of trousers, one winter green jacket and a pair of trousers. There would be no need for mistakes. The articles and sizes were clearly labeled on each and every bin.

What does he think, Adamczyk wondered, that marines are stupid. He wondered if the tailor was trying to be sarcastic. He had better watch his step if he was. Maguire would as readily put down a tailor as he would a recruit. Maybe even sooner. After all the tailor hadn't yet reached the level of a recruit. Adamczyk hoped that Maguire would say something. He would enjoy seeing the smart-aleck tailor find out who was boss.

The recruits followed the tailor's directions. After picking up their uniforms they mounted a long, raised

152

platform. The tailor moved behind them, going from man to man, checking the length of trouser legs.

Adamczyk felt the tailor's fingertips between his thighs sliding up to his crotch. The fingers seemed to remain a bit longer than was necessary to measure leg length. Then they were gone and Adamczyk felt the chalk rub against his trousers at his instep.

He probably gets his kicks on the job, Adamczyk thought. Somebody ought to check up on him. It was bad enough to have a civilian ordering around and handling a marine platoon, he didn't have to be queer to boot.

Adamczyk glanced around him at the others on the platform. The dress uniforms made a real difference. The recruits looked for the first time like real marines. Besides adjustments, all they needed now were the cloth covers for the hat frames they were wearing. The frames, a stiff black headband and leather bill with a white plastic grommet rising above the headband on a metal strut, were to hold the cloth cover, tropical or green, stretched tight and in place. Without covers, the round white grommets reminded Adamczyk of haloes.

Except for leg length, Adamczyk's tropicals were a perfect fit. He felt good in the stiff dress uniform with its brass belt buckle and shirt pockets with flaps buttoned shut. His tie was knotted and pulled tight, held to his shirt by a gold tie clip bearing the eagle, anchor and globe. The uniform made him feel, not stronger perhaps, but more solidly put together, more self-assured and secure. He wished the tailor would let them get down from the platform and check themselves in the mirror. Adamczyk was eager to get to a mirror. He wanted to see how much different he looked.

Maguire had told the recruits they could buy shooting medals their next trip to the PX. The sharpshooter's medal, Adamczyk thought, a flaring silver cross centered by the Corps' insignia, would look good above the left pocket of his uniform. He might even have a P.F.C. stripe on his sleeve. He hoped so. It would feel good to go home in the tailored uniform with his brass and shoes all shined and wearing the sharpshooter's medal and a P.F.C. stripe.

Not for himself, he thought, but for his parents. He wanted the medal and stripe so his parents would have something to be proud of. They would be so happy to see their son coming home in his dress tropicals, bigger and stronger, his face sun-tanned and healthy.

His father had been against his enlistment, yet Adamczyk was sure both of his parents would be proud of him when he came home. It had always bothered his father, even though he lied and said it didn't, that he himself had never been in the service. Adamczyk's Uncle Ted had been in the army in the Second World War and had fought in Italy and he never let Adamczyk's father forget it.

He remembered his uncle sitting at the kitchen table across from his father, holding out a key ring with a miniature license plate dangling beside the keys. "How d'ya like that? I lose these anywhere in the country and they come right back to me." His uncle turned over the tag. "See. 'Postage guaranteed. Finder deposit any mailbox.' Whoever finds'm drops them into a mailbox and the D.A.V. sends them back to me. No name and address on the key ring. Some smart guy finds'm maybe, this way he can't come by the house and make off with the car. Pretty nice, hey."

Adamczyk's father shrugged his shoulders.

"Maybe if I pulled some strings I can get you one."

"What do you mean? Anybody can get one of those."

"Only vets."

"You're nuts! They send'm out in the mail. To everybody. I got one in the mail a couple months ago. License tag and an envelope for a donation."

"Where's the tag?"

"I threw it away."

"Sure you did."

"What do I need with it?"

"You lose your keys sometime, don't you want'm back?"

"Who says I lose them?"

"Ha! Listen to him," Uncle Ted said, laughing and

154

turning to Adamczyk. "Like he never lost anything." He turned back. "I'm just trying to do you a favor is all."

"When I need one, I'll ask."

Uncle Ted jingled his keys, then slipped them into his pocket. "Well, anyhow. I know a guy. I'll see what I can do."

Adamczyk's mother had written in her last letter that Uncle Ted's boy, Steve, had been turned down by the marines. She said he'd tried to enlist in all the services, even the coast guard, but asthma and flat feet would keep him out of service altogether. He was 4-F.

Adamczyk would stop in and see his uncle when he went home on leave. Or maybe his uncle and his family would come over to the house for a visit. Whichever, it wouldn't be all his uncle's show anymore. Adamczyk would no longer have to sit quietly with his father, listening humbly while Uncle Ted rattled on about army life. He could tell a few stories of his own now. His uncle had been in combat, but only in the army, not the marines. Adamczyk felt he would still have the edge.

And poor Steve. So messed up he couldn't even get into the coast guard. He'd like to have seen Uncle Ted's face when his pride and joy came shuffling home a reject. He'd bet his uncle had called the recruiters' offices and the draft board and anyone else he felt was responsible for the only son of a decorated World War II veteran being turned down for enlistment.

"Y'all kin giddown now."

Adamczyk followed the line down the platform's narrow steps. As he passed the tailor, he avoided looking at the man's face. Back in ranks, he took off the dress uniform and got into his sweat-soaked utilities. The utility uniform depressed him. He was once again only one maggot in a herd of maggots in a battalion of maggots on an island full of maggots. Like all the others he was afraid he might not graduate. Like all the others he was unsure about actually becoming a marine. Like all the others he had a long way to go.

Yet his chances of making it were good, he reminded himself. Would the Corps spend money on dress uniforms for him if they didn't think he was going to make it?

One of Adamczyk's many new rules for self-improvement was to avoid worrying about things he could do nothing about anyhow. He caught himself now and, recalling the rule, forced from his mind the doubts surrounding his graduation. After graduation, Adamczyk thought, after graduation . . . He again pictured his homecoming, his parents' reaction, talking with Steve and Uncle Ted, going to see Father Matuzak, telling the kids he'd gone to high school with how tough P.I. was.

Adamczyk's mind faltered. The vague sense of fear and depression returned. He tried to dispell it by reviewing his successes: the History and Tradition test, the rifle range, the bayonet course, his weight gain, his having better wind and more self-confidence.

Maybe he wouldn't go see Father Matuzak. And he realized that it was the idea of that visit that had made him uneasy. He wondered why. There was no reason he shouldn't visit his old pastor. He'd wear his uniform too. He had done nothing to be ashamed of. He had gone to Mass and communion every Sunday since he'd been on the island. He'd gone to see the chaplain to talk about his problems, even though he had had to buck Maguire to do it, and he had tried since then to follow the chaplain's advice. Father Matuzak should be proud of him. And would be, Adamczyk thought. Back home on leave, he'd go to noon high Mass at Saint Stephen's. He imagined himself in his uniform walking with his mother up the center aisle with all of the people watching.

"That's it," the tailor drawled. "Y'all done."

"All right," Maguire said, not to the tailor, but to the platoon. He slid from the desk and put on his D.I. cover. "Ten-hut. Left face. Move out by squads through that hatch and form up on the hard-stand. Forward . . . harch."

Outside, the sun was high and small and white, and the scorching blacktop paving stuck to the recruits' boot soles. Maguire looked over the platoon.

"Weasel."

"Yessir."

"We're outside."

"Sir?"

"It's daylight and I can see that fucked-up face of yours."

"Yessir!" Weasel hurriedly put the bucket over his head and returned to attention, a green robot with an aluminum head.

Maguire rapped twice on the bucket with his metal-tipped swagger stick. Weasel executed a left face. "Now the rest of you shitbirds," Maguire said, "left . . . hace. Forward . . ." he raised the stick beside the gleaming bucket, then at the moment he spoke, struck a single sharp blow, "Harch!"

EIGHTEEN

It happened before Waite realized he was moving. He had been sitting on his locker box during the evening free time, thinking it was no wonder he felt upset all the time, always having to hurry to chow, hurry into ranks, hurry into the squad bay, Maguire or Midberry yelling orders every minute. He'd been only dimly aware of Fillipone trying to prod Weasel into a fight. He remembered something about Fillipone telling the others Weasel's lip was not an accident and that if Weasel would kneel down he'd show them how he'd gotten the lip. Then, suddenly, he was standing over Fillipone who was crawling backwards on the deck, nose pouring blood, hands up to block the sharp kicks at his head and ribs. It had taken four recruits to pull Waite back. Adamczyk was one of the four, grabbing at Waite's arm, his blue eyes big in surprise. Over the pounding in his ears, Waite could hear Adamczyk's hoarse whisper, "Take it easy, Joe. Take it easy. Take it easy."

Now he tried to take it easy. Night prayers over, the platoon was in the sack. Taps had sounded. Waite lay on his back, controlling his breathing and swirl of thoughts and emotions, trying to take it easy.

From beneath him, Adamczyk whispered that if he needed any help he could count on him. Waite laughed aloud and Adamczyk stopped talking.

"You scared?" Adamczyk had asked him earlier.

"Of what?"

"Fillipone. He said he'd get you, didn't you hear?"

"Shit," Waite had said, his fear nearly cramping his

throat. "That Wop's not that crazy. He knows I'll kill him if he tries anything."

Adamczyk had kept asking questions: Why had he done it? How come he didn't do it sooner? What would he do if Fillipone's buddies ganged up on him? But Waite ignored him. He wanted to be by himself and by refusing to talk he got what he wanted. Adamczyk had finally given up and left.

He hadn't been lying, Waite thought. Not exactly. It wasn't Fillipone or his gang that scared him. Just himself. He was afraid now that he'd blown up, he wouldn't be able to get the lid back on. He felt as if he had accidentally punched his fist through a dam. Water rushing through was widening the hole. Poor little Dutch boy, he thought angrily, the whole damned dam could go anytime.

Still he hoped it wasn't too late. Patching the wall might help hold it at least for a while. He had no other choice. The only way he was going to survive Maguire and the island was to keep whatever it was inside of him dammed up. If he let it loose, he realized—in a rush remembering his mother and Carolyn, his job, his whole life leading up to his lying on his back keeping himself quiet in the narrow rack in the long dark squad bay— he wouldn't even know who he was. He had always kept himself shut tight. Who could tell what would come out if he didn't?

That was what had him scared. Not getting his ass kicked by Fillipone or his bunch. Not even Maguire shit-canning him. Just himself. Waite felt as if the rack he lay on had shot straight up into the air until he was swaying with it high up in the wind. Like a flagpole sitter or high-wire artist. One wrong move and the fall would be fatal.

He was sweating and his face burned. Heat exhaustion, he thought, and was glad he was sick. They would have to put him in sick bay. The beds would be clean and the small, white room quiet and orderly. He would be taken care of. And if he played it smart and faked relapses he might be able to spend the rest of his recruit time there. As far as he was concerned, they could keep him in sick bay the rest of his life.

159

Turning onto his side he drifted off to sleep and onto a tower swaying high in the wind. He had to hold on for his life. Above him, the sun was white hot. A Parris Island sun beating him down, drying him out, boiling his brains. Yet he noticed that from time to time the sun was obscured by shadows. Clouds, Waite thought.

Then, twisting to look up, he saw the clouds were huge dark birds circling high above him. Their great, spread wings blotted out the sun in their spirals and sweeps.

As Waite watched, one bird broke away from the rest and came spiralling down. It was a vulture—a giant vulture with a long, naked neck and hungry red eyes. He should never have looked, Waite thought. He cursed his curiosity. If he hadn't looked, they wouldn't have bothered him. He should have minded his own business. Now, whatever happened, he had brought it upon himself.

He searched for something to defend himself with, but saw what he hadn't noticed before, that the platform was utterly empty and that he was stripped naked. Above him the monstrous black wings opened. He curled himself tightly into a ball and held his breath, waiting naked and frail for the iron talons to puncture his skull and body.

The great vulture lowered its tremendous weight onto him, bending Waite's ribs in against his lungs. He felt the bird settle itself. He realized then that he was not going to be carried off. He felt no talons against his skin. The great wings flapped once, twice, then tucked in along the long, dark body. The tail feathers ruffled. Waite thought he heard a deep, almost rumbling, cooing.

Oh God! She thinks I'm an egg! She's trying to hatch me!

If he'd had a fever it was gone by morning along with his fears. He woke feeling drained and empty. Throughout the march to and from morning chow, however, Waite thought out his problem. He decided there was not the least cause for panic. There was no certainty that he would blow up again. Things could run smoothly again if he only watched himself closely and tried to deal sensibly with whatever problems came up. All he had to do, he thought, his feet automatically obeying Midberry's cadence as the platoon returned to the squad bay from the mess hall, was to admit to himself what bothered him. That would prevent another build-up of tension. After getting his problems into the open, he could devise a plan of action. Maybe there would be some things that bothered him that he could do nothing about, but at least he would have given it a try. He hoped that that in itself would help him avoid the sort of explosion he'd had with Fillipone.

Throughout the long day spent at lectures on platoon tactics, night-fighting, and reconnaissance techniques, therefore, Waite concentrated on discovering the root of his problem. From the surface of his muddled thoughts, he skimmed off several incidents which had angered him: the judo instructor's crude attempts at humor, the incessant marching and standing at attention and saluting, Maguire's shouting, Maguire's frequent "thump calls," Maguire's punishment of Detar, Maguire's making Weasel wear a bucket on his head. Waite's mind gave up a score of single, irritating incidents, yet he could not seem to delve deep enough to discover why they had happened. Maguire? That seemed too easy an answer, that there was simply a personality conflict between him and Maguire. Nor could he answer why the incidents had gotten under his skin. Just his nerves? He hoped so. But even if it was only his nerves, Waite thought it best to do something about the situation rather than wait for another explosion. He decided therefore to take his complaints straight to the D.I. To Midberry, of course, not Maguire.

"Sir," Waite said, "take the Weasel for example. He's always getting hit on the head with that swagger stick."

"Doesn't hurt with a bucket on, does it?"

"Sir, maybe not. But he gets hit for screwing up at drill and if he didn't have the bucket on his head in the first place, he could see and probably wouldn't screw up so much."

"You don't really believe that," Midberry said. He smiled sadly. "You and I both know that Weasel would find a way to screw up no matter what. Right?"

"Sir, I don't know." Waite felt himself weakening. It would be so easy and comfortable to slide into the usual kidding about Weasel. But he braced himself with the knowledge that if he let his questions slip away here, they would be waiting for him back at his rack. "Yessir," he said abruptly, "I do believe it. I think Weasel could square away as well as anyone else if he had half a chance."

"What's your worry, anyhow, boy?" Midberry leaned forward as he talked as if to get a closer look at Waite. He propped his elbows on the desk, the swivel chair tilting forward. "You worried Sergeant Maguire isn't being fair? That it?"

"Sir, there just doesn't seem to be any point to it."

Midberry took his time lighting a long, black cigar. "Sergeant Maguire," he began, then coughed out a cloud of yellowish-gray smoke. He looked hard at Waite through his watering eyes, but the recruit's face was impassive, his eyes locked on a point above and beyond Midberry. Midberry laid the smoldering cigar in a metal ashtray. "Sergeant Maguire," he said with obviously strained patience, "has more years in this man's Corps than you've got weeks, understand?"

"Yessir."

"He's been turning out top-notch recruit platoons for two years. Seven first-rate platoons. And you think you know better than he does how to train recruits?"

"Sir, I'm only saying there's no point in Weasel having . . ."

"A marine has got to be able to take it; that's why the bucket. Sergeant Maguire wants to see how much the Weasel can take. He wants to see if Weasel measures up. It's for his own good."

Waite was aware of Midberry's growing exasperation, yet he was determined to push his questioning until he got a satisfactory answer. "Sir, take what?"

"Pressure! Pressure. Don't act so damned dumb, boy. You know a marine's got to be able to take it. A man gets into combat, there's tremendous pressure on him. He has to take it and keep right on going."

"With a bucket on his head?"

Midberry shot out of the chair. "Don't get smart with me, maggot! I'll have you doing pushups the rest of the goddamn day, you get smart with me. Understand?"

"Yessir!"

"When you open your rotten mouth, you say 'sir,' understand?"

"Yessir."

"You sure?"

"Sir," Waite shouted. "I understand."

Midberry paused. He picked up the dead cigar, then thought better of it and put it back in the ashtray. "Weasel in your squad?"

"Nosir."

"So what're you worrying for?"

That was a good question, Waite thought. Another good question. If he kept at it he'd have quite a list.

The recruit's hesitation was a good enough answer for Midberry. He knew from platoon tactics—he ought to, he thought, having taught the course for a year at LaJeune— that once you caught the enemy off guard, you should immediately seize the offensive. He started to speak, then hesitated. Was this the enemy?

"Sir," Waite said, "the reason I wanted . . ."

And now Waite was seizing the offensive. Yes, he was the enemy! What Midberry wanted was to put a neat stop to a discussion which had started to get out of hand, and what Waite wanted was to keep it going. Midberry cut in on the recruit "Don't you have enough to worry about in your own squad?"

"Sir, I . . . yessir."

"Adamczyk could start back-sliding anytime. He's not in the clear. In fact, he's far from being squared away. And your job's to see that he gets and stays squared-away, right?"

"Yessir, but . . ."

"Powers is sloppy on close-order drill. He could use a little extra pushing on your part. The same with Rodman. You keeping on these people?"

"Sir, I try to."

"And you didn't do a very outstanding job at the range, did you?"

"Nosir."

"You've been sloughing off ever since then, too. What's your trouble, anyhow, boy? You think you're in the home stretch now and can afford to coast a while? Or you changed your mind about getting to be a marine? What is it?"

"Nosir."

"Nosir, what?"

"Sir, my trouble is what I was trying to tell y . . . the drill instructor, I mean. All this stuff with Weasel, and the way Sergeant Maguire . . ."

"I heard all that already. Now you listen to what I'm saying." Midberry stepped around the desk. "I'm telling you for your own good. Sergeant Maguire knows what he's doing, and your buddies don't need any help from you. They can take care of themselves. So quit wasting time worrying about Weasel and Cooper and all the sad sacks in this platoon and take care of yourself and your squad. Don't start thinking you got it made. A good marine never lets up. A recruit lets up and he's through, understand?"

"Yessir."

Midberry clapped a hand onto Waite's shoulder. "Only a couple more weeks, it'll all be over."

"Yessir." Some answer, Waite thought. He waited for Midberry's hand to leave his shoulder. Maybe all a sergeant was allowed to hand out were half-ass answers. Real questions and answers were handled by the generals. Or maybe only the commandant. All questions were left up to the commandant. Everybody else got orders.

Midberry could sense the stiffness and anger in Waite's shoulder. He wished he had kept his hand to himself. He wasn't the type that could make an overt gesture like back-slapping without feeling awkward. And Waite made it worse. "You've been doing okay so far," he said. "I wouldn't want to see Maguire shit-can you, so square away, okay?" He didn't wait for an answer. "Keep your mind on your job. Buckle down."

Big brother, Waite thought. Just trying to help out a fellow marine. We all know it's tough, but what isn't? Life is tough. That's just the way things are. You can't change the world, you know. We all have to do our part. We got to stick with it. Take it on the chin and come back swinging. Give more than we take. Do the best we can. Oh, the stupid bastard! "Yessir," Waite said. "I'll try."

Midberry tried to think of something else to say. He knew, and worse he felt that Waite knew, that he had completely dodged the question. But what else could he have done? "Yes, Maguire, my immediate senior officer is a raving maniac. He really ought to be court-martialled. Why don't you and I just run him up, old buddy, Private Waite." Who was crazy? Nobody saw Maguire worrying himself about what some recruit might think of him. Or having to wipe noses for each and every maggot who got a little nervous or depressed.

Midberry let his hand drop to his side. He turned and went to the desk. He licked his tongue slowly over his teeth. That damned cigar had left a rotten taste. Behind him, he sensed Waite's silent hatred. "Dismissed," he barked. "Go on, get outta here."

"Aye aye, sir!" Waite stepped back, automatically clicking his heels and immediately wishing he hadn't, and left the hut.

He passed Adamczyk without speaking and went to the rear of the rack to sit on his locker box. What a shit Midberry was, he thought. And Maguire. And the brass. The squad bay. The mess hall. P.I. The corps.

Adamczyk twisted about on his locker box. "What's the trouble?"

Waite tried to think of a sensible way to word it. He didn't know how to get started. He felt like a fool. "I don't know," he started, then saw Adamczyk shrug and turn away.

Him too, Waite thought. Always butting in with questions, then not having the time to wait for an answer. Because he really didn't want to know. Adamczyk was a shit just like the rest of them.

Waite glared at the back of Adamczyk's head. He smacked his fist into his palm.

What was he getting so upset about? He wasn't learning anything new. Ever since he could remember he had known not to trust people. Most of the time, he couldn't even trust himself. What then had he expected of Adamczyk and Midberry? They were nothing to him. He was nothing to them. And that was just fine with him. Joe Waite could take care of himself. He could go it alone when he had to, would rather.

He felt a need to do something with his hands and took his shoe kit from his locker box. He began working polish into the leather of one of his dress shoes.

Is that why he had stayed at home so long—because he was independent? Is that why he had put up with clerking and with his stupid brother's righteousness? Why he'd strung Carolyn along? Kept his mother filled with false hopes? Sure, he was independent. As long as someone took good care of him and as long as he wasn't made to give too much of himself in return, then he was a very rugged individualist.

What if his mother had gotten fed up with him and kicked him out? By rights that's what she should have done. He wanted to be cut off from the family, she should have forced him into it all the way. She shouldn't have let him drift, living at home, half-hearted about everything, always hurting her with his detachment.

Waite saw now his staying at home had been a mistake. He had had no interest in the business. Smiling at a herd of nameless people in order to get their dirty clothes and money, that was his brother's talent, not his. What his was, he still didn't know. But he had known for years he wouldn't find what he wanted at home and he should have left as soon as he was old enough. He realized, and as with all his realizations, he thought, it came too late to do any good, that he could have been closer to his family by moving away. No matter how much his mother had stressed the family business, he had known the business had no need of him. He knew too that if he'd taken an interest in any field at all, it would have made his mother happy. All she had wanted was to see her son moving in

166

some direction, any direction which would free him from the sluggish eddy of his dutiful daily routine.

But to break the routine hypnotizing him (for he enjoyed the comfort of the routine even while he cursed it; even while he flattered himself that he was the only one smart enough to curse it), it would have been necessary for him to shake himself awake and make a concrete decision. That was what always stopped him. Not being sure what he wanted, how was he to presume to make a decision? A friend working in a lumber camp in Oregon wrote him how great the work and the country was. Waite had thought then that maybe he would go out and try his luck. But as soon as he'd started planning, doubts hit him. What if there weren't any jobs? And if there were, maybe he would hate the work as much as the dry cleaning business and so would have made the long trip for nothing. And then he would have to come back and hear his brother telling him how he had known all along that the idea was a waste of time.

It was the same as it had been in college. In less than two years, he had had four majors. First, it had been psychology. Waite had hoped that by studying the human mind he would understand his own seemingly futile, circular patterns of thought. But after learning the use of statistical methods and the charting of graphs, after watching white mice struggle wih the meaningless complexity of the tee maze (the experiment only sharpened his own sense of indirection), after taking frequent mimeographed multiple-choice examinations on which he cynically experimented with chance (circling the lettered answers on the basis of an arbitrary pattern—aabc, baba, cbab, etc.), after these disappointments he switched his major to philosophy. There, dealing with basic ideas rather than just measuring the mind's capacities, he had thought he might find his answers. In the history of philosophy course great men had passed in review: Socrates, who needled friends with endless questions, but was himself a poor provider; Plato, who hung it all on a skyhook to dodge the issue; Aristotle, like Maguire, a self-contained disciplinarian. And the others, Hobbes, Spinoza, Leibniz, Newton, Locke, Hume—who played pool, Kant—who watched the clock and whose categories deepened Waite's despair at ever understanding anything. Only Descartes in his empty furnace had come close to getting at the heart of things. Sensing things clearly—if Waite had at all understood the readings from the *Rules for the Direction of the Understanding*—was what he wanted and needed to do. Yet to pick out the simple things necessary to begin an intuition of truth was impossible in the midst of his mind's confused drift. As with everything else, he had eventually given up. In the end, Descartes and all the other great thinkers catalogued in the philosophy text, remained as aloof and impenetrable as the bronze figures of the Mount Surabachi monument.

Without much hope, he had transferred to History and, a semester later, to English, but neither ordered events nor ordered words proved much help. He had drifted from one major to another, avoiding the decision to drop out until his disinterest made it for him. He had gotten five "F"s at midterm his last semester, and without officially withdrawing he had simply quit going to classes. For he had realized the hopes he had for college were as empty as those his mother held for his future in the dry-cleaning business. Protected by a growing cynicism, he accepted as natural the fact of his failure. It was no catastrophe and brought no major change in his life. Instead of driving to classes each morning he walked the four blocks to the family cleaners. Sliding the thin plastic bags over warm, cleaned coats and suits and dresses and sweaters, he felt every bit as close to, or as far from, the answers to his questions as he had in his classes. Taking an examination or ringing up the charge for a winter coat's cleaning and pressing left him equally untouched. Running tee-maze experiments or helping his brother to figure accounts were equally boring. So what? he thought, and that became his all-purpose answer. When questions came up about putting off marriage or his fits of staring, or his long, meandering walks at night or his constant oversleeping, or anything, he would counter, "So what?"

Waite put down the shoe and picked up its mate. A scrap of T shirt covering his fingers, he gouged polish from the can. He held the rag to his nose a moment, breathing in the waxy, sweet smell of the polish. He liked the smells of shoe polish and linseed oil, of soap and brass cleaner that hung about the squad bay. They were fresh, clean smells; clear. He looked about him, then began polishing the other shoe.

He had done the best he could, he thought, his mind returning to his home and family as certainly as his fingers drew their slow circle. If the others had expected more, maybe that was their fault. They should have known he could not throw himself into the family business any more than he could commit himself to marriage. How could he make any choices or decisions involving others, when he could not even begin to decide about himself?

Even his enlistment had been someone else's idea. Waite knew that his enlisting had been an escape from his mother, brother, Carolyn, the business. He had thought that the service would make his life easier, simplify it. All he would have to do was to take orders. Somebody with stripes or bars could make his decisions for him.

Waite grinned, remembering an old joke he'd heard about the fellow who jumped from a hill into a patch of cactus and when asked why, said it had seemed like a good idea at the time. Well, it probably had. The poor damned fool.

"Shit!" Waite threw down the shoe. It hit the deck and skipped under the rack.

Adamczyk turned. He raised his red eyebrows, eyes widened, in an awkward attempt at mock surprise. "Hey," he said. "You decide to start throwing things my way, you let me know first, okay?"

"I dropped it."

"Sure."

"Any idiot could tell that."

"What? Did I say you didn't?" Adamczyk put on a sly smile.

"Did you?"

"Oh, c'mon . . ."

"Why don't you just shut your fucking mouth, huh? Just shuttup."

"Oh, brother!" Adamczyk shook his head and turned away.

Waite kept staring at him. He wished Adamczyk would have pushed it. He wanted some excuse to knock the stupid, fake grin from his face. Everything Adamczyk did or said seemed fake to Waite, and he longed to punish him for it. What a freak! A scared, skinny, stupid kid pretending he had it all in the bag. Putting up a front, a good marine, no questions, tough, squared away, ready. And who were the bastards taught him to play it that way. Not just Maguire and Midberry.

"What a goddamned zoo this place is!" Waite said aloud. He glared about him, but no one would look at him. The others were giving him a wide berth after the Fillipone fight. That left him no one to take out his anger and hatred on but himself. "Shit!"

He had known better than to argue with Midberry. He'd known damned well, or should have anyhow, that he was wasting his breath. "There is no such word as 'retreat' in a marine's vocabulary." One of Maguire's many truths. And Waite understood too that there was no such thing as a question in a marine's mind. He imagined it might be one of Maguire's rules: "There is no such thing as a question mark in a marine's punctuation arsenal." So much more so for a recruit. Asking questions wasn't part of his job. A good recruit followed orders. A good D.I. didn't listen to questions. That wasn't his job. He gave orders.

Like the orders at the mess hall—Maguire and Midberry telling the boots how to march into the hall, how to yank off their utility caps, slap them against the right thigh and fold them into the right rear trousers pocket, how to face the stainless steel counter, how to hold the metal mess trays directly in front of their brass belt buckles and parallel to the deck, how to stare at the white wall beyond the heads of the messmen, how to side-step at attention down the long serving line, the green-uniformed, sunburned, clean-shaven, staring recruits clicking their heels with each abrupt side-step. Like a line of tin ducks in a shooting gallery, Waite thought. The ducks jerked along with bright, painted eyes; clickety, clickety, clickety. And the D.I., an expert's badge pinned to his shirt, squinted down the barrel of the rifle. Bang. Ding.

No wonder his stomach was usually upset after chow. It was all the damned standing in line and staring like some goddamned dummy, then not being able to talk at the table, just hearing all the jaws chewing and the clatter of knives and forks against the metal trays, bumping elbows with the recruits, boots, maggots, shit-birds, fuck-ups wedged close on either side, having to gulp the meal and get outside in platoon formation before Maguire and Midberry finished their meal.

Sometimes, standing in line and feeling his tray jerk as a scoop of potatoes or corn or stew dropped onto it, Waite felt as though the line was moving in a huge circle and that he would hold his tray and keep his mouth shut and side-step and click his heels and stare at nothing forever.

Bang. Ding. Bang. Ding. B'ding, b'ding, b'ding, b'ding, ding!

NINETEEN

After an evening squad-tactics lecture, the recruits marched the three miles back to their area through a moonless dark dotted with street lamps. The wind from the ocean was cooling and soft and the grass plots fronting the white barracks were a cool, dark green. Midberry did not call cadence, but let the platoon keep its own pace and its silence.

Adamczyk surprised himself by keeping in step without the cadence. He closed his eyes and listened to the even chuck-chuck-chuck of heels hitting pavement. He felt good tonight, confident. Holding himself tall and straight and keeping in step was becoming almost natural to him, and he thought, despite his earlier feelings, that the training might be doing him some good after all.

"Column left, harch."

Waite missed the step, then hurriedly turned. Adamczyk stepped on his heel. Waite skipped on his right foot, came down on the left, in step.

He had been caught dreaming. He was lucky Midberry hadn't noticed. Or Waite wondered if Midberry had noticed and just not said anything. Midberry was a hard one to figure.

Waite was careful now to keep in step. He hadn't missed the command for the reason he'd been missing others lately, his worry and confusion. This time he had simply been dreaming. He'd been half-asleep.

He had not gotten much sleep the past week. And when he had managed to doze, his sleep was broken by strange, violent dreams. He was always being drowned or being buried alive. And he woke in the mornings spent from swimming or clawing at the earth all night.

Now, the cool night air and the easy rhythm of the marching had let him doze. The cords of his neck felt less tight. Maybe, he thought, he ought to take things easier. Recalling the past few weeks, he wondered if he hadn't fallen into the habit he accused Adamczyk of having—blowing up every little incident into a major catastrophe. He knew he ought to keep things in perspective. Eleven more days and it would all be over. He would be off the island and free of whatever it was, some vague silly feeling that had started to wear on his nerves and temper. Eleven more days. He would be a fool at this point to let anything come between him and graduation. Especially when he wasn't even sure what it was.

"Listen up," Midberry called, "column right, harch."

Waite, at the head of the right column, pivoted on the ball of his left foot, stepped out on his right, then cut to half steps to let the left and center column leaders come abreast of him.

All he had to do was what he had just done. Stay awake. Pay attention. Do what he was told to do when he was told to do it.

Midberry halted the platoon before the iron ladder and ordered the recruits to march single file into the squad bay. Inside, in the sudden flash of the overhead lights, the recruit blinked and stared, their eyes shrinking from the glare of their surroundings, then slowly beginning to adjust.

Maguire stood in the center of the squad bay. About him, seabags lay opened, their contents spilled onto the deck. All along the center passageway the tops of locker boxes gaped, pillows were stripped of their cases, blankets and sheets lay crumpled between racks.

Midberry stepped inside and stopped. He ordered the recruits to line up at their racks. He walked slowly through the debris toward Maguire. He glanced at the staff sergeant's thick hands, wondering what he could do if Maguire had gone berserk. He wondered too, if it came to holding down Maguire, if any of the recruits would help him. He doubted it.

"What's up?" Midberry said, faking a grin. "Burglars?"

"Goddam right. And this time I'm gonna find out who."

"Something missing?"

"My watch," Maguire said.

Oh Lord, Midberry said to himself. "Sure you didn't just lose it?"

"Shit! Like Wood lost his fourteen bucks, right?" Maguire turned to the platoon. "My watch was taken from the hut sometime this afternoon. I wanna know which one of you maggots took it."

The recruits stood silently staring into space. Midberry tried to think of a way to stall Maguire, to give him time to cool down. He tapped Maguire on the shoulder. "Hey, look. . ."

"Sergeant Midberry," Maguire said, not turning. "There are some chits for 782 gear in the hut. On the desk. They got to be filled out and sent to the gunny."

"I'll get them in the morning."

"The gunny wants'm right away. I told'm you'd take care of'm tonight."

Midberry was almost certain that if he simply refused, Maguire would not force the issue. Maguire already had his hands full. Yet Midberry realized if he did force it now, then any leverage he might have later would be lost. He decided to stick with his plan, to wait for the right time to step in. "Right," he said, and left the squad bay.

Maguire stood squarely beneath the wire-caged overhead light in the center of the squad bay. "One of you maggots has got light fingers," he said. "Now I will find out this time which one of you it is. I will find out even if it kills you."

In his mind Waite repeated slowly to himself, take it easy, take it easy. A couple more weeks. Take it easy. He fought down a surge of emotion—fear mixed with anger—and refused to entertain plans of escape or resistance. All he had to do was to take it easy. He hadn't stolen the watch so it was not his worry. He was pretty sure he could take whatever was in store for the platoon. Whether some of the others could take it—Weasel? Cooper? Adamczyk?—that was their worry, not his.

"It wasn't in any of the gear here," Maguire said, beginning his slow, predatory pacing between the two lines of recruits. "So light-fingers either ditched it outside or has it on him. Aw right, I want each of you maggots, left hand only, to unsnap the pockets of your cartridge belts." He watched carefully as the platoon carried out his order. "Hands back at your sides. And I had best not see one of you fucking clowns so much as twitch. Understand?"

"Yessir!" the platoon shouted.

Maguire turned to the recruit nearest him and began searching the boy's cartridge belt. He made the recruit turn out the pockets of his utility jacket and trousers, then take off his boots and drop his trousers and skivvie shorts. He found nothing and moved to the next man. In the fourth man's cartridge belt, Maguire found two Milky Way bars. He held them up for the platoon to see.

"Pogey bait!" Maguire said derisively. "What's the matter, Shapiro, ain't you getting enough chow at the mess hall?"

"Yessir."

"We got your fat ass on a diet so you go sneaking in pogey bait on PX calls, huh? Well?"

"Yessir."

Maguire shoved the candy bars under the hook of Shapiro's nose. "These kosher?"

"Sir, I don't know."

"Whaddya mean, you don't know? You're a Jew, ain't you?"

"Sir, not orthodox."

"What are you, ashamed?"

"Nosir."

"Then you a Jew or not?"

"YESSIR!" Shapiro screamed. "Yessir, I am!"

"Oh, proud too?" Maguire cocked a fist and Shapiro flinched. Maguire laughed. "Holy-fucking-Moses! A

175

sneaky, chicken-shit, pogey-bait-eating, proud Jewboy! What the hell you got to be so proud about anyway?"

"Sir, I . . ."

"And I'm supposed to make a marine outta something like you?"

"Sir . . ."

"Shuttup! Here, take it." Maguire handed Shapiro one of the candy bars.

"Sir?"

"Eat it. Now."

The recruit reached to strip the paper from the candy and Maguire slapped him hard across the ear.

"With the paper, dummy. With the paper."

Shapiro took a bite of the wax paper-covered candy. He chewed with difficulty, started to gag, but Maguire raised his fist and Shapiro managed to swallow.

Adamczyk watched from the corner of his eye. He had been scared as soon as Maguire had announced the inspection. He hadn't stolen the watch, but that was no comfort. He knew the whole platoon would suffer and was afraid he wouldn't be able to stand the strain. He had to lock his knees and press his arms tightly against his sides to keep from shaking. He remembered his fainting the first time the platoon had met Maguire. He had been trying to live that down and now felt himself teeter on the edge of repeating it. He sucked in a deep breath, then another.

What scared him was the rosary. Without looking, he could picture it coiled (like a snake, he thought, but Maguire would strike) in the second left-hand pocket of his cartridge belt. Seeing how Maguire was treating Shapiro spurred Adamczyk's imagination to picturing the humiliation, punishment, maybe even torture, he would suffer when Maguire discovered the rosary. He cursed himself for being so stupid. They'd all been warned their cartridge belts were strictly for carrying M-1 clips. How in God's name, Adamczyk asked himself, could he have been so dumb as to set himself up for something like this?

The martyrs suffered and died for what they believed, some part of him whispered. But they didn't carry rosaries

176

in their cartridge belts, did they? Adamczyk said. Don't be flippant, the voice answered, and he recognized it as Father Matuzak's. Adamczyk saw the old man, his face a deathly white above the black cassock, sitting at his rectory desk, his long, thin fingers intertwined across his stomach. For I know whom I have believed, the priest said.

But the chaplain, Adamczyk began, stopping at his pastor's raised eyebrows.

Peter denied his Lord three times. Father Matuzak leaned forward in the chair, resting his elbows on the desk. Adamczyk saw how much the thin face resembled a hawk's. He wondered why he had never noticed that before.

Yet Peter in the end was granted courage to bear witness. Because, the priest said, holding up a bony index finger, because he prayed. Through prayer he was granted the strength and the power. . . .

Startled by a strangling cough, Adamczyk saw Shapiro, his shoulders hunched, mouth hanging open, dribbling stringy brown chunks of chocolate onto the deck. Adamczyk's knees threatened to unlock and he looked away, staring at the white of the squad bay wall opposite him. He heard the quick smack-smack of Maguire's hand on Shapiro's face, but didn't look.

"Pig!" Maguire roared. "I oughtta make you lick it up, for chrissakes! G'wan, get a swab. Get this shit cleaned up. G'wan, move! Move!"

Adamczyk had been fool enough to think he was in the clear. He'd thought he had squared away and was actually on his way to becoming a real marine. Now he would be caught with the rosary. Just like the other times he'd vomit or faint. Everybody would laugh at him. He'd be Doubleshit again. Maybe Tripleshit; a fuck-up, a shit-bird, a maggot.

What would Maguire's reaction be? What was Maguire's reaction to anything against regulations? The only real questions were what would Maguire do to him and how long would it last and could he take it? Adamczyk imagined Maguire strangling him with the rosary, or making him stand as if he were crucified, arms outstretched, until he passed out. What he had to do . . . he began. What did he have to do? Was he bound to stick up for what he believed in even if it made no difference to anyone? What good was it going to do to let Maguire find the rosary and ridicule it in front of everyone? Wouldn't he, Adamczyk thought, the pace of his thoughts quickening, one idea tripping on the heels of another, wouldn't he be doing more of a service to his religion by hiding the rosary from Maguire? After all it wasn't as if Maguire was some communist dictator who had taken over and was executing anyone who professed a Christian belief. As it was, it all boiled down to the fact that he, Adamczyk, a Marine Corps recruit, had ignored the U.S.M.C. regulations he had sworn to obey. He was guilty of concealing unauthorized gear in a government issue cartridge belt. How serious his mistake would be to Midberry, Adamczyk didn't know. But to Maguire every mistake seemed deadly serious.

As if it had not been there before, Adamczyk suddenly became aware of the big, silver-painted, corrugated-steel shitcan in front of him. No more than six feet from him, at a slight angle to the left, it would be an easy throw.

The idea of ditching his rosary in a shitcan brought back the image of Father Matuzak. A sacrilege, the priest began saying, his face ghostly in the gloom of the confessional. Adamczyk pushed aside the heavy, velvet curtain and left the box. Father Matuzak, however, was standing in the doorway leading outside from Saint Stephen's side altar. A serious offense, he said, as Adamczyk turned and went out the front way instead, swinging shut behind him the heavy wooden doors.

If someone tried to make him publicly deny his faith, Adamczyk told himself, remembering a fifth grade religion text, *Lives of the Saints*—Saint Stephen stoned, Saint John's bloody head served up on a silver platter, Saint Peter spiked upside down to a wooden X—if it were a matter of public denial, he was certain he would refuse. No matter what they did to him, yank out his fingernails, pluck out his eyes, castrate him, burn him, stone him, boil him in oil, he would refuse. He knew it. The martyrs had endured and so could he. If he was called to. If he

178

was faced with a definite challenge and clear-cut choice. But there was neither sense nor virtue in exaggerating a minor incident into a major test of faith. Adamczyk nearly laughed. He felt there was a world of difference between a saint and a fool.

He inched his hand up to his cartridge belt. Crooking a finger into the second pocket, he hooked a loop of the coiled rosary and pulled. His hand slid back to his side, the rosary clenched in his fist.

He looked at the can again and noticed Weasel watching him intently. Oh no, Adamczyk thought, he thinks it's the watch. He let the crucifix and first few beads dangle from his hand. He nodded for Weasel to look and was relieved to see what seemed to be a slight smile warping Weasel's thick lower lip.

Behind his back, he passed the balled-up rosary to his right hand. He would have to be careful to loft it so it didn't string out and fall short or catch on the rim of the can. He checked the distance again. How could he miss?

Adamczyk waited, the plastic beads and metal crucifix bunched in the curl of his sweaty palm. Every few seconds he flicked his eyes to check on Maguire. When Maguire had reached the last recruit in the opposite line, Adamczyk, his heart galloping, opened his right hand and, keeping his body perfectly straight, tossed the rosary in a slight arc into the open mouth of the shitcan. Plop. A direct hit. It hadn't come near the can's rim and Maguire had noticed nothing. Adamczyk was elated. He had done it. No matter that he still had to face the general punishment, his fear was now controllable. No matter that despite his reasoning he still felt guilty about the rosary, he would have felt guilty whatever he had decided to do. What was important was that now Maguire had no cause to pick especially on him. Now the weight of tension seemed to have fallen from his arms and legs as if it had been shackles. Adamczyk breathed more easily. He felt freed.

Maguire inspected each recruit and found nothing. "Aw right," he said, "your drill instructor is no longer looking to find the watch. He is looking to find a confession now. And it would sure as hell save everybody a lot of trouble if light-fingers would own up. I'm sure the whole platoon would appreciate that."

Maguire waited, arms akimbo, rocking back and forth on the balls of his feet. The squad bay was silent except for a floor board creaking beneath Maguire's weight.

Adamczyk offered two quick 'Hail Mary's' that someone would confess. Even if no one had taken the damned watch, Adamczyk thought, one recruit taking the blame would be better than all of them being punished. But he couldn't do it. He was still something of a fuck-up, trying to work his way up. One of the squared-away ones could do it though. One of them could confess and probably still graduate. Yet Adamczyk knew that none of the others, squared-away or not, had the guts to shoulder the blame and he hated them for it. Squad bay? More a chicken coop, he thought. *Esprit de Corps?* Sure, and it translated "Every maggot for himself." Waite had been right all along. Everybody looked out for number one. One was as high as any of them could count.

"Sir."

Adamczyk looked up, but could not at first tell who it was had spoken. His hopes rose. Somebody was going to do it after all. Maybe it was even the actual thief. It would make sense. Why put it off? Sooner or later, Maguire was bound to catch him.

"S . . . sir, private Lo . . . Logan requests p . . . permission to . . . speak. . . ."

Adamczyk saw Weasel take a step forward. Who would have thought it would be him? Or that he had the guts to own up? Adamczyk was thinking that Weasel didn't seem the type to play hero, when he felt a cold lump of fear knot in his belly. The son of a bitch, he said to himself. What does he think he'll get out of it?

"Shoot," Maguire said.

"S . . . sssir," Weasel managed, "did the d . . . dddrrill innnnstructor f . . . forget the sss . . . ss . . shitcan?"

"You see somebody ditch it there?"

"Nnnosssir. I . . . I thought . . . mmmaybe . . ." Weasel stopped, his mouth working, the lower lip refusing to cooperate.

"Aw right." Maguire looked at the recruits near the shitcan. "Waite."

"Yessir."

"Dump it on the deck."

"Yessir."

Waite cleared a space and emptied the contents of the can onto the deck. He set down the can and returned to attention before his rack. Maguire spread the trash out with his foot. Adamczyk's body went rigid as he watched the pile break down into crumpled sheets of note paper and U.S.M.C. stationery, envelopes, oil-stained bore-cleaning patches, two empty bore cleaner cans, a sock, a knotted shoelace and the rosary.

"No watch," Maguire said to Logan.

"Sssir, I ju . . . just thought that . . . mmmaybe . . ."
His lip trembled again and his voice trailed off into silence.

Maguire looked at Logan for a long moment, then told him to get back to his rack. He looked down again at the scattered trash. Adamczyk bit the tip of his tongue. He tried to make his breathing sound regular and relaxed.

Kicking aside the rosary, Maguire shouted, "You wanna play games? Aw right, we'll play games! Get all your gear back into your seabags. Right now. Get hot!"

TWENTY

Hauling loaded seabags on their shoulders, the recruits ran heavily in an oblong circle the length of the long squad bay. Maguire goddamned any who showed signs of slowing, kicking at them as they passed. He caught Cooper with a boot in the ass that sent the recruit sprawling. Cooper scrambled to his feet at Maguire's rush and, already running, hoisted the lumpy seabag back onto his shoulder.

On the fifth trip around, Weasel dropped his seabag. Maguire slapped him on the back of the head. The recruit struggled with the bag, ran a few feet, dropped it again and, trying to pick it up without stopping, tripped. Maguire ordered Weasel to attention and told the others to keep running.

"You're gonna keep falling," Maguire said, "then we'll have t'figure a way to keep you from hurting yourself. I mean, we wouldn't want you to mess up those handsome looks, would we?"

"Nosir."

"Get your bucket."

"Yessir." Weasel got the silver-painted bucket from behind his rack.

"Put it on."

"Yessir."

"Pick up your seabag."

"Yessir."

"All right, herd . . . whoa! Whoa!"

The recruits shuffled and stamped to a halt. They sagged under the weight of their seabags, breathing hard.

"You pussies are outta shape," Maguire said. "You're already puffing and panting like some W.M. her first time getting the meat put to her. Hell, we only just got started! You tired?"

"Nosir!" the recruits shouted, sweat streaming down their flushed faces.

"You wanna quit already?"

"Nosir."

"Maybe I'm being too hard on you, sweethearts?"

"Nosir."

"Maybe this training's too tough for you."

"Nosir."

"What?"

"NO SIR!"

"A marine is tough, maggots. Tough."

"Yessir."

"A marine can take it."

"Yessir."

"Can you maggots take it?"

"Yessir."

"Can't hear you."

"YES SIR!"

"You sure? You sure you can take it?"

"YES SIR!"

"Absolutely?"

"YES SIR!"

"What?"

"YES SIR!" the platoon screamed.

"We'll see," Maguire said. He took Weasel by the arm and led the bucket-blinded recruit to a place in line. "Just put your hand on the seabag in front of you. Turn when it does. All right, herd, let's go. Move out."

The recruits broke into a trot. By the second turn, Weasel had lost his hold on the seabag and crashed head-on into the wall. He fell backwards, dropping his bag, the bucket clattering beneath a rack. The other recruits kept running, stepping around or jumping over Weasel.

"Didn't I tell you t'keep hold that fucking bag!" Maguire yelled.

"Yessir."

"Can't you do anything right?"

183

"Yessir."

"Sure you can. Sure you can. That's why you're still on your ass, right?"

"Sir . . ."

"You would fuck-up a wet dream, you know that?"

Weasel had gotten to his feet and was standing at attention. "Yes sir!" he shouted.

Waite passed Maguire and Weasel. Weasel's face was streaked with sweat. Waite wondered how far Maguire was going to push him. Did he want Weasel to crack? Did he want to get rid of him because he couldn't stand his face? But so what, whatever Maguire's reasons, whatever his intentions, no one in the squad bay was going to play hero. Weasel's problems were Weasel's problems. The seabag strap was cutting into his shoulder and Waite shifted the weight closer to his neck. He shook his head sharply to fling the sweat, the thrown drops white in the light, from his forehead. Just run, he told himself. Don't think. Run.

Weasel was back in line, running clumsily with the seabag on his shoulder and the bucket on his head. He clung with his left hand to the end of a belt Maguire had tied to the belt of another recruit.

Adamczyk glanced at Weasel from across the passageway. Served him right, he thought. He wanted to get somebody else in trouble and it backfired. He got what he was asking for. He should have known enough to keep his mouth shut.

Adamczyk still wasn't sure what Weasel had hoped to get out of telling Maguire about the shitcan. Had he actually thought the watch might be in there? Who would ditch it in such an obvious place? Weasel had probably been hoping the rosary would take Maguire's mind off the watch, make good old Doubleshit the scapegoat. Like all the rest of them, Weasel had been trying to save his own skin by running up someone else. It was especially that way, it seemed to Adamczyk, with guys like Weasel and Cooper, the ten percent. They were so scared of getting shit-canned, they grabbed any chance, however slim, to get points squealing on the others. At least, whatever he had done, Adamczyk thought, recalling the His-

184

tory and Tradition test and the rifle range, he had done on his own. He didn't get his points playing stoolie. If he made it through graduation, he'd have the satisfaction of having done it with nobody's help and at nobody else's expense.

The pace of running, despite Maguire's shouts and threats, had started to slow. Weasel had fallen two more times and a number of recruits were beginning to stagger when Midberry returned to the squad bay.

"They're done," he told Maguire.

"What?"

"The chits for 782 gear."

"Yeh?" Maguire's attention was on the recruits. "Keep it up, goddam it! Wood, you drop that bag again and I'll drop your ass. Cooper, quit your whining and run. All of you, pick it up! You're slowing down!"

Midberry asked how long the recruits had been running. Maguire turned. "Don't start."

"Start what?"

"Begging off for'm. Making excuses for the mob. One of these sneaky sonsabitches knows what happened to that watch and I'll be damned if I ease off till I find which one."

"I know how you feel, but . . ."

"And don't try telling me it's a personal thing, either, cause you oughtta know better. There's nothing personal about it. It wouldn't make no difference to me whose watch it was. You can't have a thief in a platoon. It breaks down trust. Marines have got to trust each other if they're gonna be any good in combat." Maguire paused. "Just like it is with a team of D.I.s. They've got to be able to count on one another if they're gonna work out together."

The abrupt attack surprised Midberry. He felt he ought to say something to square himself or to regain the initiative, but could think of nothing. Finally, he asked Maguire if he hadn't found the watch yet. Maguire didn't answer and Midberry despised himself for having asked such a damned stupid question. The platoon was still running. The watch had obviously not turned up yet.

Midberry left Maguire and went to sit on the corner of the rifle-cleaning table. Maguire's determination disturbed him. He wondered what he could possibly say or do to stop Maguire this time. He wouldn't be able to try the telephone trick again. Maguire knew he wouldn't really go through with it. Not now. Midberry had strung along too far to turn Maguire in without turning himself in too.

He watched the recruits as they jogged past him. Many were half-stumbling and their faces were flushed and sweaty. Where the seabag straps cut across their hands, their knuckles and fingers were white. The thought struck Midberry that maybe the time to move had come. Yet he had no plan. Despite his earlier resolution and confidence, he felt paralyzed. He wished he were off duty. He considered simply leaving and letting Maguire run things his own way. That was what was happening anyway. Except he felt guiltier having to watch. What the hell! He wasn't the one making them run. If it was up to him, he'd stop it. If he was the S.D.I., things would be different.

"All right, herd," Maguire said suddenly, "get back to your racks. Put up your seabags."

Midberry had a faint hope that maybe his just being there was a reminder to Maguire of what had happened the last time, maybe that would be enough to set limits.

"And get your weapons. C'mon, c'mon, step on it. Get'm at the order. Ten-hut."

Midberry slid from the table and went to Maguire. "Why don't I drill them on the manual for a while?" He tried to make his voice sound casual. "You take a break. You deserve it."

"Shit." Maguire began calling commands for the manual of arms. The recruits slapped their weapons, moving them sharply from shoulder to shoulder, down to the order, back to port, back to the order.

"Present . . . harms." Maguire's command was followed by two sharp slaps—smack, pause, smack—as the recruits' hands hit the stocks in unison.

Midberry stood dazed in back of Maguire. His being there wouldn't be enough. He'd have to hit Maguire over the head with something to stop him now. Maguire seemed to have completely forgotten the time before. Had Midberry exaggerated in his own mind the night of his victory?

186

Had he given himself credit for more power over Maguire than he actually had. If so, he was back where he started.

His mind occupied with his new doubts, Midberry was startled by the blur of the boot and the body pitching forward onto the deck, the heavy thump of the body and the rifle's clatter.

Maguire stood over the writhing recruit as Midberry knelt. Too late, Midberry was thinking, cursing his own cowardice and stupidity. He'd let it go too far. Now this.

"He's faking," Maguire said. "I kicked his weapon. The butt of his weapon."

The recruit was groaning and whimpering, his body curled tightly. Midberry tugged him onto his side. The boy's eyes were shut tightly and his mouth gaped.

Midberry remembered his first morning in command of the platoon. He remembered Cooper dusting the desk, the boy's fear so obvious it left a smell in the room when he'd gone. Midberry had known then that Cooper would never make it; that sooner or later something would happen to him.

Cooper was thrashing his feet, scissoring his legs, his whine wet and throaty like a dog's.

"The little bastard's faking it."

"Hold his feet," Midberry said.

Maguire anchoring the feet, Midberry loosened the recruit's belt and gently pulled down the trousers and skivvie shorts. Cooper's breathing snagged. He clutched at his groin, but Midberry forced the boy's hands away from the purpling, swelling testicles.

"Goddam," Maguire hissed. "The little bastard."

Midberry looked at Maguire, but held back. Later, he warned himself. There'd come a time. He'd get his chance. "Fillipone," he called. "Waite, Neal. Get over here."

The three squad leaders helped lift Cooper, moaning and crying, from the deck. Maguire went ahead of the group and pushed open the squad bay doors.

"Go on," Midberry told him, "get a corpsman, will you." Cooper tried to pull away and Midberry tightened his grip on the boy's skinny arm. "For Chrissakes," he said, "get a corpsman!"

187

Midberry realized fully now that he had absolutely no power whatever over Maguire. The Maguire he had thought he controlled was no more than a hopeful fiction his mind had created for its own comfort. He had had to face that fact, finally, in the hut when the corspmen had left with Cooper. Maguire suggested that Midberry make sure the recruits near Cooper would testify his rupture was an accident, and Midberry objected that the decision was one the recruits ought to make for themselves.

Maguire laughed. "Look, I went along with your trying to play nice guy so long as it didn't get in the way. Now things're different. The brass is gonna be down here peeking into corners and under rugs and anywhere they think they might smell a stink. I don't want any chance of a slipup on our part. These maggots are gonna get hit with a lot of questions and they're gonna get spooked and, when that happens, they'll start looking for a weak spot, somebody they think will tell'm how to smooth things over. That's sure to be you. Naw, don't shake your head, you and me both know that's what'll happen. And so far, so good. I want'm to come to you, see? Better you than the brass. But I don't want you sympathizing with'm so much they think you're taking sides with'm, understand? I want you to make damned sure they keep on doing just what they're told to do, understand?"

Midberry didn't argue with Maguire, but neither did he move to carry out Maguire's "suggestion." He stood by the window, paring his fingernails with his key ring knife.

"It took me thirteen years to earn these." Maguire patted the staff sergeant's stripes and rocker on his sleeve.

"I sure as shit don't figure on starting over again as a P.F.C. hauling a B.A.R. It'll happen to you too, don't think it won't. Once the brass gets hot on something like this they're not gonna stop till they nail down everything in sight. Hell, that's how these chicken-shit lewies and captains buck for rank."

"I don't know," Midberry said.

"You think you're gonna like being a P.F.C. again?"

"No."

"Maybe if you're lucky they'll let you be a fire team leader. That what you want?"

"You know that's not what I'm . . ."

"See, there ain't no ifs, ands or buts about it. I told you plain what's got to be done and what you're gonna do. Lemme tell you something else, buster, being a D.I.'s like being pregnant or dead, you either are or you aren't. No halfway to it. None. And you had best get that into your head right now!"

Midberry looked around him, he didn't know for what, then swung open the squad bay hatch.

"Ten-hut!" The flurry of movement ended with the recruits at attention before their racks. Hands clasped behind him, Midberry slowly walked into the squad bay. He watched his feet, one brightly-polished black dress shoe, then the other, move toward the center of the passageway. He stopped. The overhead light became two white dots on the toes of his shoes.

"At ease, people."

Okay, he thought, so here you are. Here's where it brought you. Wayne Midberry. Sergeant Midberry. The J.D.I.

"You people are maybe wondering about Cooper," he began. "Cooper is all right. He's over in sick bay and is getting good care. The corpsman told me he thinks Cooper'll be fine. He just needs some rest."

Sure, Waite thought. And a new set of balls. Like the rest of us.

"Now you are all grown men and I want to level with you. You came here to be marines and there's a lot you got to learn. One thing you learned and are maybe still

189

learning is that the training here is no pushover. It's tough. It's got to be tough if you're gonna be tough. And anytime you get seventy people going through what you're going through, somebody is bound to get hurt. Accidents are bound to happen. There's no way anybody can stop things like this—like Cooper, I mean. Everyone's sorry it happened, but it did and that's that.

"And remember what I said, the training is hard cause you gotta be hard. Maybe this thing doesn't happen so much in the Army or Navy, but look what they turn out. It happened here because you people want to be marines. All the marines ever came before you went through this very same training and all the marines come after you will too. That's what it takes to be a marine. It's something a marine can be proud of knowing he made it."

Midberry paused to let his words sink in, then put in the clincher. "Cooper is going to be all right, so there's no sense anybody here worrying about him. We got a goal. It's like you gotta platoon charging a hill and half the platoon gets hit. Now if the other half stops to help or to start worrying about the wounded right then, then the whole platoon gets it. There's corpsmen to take care of the others. The platoon's job is to take the hill, not to stop till it's taken. So what this platoon has got to get its mind back onto is training. We got to keep right on going. We gotta lot to get done yet before final field. That's the last test, the big one. And I'm pretty damned sure there's nobody here wants to flunk that test and stick around here a couple more weeks. Or am I wrong?"

The platoon answered "Nosir!" and Midberry thought that although the answer could have been louder and more affirmative, at least he'd detected no outright anger or resistance. Maguire had told him the platoon would come through it all right, that what the recruits were worried about was not what had happened to Cooper, but what might happen to them. "All these maggots want right now," Maguire had said, "is to get off this rock. They're too close to graduating to do anything that might screw it up. You remind'm of that, that's all you got to do. Keep that in their heads—graduation. They'll come along all right. I seen it happen before. I know." Midberry recognized now that he hadn't at the time believed Maguire. He'd been afraid that there would certainly be a rush to turn the D.I.s in to the brass, and had come into the squad bay expecting a sort of mutiny. Now, looking at the recruits, it seemed that Maguire had again been right; that Midberry had let his imagination run away with him again.

"I want to see Waite, Adamczyk, Logan, Moore, Brashers and Taylor in the hut. The rest of you people go on about your business. I'm gonna be checking weapons tonight so you had best make sure they're clean. And I want no talking or milling around in here either. Okay, get hot."

The six recruits followed Midberry from the squad bay into the hut. They stood at attention in front of the folding cot, shoulder to shoulder in the small room. Midberry told them to stand at ease.

Waite glanced at the others. They all looked determined. And Waite knew damned well determined about what. The recruits stood there hard and sure, himself included, courageously determined to get off the island in one piece. They were bound and determined to stick together. One for all and all for one. Except for Cooper. Cooper no longer counted.

Waite covertly studied Adamczyk. No matter how hard the redhead tried, he still looked just like a scared kid. Waite wondered what Adamczyk had seen. Anything? After it had happened, Adamczyk hadn't wanted to talk about it. Still, Waite thought he had seen the same thing all of them had—Maguire suddenly kicking Cooper in the groin. Not that it mattered. None of them would admit it, not to each other, not even to themselves, perhaps. Why should they? "You stick your chin out," Waite told himself, "you'll get hurt." Maguire had told them that, he thought at first, trying to place the words, then remembered they were his own. That's what he had told Adamczyk when Klein had cracked up. Waite's wisdom, he thought bitterly. Yet wasn't it true? Wasn't it even more true now than before? Stick your chin out now and you'd get your head chopped off. That's why the six of them were in the hut, to see who was going to keep his head.

Midberry sat in the desk-chair and looked up at the waiting recruits. "All of you racked near Cooper. You should have seen Sergeant Maguire kick at Cooper's weapon, right?"

"Yessir," the recruits answered.

"And when Cooper pulled back you saw him hit himself with the butt of his weapon, right?"

"Yessir."

"Sergeant Maguire was trying to adjust the position of private Cooper's weapon. The injury was an accident. Is that right?"

"Yessir."

"Adamczyk?"

"Sir?"

"Just answer the question, boy, it's not that hard to understand, is it? Was it an accident or not?"

"Yessir."

"What?"

"Sir, it was an accident."

"You're sure about that?"

"Yessir."

"Taylor?"

"Yessir."

Midberry got the same answers from the others. Maguire had them pegged, he thought. Right down the line. *Semper Fidelis.* "Waite?"

"Yessir."

"You don't sound very positive."

"Sir, I couldn't see so good. It happened so quick."

"What did?"

"Sir, the . . . accident."

"You trying to tell me it might've been on purpose? That it wasn't an accident? What? Speak up, will you?"

Waite hesitated. He could sense the growing tension of the other recruits. Every one of them in the hut, he thought, had passed the tests of the confidence course, the rifle range; they knew how to run, shoot, fight with a bayonet or a knife, they could throw a man or break his arms and legs, poke out his eyes, strangle him, rupture

192

. . . oh yes, they had learned that too. Kick the bastard in the balls, that was part of the training. The others had learned it all. Midberry knew it all too. Trained killers. And here they were ready to wet their pants they were so scared he was going to open his mouth. Sir, that sadistic sonuvabitch Maguire simply hauled off and kicked poor Cooper in the nuts! We all saw it! That was all one of them had to say. There they stood, peeing their U.S.M.C. utilities. Oh no, sir, he's wrong, the cowardly chorus sang, we saw nothing of the sort. Sir, it was an accident, sir. Sir, we're certain, sir. "Sir," Waite said, "it was an accident."

"You're a squad leader, boy. You are in a position of responsibility. So you had best make damned sure right now you know what you're saying. You think it was an accident or not?"

Waite let his eyes slide toward Midberry's, then forced himself to stare at the wall. The tone of Midberry's voice had thrown him off-balance. It seemed to him that Midberry was actually asking; as if he himself weren't sure. Waite knew, though, it could be a trick to catch him off guard. A D.I.'s talent was finding out which recruits couldn't be trusted. Why should Midberry be different? And a recruit's talent was going along no matter what, taking orders, like it or not, being careful not to make waves. Why should he be different?

"Sir, I am positive. Cooper pulled back and hit himself."

Midberry made a slight hissing sound as he suddenly swiveled about and rose from the chair. He went to the window and stood looking out.

What is he, disappointed? Waite wondered. Had Midberry really wanted the truth? But Waite warned himself against letting down his guard. The time he had complained to Midberry about the way Maguire treated Weasel, Midberry had shut him up and that was exactly what he would do now. No matter how Midberry might act, he was a D.I. Pity the poor sap who fell for his tricks.

"All you people say the same thing? It was clearly and positively an accident?" Midberry hadn't turned.

"Yessir."

"What?"

"YESSIR!"

Midberry turned, nodding his head. "All right," he said. "All right. Good. Then that's clear."

It was clear that Maguire had been right, Midberry thought. It was clear that the recruits, whatever might have happened, would stick to the official story. What wasn't clear were his own feelings. He felt disappointed, yet at the same time relieved. He wasn't sure what disappointed him. Maguire's being right again? The recruits' cowardice? His having nothing to hold over Maguire's head? Nothing to give himself some leverage to offset Maguire's control? But he was uncomfortably certain why he felt relieved. A recruit claiming he had seen Maguire simply kick Cooper in the groin would have forced Midberry smack into the middle. He would have had to make a choice then—turn Maguire in or shut the recruit up. And he wasn't sure which he would have done. What could he have done? Would he really have had any choice or was he only kidding himself? Maguire was his superior officer. Therefore, he owed Maguire loyalty. And what did he owe the recruits? And himself? Hell, he thought, it hadn't happened, that was all. There was no sense worrying about what he might have done in a situation that didn't exist. A situation that thanks to the recruits wouldn't exist. They had made their decision and would stick to it. And Midberry reminded himself that he had made his too, a long time ago. No one had forced him into the D.I.'s job. He had been glad to get it. Now was no time to change his mind. The time to quit the Corps, he had been taught during his own boot camp training, is before the war starts, not after.

"Get back to the squad bay and line up at your racks," Midberry told the six recruits. He followed them out of the hut and into the squad bay.

"There will be an official investigation of the accident," Midberry told the platoon. "There will be brass coming down here to talk to each and every one of you and they'll be trying their damnedest to get you to say something they can use to cause trouble. That's their job. They got all kinds of tricks, too. Maybe they'll try to act like they're your friends; tell you how they'll get you off the island early or get you into another platoon, even that they'll see you make P.F.C. if you play along. They'll ask you about everything, too, not just about what happened to Cooper. They'll wanna know how the D.I.s treat you, whether or not they ever hit you, just how they punish you, everything. So you people just remember one thing: the brass is not one stinking bit interested in what happens to you. They're not part of this platoon. They haven't been here living and training together as a platoon for the last eleven weeks. They'll use you, that's all. All they want is to run up a D.I. so they can grab up another promotion. No matter what any of them tells you then, you keep it in mind that if one of you, just one is all it takes, says a single thing they can use for a court martial, you will all be witnesses. And these trials sometimes go on for a week or more, maybe even a month. That's another whole month on the island. When it's over, you might not have a D.I. and then you'll have to be split up and stuck into other platoons. Now the brass doesn't worry about whether or not the platoon you get put into is as far along as this one, so that's maybe another couple weeks on the island. I doubt if anybody here's itching to put in another four to six weeks training."

"NOSSIR!"

"Then all you have to do is stick to your story. You tell them nothing and we'll all ride this out together. Understand?"

"Yessir."

Together, Adamczyk thought. That was the first time he had noticed either Maguire or Midberry speak of the platoon as if everyone was a part of it. It made him feel proud, gave him a feeling of belonging. It made him feel that he and the others were finally being recognized as marines, not maggots, that the D.I.s felt the recruits had reached the point where they could be trusted. Cooper's accident seemed to Adamczyk to have turned things around. The D.I.s were in a spot now and had to depend upon the recruits for help. They were no longer D.I. and boot. Now they were all simply marines.

"What platoon is this?" Midberry asked suddenly, raising his voice.

"Sir!" the recruits shouted, "Plah-toon one ninety-seven, sir!"

Midberry was following Maguire's instructions faithfully, and he knew now from the surge of emotion he sensed in the recruits that the method was working. Maguire certainly knew how to run a platoon. Maguire understood thoroughly the workings of the recruit mind.

"What's the best platoon on this island?"

"Sir! PLAH-TOON WAN NINE-TEEE SEVEN!"

"What platoon's going to walk off with the honors at final field?"

"Sir, PLAH-TOON WAN NINE-TEEE SEVEN!"

"Which platoon on this island has got the best marines in it?"

"Sir, PLAH-TOON WAN NINE-TEEE SEVEN!"

"You people proud of this platoon?"

"Yessir."

"How proud? Really proud?"

"Yessir."

"Are you sure?"

"YESSIR!"

"Who's gonna come down here asking questions and trying to stir up trouble for us?"

"Sir, the brass."

"They're gonna try to get us to turn against each other. They learn that at Quantico, sitting on their asses in dress uniforms in air-conditioned lecture halls—divide and conquer. They gonna divide us?"

"NOSSIR!"

"Conquer us?"

"NOSSIR!"

"Or we gonna stick together and keep our mouths shut?"

"YESSIR!"

"We gonna show'm you don't learn what makes a marine platoon run by sitting around with clean fingernails in an air-conditioned room?"

"YESSIR!"

"We gonna show'm what real marines are?"

"Yessir."

196

"That a real marine takes everything gets thrown at him and comes back for more. That what we're gonna show them?"

"Yessir!"

"That real marines stick together?"

"Yessir."

"That Platoon One-Ninety-Seven, Company B, 1st Battalion, R.T.R. does not need any captain or chicken lewie's shiny shoulder to cry on? That we can damned well take care of ourselves?"

"YESSIR!"

"Who's gonna try to make trouble for this platoon?"

"Sir! The brass!"

"Who are we not gonna tell one stinking thing?"

"Sir! The brass!"

"All right." Midberry adjusted the D.I. cover on his head and wiped the beaded sweat from his forehead. "All right." He took a long, deep breath. "You people got those weapons cleaned?"

"Yessir."

"You sure?"

"Yessir!"

Midberry glanced at his watch. "You got ninety minutes till sack time. I'm gonna leave the weapons inspection go tonight. . . ." He stopped at a murmur from the recruits, and it died immediately. "I'm gonna give you the rest of the evening as free time. Now," he said quickly, an index finger pointing the warning, "I'd best not hear a bunch of noise in here. You can move around and talk, write letters, whatever, but keep it down, understand?"

"YESSIR!" the platoon roared. A few voices added, "Thank you, sir."

"YOU!"

The recruits went suddenly silent, the visible strain returning to their faces.

"Thank you, sir? Thank you, sir? You? Shit!" Midberry hesitated, then grinned broadly. "Well, hell, go on. It's free time, isn't it? Don't waste it standing around like a bunch of goddam dummies."

"YESSIR!"

"Sis, boom, bah," Waite said as the double doors swung shut behind Midberry.

Adamczyk looked at Waite, started to speak, then changed his mind. He makes fun of everything, Adamczyk thought. How could someone like Waite understand how the platoon felt? He doesn't know how anybody else feels. He doesn't even belong to the platoon. Not down deep, he doesn't, even though he's a squad leader. Down deep, he doesn't belong to anything.

"What're you gawking at?" Waite asked.

"Nothing," Adamczyk said.

TWENTY TWO

"What am I supposed to do?" Adamczyk said. "Just tell me that. You're the one's got all the answers, right?"

Waite, outwardly calm, finished threading a needle. He carefully knotted the ends of the double green thread. "Can you hand me that jacket. I gotta rip in my pocket."

Adamczyk twisted around on the locker box and took the utility jacket from the upper bunk. He gave it to Waite. "You gonna answer me?"

"All I asked was what you saw. I just wanted to know what you thought happened. You don't want to talk about it, that's your business."

"Oh sure." Adamczyk sat looking at the deck, one by one cracking the knuckles of his left hand, then his right. "Sure. You don't think I know what you're trying. . . . What a laugh! I know what you mean all right."

"So what're you getting so steamed up about?"

"I'm not. I'm just not falling for any tricks, that's all. Not yours or anybody else's."

"Damn!" Waite jerked up his hand. A drop of blood welled onto the tip of his index finger. He sucked at it. "What kinda trick? What do you think I'm trying to pull?"

"You know."

"No. Tell me."

"Come off it, will you? You want me to stick my neck out, that's all. Act buddy-buddy and all so I'll do the dirty work. Sure. And then you can sit back while I get shit-canned. Like when I tried to get somebody to do something about Klein. You ready to help out then?" Adamczyk laughed again.

The laugh seemed nervous and forced to Waite. But he didn't say anything.

"I'm not so dumb as I used to be, y'know," Adamczyk said.

"And that's what you think?"

"Think, nothing. I know it."

"No," Waite said, "I mean about me trying to set you up."

"Why not?"

"Why should I?"

Adamczyk waved a hand.

Waite tried again. "That what you'd do? I mean, say it was me that stuck my neck out, what would you do?"

"There's a helluva lot of difference between you and me," Adamczyk said. "Let me tell you, one hell of a lot!"

"What would you do?"

"Look, don't hand me that crap!" Adamczyk got up. He moved as if to walk away, then stopped. "What're you trying to do anyway? Why make out like you're gonna do something about Cooper? You think I don't know you better than that? Shit! Do me a favor, okay? Just knock off trying to bullshit me, okay?" Adamczyk jammed his hands into the back pockets of his utility trousers. Again he turned to leave and then stopped. "You wanna know what I saw, huh? Okay, I'll tell you."

Waite looked up. Adamczyk gave him a thin hard smile and leaned cockily against the rack.

"What you saw," Adamczyk said, "that's what. I saw exactly the same thing you did. Okay? That answer your question?"

"If you really did, then maybe the others did too."

"What do you mean, maybe? Sure, they saw what happened. We all did. So what? So what if the whole platoon saw it? Nobody's gonna say anything."

"Maybe not."

"Maybe shit. Nobody, that's who. Not you or me or anybody else with any brains in his head. Even if one of us did talk, even if both of us did, it wouldn't do any good. Nobody'd back us up. You know that. You saw those other guys today, Brashers and Taylor. Hell, we'd get shit-canned is all."

Almost the same words, Waite thought. It was like listening to a recording of himself. What a joke it was, getting back exactly what he had dished out. His smile grew, then he laughed, shaking his head.

"What's so funny?" Adamczyk asked.

"You," Waite said. "And me. This whole thing."

"How come I'm so funny all of a sudden?"

Waite's laugh trailed off. He looked at Adamczyk, then took up the threaded needle. "Nothing," he said. "Forget it, okay? It was more me than you anyhow." He stuck the needle through the heavy cloth of the utility jacket, then jerked the thread through after it.

Adamczyk took hold of Waite's arm. "I said I wanna know how come I'm so funny?"

"You know what your trouble is?" Waite said. "You got no sense of humor. You take everything way too serious." He continued stitching together the torn pocket. "That's not good for you either. You can get hurt taking everything too serious."

Adamczyk's hand still held Waite's arm. He watched Waite continue his sewing. What in hell is he trying to pull? Adamczyk wondered. He couldn't figure it. First, Waite is buddy-buddy, then all serious about Cooper, and the next thing he's laughing. Had Waite been stringing him along; just seeing how far he could get him to go? That would be like him all right. Always playing it close, making fools out of other guys, getting somebody else to do the dirty work so he could sit back and laugh. Sure, Waite had a sense of humor. Everything and everybody was a joke to him. He could go on talking about Cooper all night. It didn't bother him. He wasn't going to do anything about it, so why not talk about it? Why not get somebody else worked up about it?

Waite reached over and pried Adamczyk's hand from his arm. "I said forget it, all right? I was just talking. Now go on, will you."

Sure it had been a joke. Adamczyk cursed his own stupidity for not having seen through it a lot earlier. He'd let himself be taken in, listening to the talk about Maguire and Cooper and all the time Waite was talking tough, he'd been sewing up his pocket to look good at the next inspection. All that time he had been getting his kicks making a fool out of good old Doubleshit. No wonder he couldn't keep from laughing.

"I'm busy," Waite said, "Don't you have anything . . ."

"You fucking phoney!" Adamczyk ripped the utility jacket from Waite and threw it on the deck. "You goddam phoney! That's all you are, you know it? A goddam phoney!"

Waite had not gotten up. "Give me the jacket."

"All you do is talk, you know that? All talk, that's all."

"Pick up the jacket," Waite said, "or I'll make you do it."

"Sure, sure. Big bad ass, aren't you? Gonna show everybody how tough you are. If you got so much guts, why waste time talking to me? Why don't you go straight to Maguire, huh? Oh no, cause you're too chicken-shit . . ."

"If I have to get up," Waite said, "I'm gonna kick your ass for you good. I mean it."

"Big man! All you do . . ."

"Last time I'm asking you. Gimme the jacket."

Waite stretched out a hand and waited. Adamczyk didn't move. He knew without looking that the others had formed a loose circle about the rack. His anger drained out of him and left him feeling weak and sick. Why hadn't he let it go?

"Shit!" he said suddenly, scooping up the jacket and flinging it at Waite. "You're not worth the trouble."

As he pushed his way out of the circle, he heard the others laughing. Somebody punched his arm as he passed: "Who-ee! Ain't Doubleshit a mean one!" Adamczyk went to the rear of his rack and looked out the screened window. He was aware of more remarks and laughter, then bit by bit the general muted drone of voices returned, and Adamczyk let out a long, slow breath.

He had gotten out of it, but he hadn't fooled anyone. They all knew he was yellow. His trying to bluff had only made it worse. Doubleshit. Chickenshit. Goof-ball. Odd-ball. Shitbird. Fuck-up. Why shouldn't Waite laugh at him. The rest of the platoon did. Maguire and Midberry too. No matter what he did, he was still a joke to them. Like Weasel and Cooper, he was one of the ten percent.

202

He knew for certain that everyone was betting he'd wash out. He just didn't pack the gear. He didn't measure up.

"Jesus Christ," Adamczyk whispered. He pressed a fist down hard against the wooden sill. The coarse-grained wood cut against the ball of his fist, and he welcomed the pain. He could feel his eyes burning with tears and his throat gagged at the taste of himself. He ought to shoot himself and be done with it. He ought to just run out of the squad bay and toss himself into the bay, let the sharks get him. Why not?

He stood for a long while against the window, his mind worrying his bitter self-hatred. Behind him, he could hear Waite getting his shower gear from his locker. God, Adamczyk thought, how he hated Waite. How he hated them all, D.I.s and maggots alike. All of them were trying to keep him from making it. And he knew why, too. They'd never liked him. Right from the start they had made fun of his praying and his red hair and of anything else he said or did. They didn't want him to belong to the platoon no matter what he did. Didn't the rifle range and History and Tradition test prove that? They knew he was scared and so wouldn't give him a chance. That's why everybody was always on him—to break him down. He was sure there were others just as scared as he was; at least, he suspected there were. Like Waite, the other recruits were so scared stiff of Maguire that they got attention off themselves by picking on someone they knew they could take.

Adamczyk rubbed his eyes dry on the sleeve of his jacket. He studied his fist, doubling and redoubling it. It would have been stupid for him to have fought Waite. That's what they all wanted; get him to sick bay so he'd have to be set back. Why should he have to prove anything to them anyhow? He could fight Waite after graduation if he wanted to. He would pick his own time and place when he was ready, not when they were ready for him. He had been too smart to fall into their trap. He would stay too smart for them too. All he had to do was to concentrate on graduating. Graduating would show everyone once and for all that he had his own kind of toughness. Maybe he wasn't a fighter; he couldn't help that. But he could take whatever they threw at him and come back for more. He could refuse to be broken down. He could endure and graduate.

And he would graduate, he thought. No matter what.

TWENTY THREE

The realization of how close he had come to the edge that afternoon frightened and angered him. Midberry wondered what was wrong with him? He knew his job. Why couldn't he seem to simply go ahead and do it like hundreds of other D.I.s? That he was younger than Maguire was no excuse. He had had his doubts from the beginning that he was cut out for the work, but had tried to ignore them by putting the responsibility onto the brass's shoulders. The corps had made him a D.I., he had told himself over and over again, therefore he must have met the job's requirements. But he could no longer escape admitting that no matter what anyone else thought, he knew he was handling it wrong. At least, he felt he was doing it wrong. It seemed to him that he did everything wrong. There was no reason in the world he should have let Waite talk to him as he had. What other D.I. would have listened to a recruit rattle off complaints like some prosecuting officer trying the Senior D.I.? Not Kiernan, Midberry knew. Nor Schramm or Cruthis. None of them. None but bleeding heart Midberry. It was the way he had acted since he joined the platoon. And Maguire had warned him right off that it would bring him trouble.

"Yew wanna nother one, sahge?"

Midberry pushed the empty fishbowl mug toward the bartender. He opened the blade of his key ring knife and intently pared the nail of his left little finger. The mug was placed before him again. Foam welled over the brim and down the bellied sides to puddle on the bar's red formica top.

"Shee-it," the bartender said. He took the dish towel from his shoulder and wiped dry the bar. "Sawry, sahge."

"Okay."

"Place so gawddamned dead ah'm losing my touch." The bartender grinned, the gold caps of his front teeth shining. He leaned against the bar, balanced on the sharp point of an elbow. "Guess with final field and all coming up, there ain't much tahm fer lifting a few."

Midberry shook his head.

"Jes look at this place." He swept the near-empty N.C.O. club with a look of disgust. "Hell, hardly anybody even to talk to."

Midberry folded the blade and put the knife and keys back into the pocket of his tropical trousers. He drank from his beer. He kept his eyes on the bar. He wished the club were more crowded. The bartender then could have someone else to talk to. But there was only one couple —a gunny sergeant and a woman—at a booth in a dim far corner of the club. Midberry did not want to talk. He felt he had talked enough that day for the next couple of weeks. The same with thinking. What he wanted most now was to be completely alone, completely quiet, and completely drunk.

"Them's the long nahts, the ones there ain't nobody t'talk to."

Midberry looked up. The bartender was mooning out at the empty tables and booths, idly working a toothpick into the crevice between his capped, front teeth. His sallow face and the way he hunched his lank frame against the bar made him seem dying and lost. His grayish-black hair was cut marine style; crew-cut on top, nearly shaven at the sides. Yet the man wasn't a marine. Midberry recognized him as one of the civilian clerks who worked during the day at the Base PX.

Midberry finished his beer and the bartender refilled the mug.

"Guess yer buddy's got the duty tonaht."

Buddy? Midberry nodded. It was easier agreeing than trying to explain about himself and Maguire. He took a swallow of beer and noted his stomach getting sour. It struck him funny to even hear Maguire called his "buddy," and he smiled. Trying to be buddies with Maguire, Midberry thought, would be about like trying to shake hands with the figures of the Surabachi monument. He pictured himself climbing the base of the monument. There was Maguire, twenty-feet tall, cast in bronze. Midberry seized a single, huge, cold hand and tried to shake it. It wouldn't budge.

"Well, that's good," the bartender said. "Y'need to spell one another. Ever man's got t'have hisself a little tahm off."

Midberry nodded.

"Thet D.I. job surely is no snap, is it?"

Midberry shook his head.

"Thet's what ah hear. Some of the boys come in here nahts and talk about it. Lemme tell y'all, thet's a job ah wouldn't have for the whole world."

Midberry laughed, thinking of the bartender in tropicals and a Smokey the Bear cover.

"Y'all see what ah mean, right? Too much responsibility. Too much pressure. Shee-it, thet's why everybody looks up to you boys. Don't think people don't know. They know the D.I.s gotta be a bit more special than the rest."

Midberry shrugged.

"Oh y'ain't got t'say nothing. Everybody knows it. Some of these big ol' sahgints come in here, the ones working mess duty or supply, you understand, and they start in putting down D.I.s. Y'know what ah tell'm? Ah tell'm—shee-it, y'all jes itching to wear one of them Smokey hats yourself and y'all jes pissin and moanin cause y'don't pack the gear. Thet's the truth. Thet's jes what ah tell'm."

Midberry swished the beer around in his mug, then drank. That's what he had told Waite, that if Waite talked it was proof he didn't pack the gear. Cooper hadn't packed the gear either, Midberry thought. That's why Maguire said it made no real difference what had happened to Cooper. The recruit would never have lasted anyhow. He wasn't cut out to be a marine. Something would have happened to him sooner or later. It was bound to. "He just didn't pack the gear," Maguire said. "So by luck or accident maybe, or maybe cause we babied him along,

207

he could've slipped through. Then what, huh? He gets into combat and gets himself and maybe his whole squad or platoon zapped. Figure it this way—better for him to have a sore set of balls than to get his ass shot off by some gook someday cause he fucked-up."

"Ah like to rib these desk jockeys sometimes, y'know. Ah ask'm first jes who's the world's best fighting men, and they right out tell me a marine is hands down. Then ah ask'm how come, and they say cause of the training. Then ah ask'm who does the training, and they start to crawfish out of it, but ah got'm and tell'm then if the gyrene is the toughest fighting man, then it looks to me like a D.I.'s got to be the toughest of the toughest." The bartender hooted and laughed. He tossed away the splintered toothpick and leaned both elbows on the bar. "Whoo! I mean to tell you thet really burns'm. But there ain't nothin they can say, and ah jes laughs."

The bartender left Midberry to take two drinks to the gunny sergeant in the rear booth. Midberry drew a finger through the beer puddled at the base of his mug. He traced a series of o's on the red bartop. His finger stalled, and he sat staring at the bar, his mind satisfactorily blank.

The bartender tore open a dime bag of potato chips and put the split bag on the bar. Munching chips, he motioned for Midberry to help himself. Midberry shook his head.

"What ah was meaning to say before was, it's the D.I.s make the Corps what it is."

Midberry looked up. He frowned, trying to read the bartender's meaning in the man's yellowish, grinning face.

"Ah mean it, all right. Ah'm not trying to bullshit y'all. Way ah figure, the Corps'd be a pretty soft outfit if it wasn't fer boys lahk yourself making sure these boots git whipped into shape. That's jest what ah tell them supply sergeants and all too. The D.I. he's the man. Yessir. He's the man what's running this show."

Midberry glared for a moment at the bartender, then looked down at the bar. Goddamned dumb ridgerunner, he thought. What the hell does he know about D.I.s and the Corps? Sucking around so he can act bigtime. The D.I.'s friend, putting down everybody else. What a freak.

208

He's probably always wanted to join the Corps and couldn't pass the physical. God damned crazy dumb ridgerunner hillbilly freak.

A hand clapped Midberry's shoulder. Kiernan, the J.D.I. of a neighboring platoon, sat beside Midberry at the bar.

"Evenin, sah-gint Kiernan."

"How's about a beer, Billy."

"Yessir. Raht away."

Midberry wished Kiernan would sit somewhere else. Then Kiernan and the bartender could talk about the glory of the Corps all they wanted.

"How things going with you, Wayne?"

"Oh." Midberry drank from his beer while he carefully thought over the possible answers he could give. His mind wandered and he lost track of the answers.

"You okay?" Kiernan was staring at him.

"Fine. Little tired is all." Midberry tried a casual smile. The bartender, setting Kiernan's beer on the bar, smiled back.

"What kinda chow you got, Billy-boy?"

"Well . . ." The bartender considered the issue. "Grill's closed, y'see. Too bad y'didn't stop in earlier. I could've fixed y'up a nice hamburger or grilled cheese or something. Now, guess all ah got's chips or popcohn, uh . . ." He bent to look beneath the bar. "And cohn curls or cheese twis . . . and uh, por skins."

"FORE SKINS!" Kiernan roared. "Jesus Christ, what kind of place is this?"

"Por skins," the bartender said.

"Y'hear that? Hey, Wayne? Foreskins?"

"Aw c'mon now, sahge." The bartender's face disappeared again behind the bar, then surfaced. He held up a dime bag of fried porkskins. "Y'all quit pulling my laig. Por skins, see."

"Okay, Billy-boy. Lemme have a bag, will you? I thought sure you said foreskins though. Must be cause I got so many kykes in my platoon. Abie this and Sammy that. Jesus Christ, New York City must be empty." Kiernan chewed a mouthful of pork skins. "Usually they wait till winter."

"Howsat?" the bartender asked.

"Well, it's not just the kykes; all those greasy little New York—New Jersey tough guys. And the coons too. Come winter, they figure they had best find a place off the streets. So we get'm down here."

"They cause y'all a lot of trouble, huh?"

"Not after you take their switchblades away."

"Shee-it!" The bartender laughed. He looked at Midberry. "Y'all git any lahk that in your bunch, sahge?"

"Hm?"

"With switchblades I mean."

"Oh, some," Midberry said.

"Y'have much trouble with'm?"

Midberry shrugged.

"Trouble?" Kiernan said. "You're asking the wrong man, Billy-boy. Don't you know who he works with? Jimmy Maguire."

The bartender's smile grew. He nodded his head jerkily, chewing and swallowing a mouthful of chips before he spoke. "Awl raht," he said. "Thet is awl raht. Yessir. I member hearing about the time Maguire hung thet boy, some smart-ass black boy from Chicago, wasn't it?" Kiernan nodded. The bartender went on. "Black boy always lippin' off and finally Maguire jes up and hung'm from a pipe till thet nigger's eyes looked like a couple hard-boiled aigs and his ol tongue was awigglin and awagglin like a snake's. Then some shavetail tried to raise a stink about it and thet whole platoon, to a man ceptin the black boy, stuck right with Maguire. Not a pissin' thing the brass could do. Thet's the way I heard it anyhow."

"You heard right," Kiernan said. "Maguire's something, I tell you. The best damned D.I. on the island and one damned good marine. Hell, once some kid banged him over the head with a rifle and put Jimmy into sick bay. You think he shit-canned that kid?"

"No," Midberry said. "He kicked his ass good and kept him on."

"You heard it, huh?"

"Cause a boy with that much guts was bound to make

210

a good marine." Midberry banged his fist on the bar. "Fucking-a-right!"

"And you know what he tells me?" Kiernan said. "What he says was the thing about it that bothered him the most?"

"What?" the bartender asked.

"You hear this, Wayne?"

"Go ahead."

"Well, Jimmy gets out of sick bay with his head all stitched up and he takes good care of this kid. Afterwards, he's talking to me one night and he tells me the thing really got to'm about it was the kid's swing. He says after all that training on the bayonet range, the kid still swung his rifle like a ball bat! And he says that's what hurt him the worst!"

"No foolin'?"

"He's something, I'll tell you. Best damned D.I. on the island and the brass goes and tries to bust him. Trying to bust a man's won D.I.-of-the-month award twice one year and whose platoons placed first in final field and drill comps three out of four times."

"Shee-it."

"Crazy," Kiernan said. "Those chicken-shit lewies'd run up their old lady if they thought it'd get'm some silver bars on their shoulders."

Kiernan shoved his empty glass forward. "Finish that," he told Midberry. "I'll buy you one."

Midberry drank his beer. The bartender took the two empties to the tap.

"Hear you got a little trouble with your herd," Kiernan said, his voice lowered. "Don't you worry. Maguire can handle it okay."

The bartender brought back the beer, and Kiernan patted Midberry on the shoulder and grinned. "Here we go. Drink up."

"Thet story true about Sahgint Maguire getting his stripes in Korea?"

"About Chosin? Sure. He's got the citation to prove it."

"Ah s'pose y'all know thet story already, sahgint?"

Though he didn't, Midberry said he did. What was this,

211

Maguire's local fan club? He drank his beer and got up to leave.

"What's the hurry?"

"Duty tomorrow."

"Stick around. I'll walk back with you."

"Wanna turn in." Midberry bumped against a bar stool and caught his balance.

"Sure you can make it back by yourself?" Kiernan asked.

"Sure," Midberry said. "I'm fine." He shouldered open the door and stepped out onto the cement stoop. The door swung shut. There was no wind and the night air was warm and muggy. Midberry carefully staggered the two hundred yards to his quarters, maintaining his shaky balance until he reached his rack, then sprawling across the made bunk in his tropicals and dress shoes, fell asleep immediately.

TWENTY FOUR

The news from his mother startled Adamczyk and he sat on his locker box re-reading the letter as if he hadn't understood it the first time. His cousin Steve had drowned. Three days before the police had dragged Steve's body from Maumee Bay. They thought he must have been in the water since the night before. No one could understand why he would have been down by the Bay at night. He didn't know how to swim. He'd told his parents he was going for a ride. The police had ruled it a suicide. But, the letter said, Uncle Ted said absolutely it could not have been a suicide and that if he had to he would take it to court to get the coroner's report changed. He said he was not going to let a bunch of crooked cops sweep it under the rug. "But why would anyone ever want to hurt Steve?" Adamczyk's mother asked him in the letter. She said she couldn't believe anyone would do such a thing. Yet she still couldn't understand why Steve would want to hurt his parents like that. Steve had always been such a quiet boy and so polite. It was more than she could understand. "You ought to write to your uncle," she wrote. "His nerves are so terrible. It would be nice."

Adamczyk wished his mother would not have written him about it. Here, there was nothing at all he could do to help. Except maybe to feel sorry for Steve and for his uncle. And what good did that do?

Folding the letter back into the small pink envelope, he put it into his locker box. There was no one he could talk to about it, so he simply sat on his locker box again, staring down at the bright toes of his boots. He tried to form a picture of his cousin in his mind, but the face was

213

blurred and shadowy. He could not remember just what Steve had looked like. His cousin seemed far away and somehow unreal, as if he had been a character in a movie or a dream. Adamczyk thought the way he felt was probably because of Steve's death, and it seemed to him a natural way to feel. Then, thinking of his uncle and of what he might write to help cheer him up, Adamczyk discovered he could form no clear image of him either. It was the same with his parents. He couldn't understand it. He wrote home every chance he got and carefully read and re-read the letters he received, yet home and his parents, his uncle, everything he had once known seemed unreal to him now. All that was another world, another life, like the vague memories he had of early childhood. Once it had seemed real, now it had thinned and faded. What was real now was Parris Island and himself as a marine recruit, not as a son or nephew or altar boy. Adamczyk felt he had grown so much—matured, he thought—since he had left home that it made the eleven weeks he'd been on the island seem like years. He felt years older. He felt too as if he had never known any other life than the one he knew now. Sometimes it seemed he had been born on the island and that he would die on it too. The only vivid memories he held were of the island. He could with no trouble picture the faces of Maguire and Midberry, of the captain, of Waite, of the other recruits in the platoon. He recalled his placing first in the History and Tradition test and his performance on the rifle range. The confidence course, bayonet range, tactics lectures, judo sessions, all these came to mind seeming to Adamczyk, now that he was in the final week of training, like so many hurdles he had managed to jump. They were all behind him. All that lay ahead was the final field inspection. Eleven weeks ago, graduation as a marine had seemed impossible. Now, Adamczyk thought, he was heading hell-bent down the final stretch and would let nothing stop him.

He remembered that morning how close he had felt to his goal. The platoon had picked up its tailored tropicals. A uniform inspection had been held by the D.I.s, and Adamczyk had received not one criticism on his appearance. His tropicals fit perfectly and he had felt very solid and confident standing in ranks in the bright sunlight, rigid at attention, his face tanned and clean-shaven, his brass belt buckle and tie clip with its eagle, anchor and globe shining, his black dress shoes and leather bill of his cover spit-polished. And it came as a pleasant shock when Maguire warned the recruits to take good care of their tropicals, as they would wear them in a few days for a graduation ceremony dress rehearsal. Having gotten that far, Adamczyk thought, what could stop him?

He imagined the platoon's graduation day. There would be speeches and the base band playing the Marine Corps Hymn, the platoon marching and standing at attention with all the other graduation platoons, and all the recruits in their tropicals, finally marines.

He sat day-dreaming about graduation until Maguire came in and put the platoon to bed. Even then in the rack his mind played with a mixture of memories and plans. And it was while imagining his return home that Adamczyk remembered Steve. He felt guilty at first for forgetting his cousin's death, then thought of where he was and of how being on and getting off the island was the first worry, naturally, of each and every recruit. He felt sorry for Steve but there was nothing else he could do. What happened, happened. A man had to take life as it came and be able to keep going. Adamczyk had learned that lesson on the island. It was something he was not about to let himself forget.

Dozing off, his mind drifting between his bunk and the parade field where graduation ceremonies were in progress, Adamczyk thought he heard someone order him from his bunk. He answered 'yessir' but could not make his body respond. In a minute, he thought. In a minute. Far off he heard springs squeak. He tried to listen, then lost track of the sound and let himself slide into sleep, his cousin Steve swimming with long slow, sure strokes into his dream.

Waite stood, his eyes blinking in the light, fighting down the panic which urged him to break and run. He deliberately kept from looking at Maguire as the D.I. paced

215

before him in the small hut. The long silence wore on Waite's nerves, and although he wore his skivvies, he felt oddly naked. He had never known himself to be this afraid. Maybe Midberry was right then. Maybe at bottom that's all there was to it, fear.

"All those reasons you're giving me," Midberry had said that afternoon in the hut, "how much you're worried about Klein and Cooper and all. Bullshit. Don't kid yourself, boy. You're no different than all the others. The only one you're worried about is yourself. How come you weren't so quick to get upset when I called you in here and asked you about Cooper? Everything was fine then. So why now?"

"Sir," Waite had tried to answer. "Then I wasn't sure."

"Sure, hell! I'll tell you what it was. Then it was only Cooper. Now it might be you. You're scared you'll break, that's all; worried the investigators might make you talk. So you come looking for a way to get off the hook. What do you want me to do, run interference for you? Side with you against Sergeant Maguire?"

"Sir, I don't know exactly."

"You just wanted a little advice, is that it?"

"Yessir. I guess so."

"All right. Keep your mouth shut. Do what you're told. That's all you got to do. Nothing else. Keep your mouth shut and do what you're told. All right?"

And that's where he had made his mistake, Waite thought. That's where he had failed to see just how far out on a limb he was crawling. Instead of saying yessir and meaning it and sticking to it, he had kept asking questions. Ignoring Midberry's obvious anger he had asked one more question, then another and another as if he was drawn to the edge despite his fear of heights. He had not been able to keep himself from inching further and further out. And now here was Maguire with the saw.

"You tell me, maggot, and it had best be good," Maguire said, "just who the fuck you think you are to tell anybody how to run this platoon?"

"Sir, I don't know. . . ." Waite tried hard to come up with something which would make sense to Maguire. He would have to tell him something. "Sir, I just felt, I don't know, that the drill instructor . . . well, sir . . . I didn't think that Detar should've had to crawl like that, cutting up his knees and . . ."

"What about Cooper?"

"Sir?"

"Sir, shit. You like what happened to Cooper?"

"Nosir."

"If you were the D.I. would you have done it?"

"Nosir."

"You wouldn't, huh?" Maguire stepped past Waite, then spun about and slapped the recruit hard across the face. Waite started back, his hands coming up. Then he forced his hands to his sides and froze at attention. He knew he was no match for Maguire.

"What wouldn't you do, maggot? You wouldn't have kicked Cooper in the nuts, right?"

"Nosir."

"But your drill instructor did, right?"

Waite could not think of an answer. Maguire told him he damned well better speak up, and Waite thought hard but not quickly enough. Maguire slapped him again. Waite kept at attention. The hut seemed very quiet. Waite could hear the rasp of Maguire's breathing and the squeak of his shoes as the D.I. resumed his pacing.

Waite thought of the rest of the recruits safely asleep in their bunks. "All you got to do is keep your mouth shut and do what you're told." Waite wished he had taken Midberry's advice. All he had done now was to make trouble for himself. Nothing else would come of it. He had known that from the start. He could be in rack right now, he thought, asleep, nothing to bother him. But no, he'd had to open his big, dumb mouth to Midberry. Midberry, that phoney bastard.

"That what you're gonna tell the investigators tomorrow? That your drill instructor kicked Cooper in the nuts?"

"No sir," Waite said. He knew Maguire was watching him closely and that the D.I. thought he was lying, but

217

he meant it. He would tell the brass only what he had been told to tell them. Let somebody else play hero. He had made a mistake getting himself out on a limb, but he hoped there was still time to get back in. "Nosir," he said again. "I'll tell them it was an accident."

"You mean you'd lie to an officer? They can put you in the brig for that, y'know."

"Sir, I won't lie. I'll tell them the truth. It was an accident."

"You sure of that?"

"Yessir."

"How sure?"

"Sir, very sure. Positive."

"How come you weren't so sure about it this afternoon?"

"Sir, I was always sure about Cooper and the accident. I never said anything about that. I'm sure Sergeant Midberry would back me on that."

"Oh, really? You know I don't like liars, don't you, maggot?"

"Yessir."

"And you're trying to tell me you didn't say anything about Cooper?"

"Yessir."

"Well, that's not what Sergeant Midberry told me, maggot. You know that?"

"Nosir."

"You think he's lying?"

"Nosir."

"How you figure it then? He tells me one thing, you tell me another."

"Sir, maybe there's some confusion about what I said."

"You gonna tell me now you didn't complain about the way I'm running this herd? About my beating heads?"

Waite hesitated. If he lied about everything, Maguire would believe nothing. But he could confess to everything else except saying anything about Cooper and maybe still get out of the hut with all of his teeth. "Nosir."

"You complained, huh?"

"Yessir."

Maguire's open hand cracked against Waite's cheek, then the backhand against the other cheek. Waite held his ground.

"What fucking right you got, huh? What right you figure you, nothing but a candy-ass boot, had to tell your drill instructor how to run a platoon?"

"Sir, none."

"What the hell you do it for then?"

Waite had seen other recruits make the mistake of trying to apologize for their errors. There was nothing that angered Maguire more. "No excuse, sir," Waite said. Stiff upper lip, he thought. The tough marine, that's what Maguire wanted to see, and whatever Maguire wants, that's what he'll get.

"You wanna know something, maggot?" Maguire said, stepping in close to face Waite. "You make me sick. That's right. You turn my goddam gut, you and your whining."

Maguire slapped him again, once on both cheeks, then as if it was an afterthought, once more, harder. Better a sore face, Waite thought, than to end up like Cooper. He wondered what would happen if Maguire kept at it until he got himself worked up to the point he couldn't stop? No one else would stop it. Or could. Waite's mouth was dry and tasted bitter, and the hut seemed so small it would suffocate him.

"Upset about a little harrassment. You, a squad leader that should know better. Shit. Nobody ever tell you a marine's got to learn to take it? You think I go around kicking ass cause it's a hobby of mine? Huh? Answer me when I ask you a question."

"Nosir. I don't think that."

"You don't think," Maguire said, his lip twisting into a snarl. "You don't think. That's your trouble, candy-ass, you just don't think. Before you start shooting off your mouth you oughtta siddown and think about just why a boot has to go through this training. Then maybe you'd see why this place ain't run like the Conrad Hilton. But no, you don't think. No, you just talk. Whine. Pissin and moanin cause you're weak, that's why. You're chicken-shit, you know that?"

"Yessir."

"That's why you come running to Midberry behind my back. You were hoping he'd help you find an easy way out, weren't you?"

"Yessir."

"Sure you were. You maggots are all alike, every fucking one of you. Always looking for somebody to baby you. Shit."

Maguire stopped pacing and glared at Waite. He went to the desk and took a pack of cigarettes from the top drawer. Lighting one, he sat on the edge of the desk. Suddenly he tossed the cigarette into the waste basket, and leaned forward to yank up his left trouser leg. "Look here," he said. "C'mon, c'mon, I ain't trying to trick you, goddamit, look."

Waite lowered his eyes to look at Maguire's knee. There was a thick pink scar half-circling the knee cap. The area about the scar was sunken as if bone were missing. Maguire pulled the trouser leg back down and Waite fixed his stare back on the wall.

"Got that at the frozen Chosin when you were still in high school, sweetheart. Took a gook's bullet right through my fucking knee, but I walked outta there anyhow. You know why?"

"Nosir."

"Cause if I didn't, I'd die. Simple as that. That's just the way it is in combat, candy-asses don't last. You either pack the gear or you end up dead. What d'you think, that I could go running up to somebody and say 'Gee, I gotta pretty bad leg here and I thought maybe I might get excused from duty.' Or that I could ask the gooks to take it a little easier on me seeing as how I had a sore knee?"

"Nosir."

"But you want me to take it easy on your ass, don't you? Well, let me tell you something, boy. My job is to see that you are a marine fit for combat and that's just what I'm gonna do if I have to kick seventy young asses black and blue every morning, noon and night, and a couple of times in between. You understand that?"

"Yessir."

"The Corps is no place for pussies, understand?"

"Yessir."

"If a maggot can't take it, then we had best find that out here and now rather than wait till he gets hisself killed in combat. You know what I did for Cooper? Klein and Detar too?"

"Nosir."

"Saved their lives, that's what. Kept'm from getting killed just the same as if I'd rescued them under fire. You find out a maggot's weak and you shitcan him, you just saved his life. Because I'll tell you this, a weak man will sooner or later make a mistake and maybe get himself killed. You think about that. The next time you feel like shooting off your mouth you think about that first, understand?"

"Yessir." And he really would, Waite thought. He tried to remember the details of what had happened to Klein and Detar and Cooper. Maybe he had judged the situation wrong and Maguire was right after all. Maybe Maguire was only doing his job. Maybe everything he did was in the long run in the recruits' best interests.

"Something else y'oughtta think about, too," Maguire said.

"Yessir?"

The punch came as a surprise and bent Waite double, knocking the wind out of him. Maguire straightened him with an uppercut that bounced Waite against the wall. Waite sat down hard. He held his stomach, trying to catch his breath. Suddenly, remembering his training, he crooked his right arm over his head.

"Shit! You're way too slow, maggot. If I'd a mind to stomp your young ass, it would've been all over by the time you got around to putting your arm up. How come? Didn't you have judo like the rest of the herd?"

"Yessir," Waite managed.

"You didn't learn very fucking much, did you?"

"Nosir."

"You're not much fucking good as a marine then, are you?"

"Nosir."

"What do you figure you're good for? Anything?"

"Sir," Waite said, "I don't know." That morning he had been so sure. Now he wasn't sure about anything.

221

He didn't even have the guts to stand up. Maybe, he thought, he was just chicken-shit like Midberry and Maguire said. Why hadn't he come straight to Maguire otherwise? Because he had figured Midberry as a soft touch. Had that been all he was looking for—an easy way out? Like at home walking out on anything as soon as it got tough? It was different though on the island. There weren't any places to hide here. Not even behind Midberry's skirts. He had found that out the hard way.

"Get up."

Waite got to his feet. He tried to keep his eyes from straying to Maguire's hands. If he acted afraid or flinched, he knew it would get worse.

"What're you gonna tell the investigators tomorrow?"

"Sir, nothing."

"You sure this time?"

"Yessir."

"Not gonna change your mind?"

"Nosir."

"I think maybe you're lying."

"Nosir. I won't tell a thing."

"You know what happens to maggots that squeal?"

"Nosir."

"The other maggots don't like it one bit. A court martial holds everybody up a week or so, see. It gets pretty tough living in a squad bay with a bunch of maggots that hate your guts. Course, the brass sometimes feels sorry for the boot who turned in his D.I., so they get him transferred to another platoon. Trouble with that is, D.I.s are kinda clannish, and all sorts of things, accidents, seem to happen to maggots that talk too much; like they was unlucky or something. Sergeant Kiernan, across the way here, he had a big mouth transferred into his mob just last month. You know it wasn't more'n a week later the poor sonuvabitch was in sick bay with a concussion. Fell in the head taking a shower. No questions about it either. There must've been six, seven of his buddies seen him fall. It's something to think about, ain't it?"

"Yessir."

"You think you might forget though tomorrow and start talking before you remember not to?"

"Nosir," Waite said. He knew what came next. He'd seen Maguire play with other recruits like this. "Nosir, I'm sure I won't forget."

"I don't think you will either." Maguire grabbed Waite by the neck and, tripping him, threw him to the deck. "You'll have tonight to remind you, won't you?"

"Yessir."

"Gimme twenty-five."

Waite spread his hands and began doing push-ups, counting off loud and clear. He had gotten to sixteen before Maguire put a boot on the back of his head and banged his face against the deck.

"What're you gonna say tomorrow?"

"Sir," Waite said, twisting his face to one side to speak. "Nothing."

"Sure about that?"

"Yessir."

Waite felt the boot leave his head.

"Finish up."

After the push-ups, Maguire made Waite do sit-ups, leg-squats, jumping jacks, more push-ups, and then duck-walk again and again along the four walls of the hut. Sweat poured from Waite's face and he grunted as he moved about in a squatting position, his hands locked behind his head, getting one leg and then the other forward, a pain in his groin like his skin tearing in two.

"Quit your whining."

"Yessir," Waite gasped.

"Think you can remember now to keep your rotten fucking mouth shut?"

"Yessir."

"You forget and you will wish to hell you'd never been born, you understand?"

"Yessir." Waite thought he'd scream at the burning in his groin. He bit his lip. He said he wouldn't forget and wouldn't tell anyone anything.

"Get up."

Waite slowly straightened. He stood unsteadily at attention. Outside the hut he heard the firewatch passing. There was a moment's quiet, then the footsteps passed going the other way.

"All right," Maguire said. "Get back to your rack."

"Yessir," Waite said. He left the hut, glancing furtively back to see Maguire as a dark shadow watching him from the hut's open hatch, and went slowly and quietly into the squad bay and to his rack. Adamczyk was snoring. Waite slipped off his shower shoes and carefully, painfully, hoisted himself into the top bunk. The fire in his groin flared momentarily. Waite lay on his back and let his mind slowly realize his body's many aches. He could feel his lower lip swelling. Sweat streamed down his forehead and cheeks and dampened the pillow hot against the back of his head.

It could have been worse, he thought. He congratulated himself that he was still in one piece. All things considered, especially his own stupidity, he hadn't come off badly at all.

And he had learned his lesson well. It wouldn't happen again.

Waite mopped his face with a corner of the sheet. He closed his eyes and felt the slow deep pain throbbing in his head. In the distance he heard the shout of a sentry's report: "Sir! O two hundred hours and all's well!"

TWENTY FIVE

"Yessir," Midberry said, jumping up from the desk chair and saluting the first lieutenant entering the hut. The lieutenant returned the salute, sharply. "You're from the provost marshall's, sir?"

"Affirmative." The lieutenant looked about the hut, his hands clasped behind him. He wore a holstered .38 revolver. Midberry noticed that the revolver had white grips.

"You're Sergeant Midberry, right?"

"Yessir."

"Staff Sergeant Maguire's not in this morning?"

"Sir, he's late. He said he'd be in by eight."

The lieutenant nodded.

"I could call him at home, sir."

"No," the lieutenant said. He spoke slowly as if each word was the result of careful deliberation.

That won't be necessary, sergeant, Midberry thought.

"That won't be necessary, sergeant. I'd like to talk with you first anyway."

"Yessir. Of course." Midberry wondered how much the lieutenant knew about the way D.I.s worked together. Did he think he could get him to talk behind Maguire's back? Maybe the lieutenant had heard there was some sort of trouble between Maguire and himself?

"Some people think Staff Sergeant Maguire's the best D.I. on the island."

Midberry wished the lieutenant would quit his marching about. "Oh yessir," he said. "He's thought pretty highly of. Would you like a chair, sir?"

"Negative. This is your first platoon, isn't it, sergeant?"

"Yessir." A T.V. lawyer, Midberry thought. Asking questions he already knows the answers to. Suddenly, it struck Midberry that the way he felt about the lieutenant might well be the way the recruits felt about him. Did he put up too much of a false front too? He didn't try to. But could anyone be sure how others saw him? Maybe the lieutenant was just trying to do his job. Maybe the martinet pose was just his way of hiding his nervousness. He's probably scared silly, Midberry thought; a green lieutenant coming in all by his lonesome to investigate a man supposed to be the ideal D.I.

"It must be a real experience working with someone like Staff Sergeant Maguire on your first platoon."

"Yessir. It is."

"He must be able to teach you a great deal about being a D.I."

"Yessir. He can."

The lieutenant glanced at Midberry, then away. He brought a hand from behind his back and stroked his narrow chin. Midberry waited for him to say something else, but the lieutenant just stood looking at the deck, silent.

"Sir, would the lieutenant care for a cup of coffee?"

The lieutenant shook his head.

"Sergeant Maguire ought to be here by now. I could check with his wife. No trouble at all." Midberry picked up the phone.

"No," the lieutenant said. "I'll wait. Listen, if you do have some coffee made, sergeant . . . if it's no trouble, I mean."

So the lieutenant was scared. "I was going to make myself some anyhow."

Midberry put water on to boil and spooned instant coffee into two cups. The lieutenant sat in the chair beside the hut's single window.

"Sergeant?"

"Yessir."

"Nobody likes these cases. I think everybody concerned would be glad if we could just ignore it. Unfortunately we have to consider public opinion. The papers are very quick to pick up cases involving brutality charges. That's

226

why we try to get things ironed out as quick as we can, before some crusading reporter gets wind of it."

"Yessir."

"What I'm trying to say is that no one is out to crucify Staff Sergeant Maguire. This is to be an investigation, not a purge. I intend to find out the facts of the matter and I certainly hope those facts will prove insufficient as grounds for any disciplinary action. I just want that understood."

Midberry filled the cups and handed one to the lieutenant. "Yessir," he said. "Everybody here's got a job to do."

"Exactly," the lieutenant said. He smiled and sipped at his coffee. "Anyway, I wanted that out in the open. I don't really think it should take very long. You can give me the names of the recruits near this Cooper boy when the incident occured, and I'll check out their stories. I'd say that ought to do it." The lieutenant took another sip of coffee. "There won't be any trouble with their stories, will there?"

Midberry stopped short on the brink of answering "nosir." How would he know if the stories checked out unless he had helped rehearse them? "I don't think so, sir. We'll find out when you start the questioning, I guess."

"What I meant was, there's always the chance some recruit has a grudge against the D.I. and will try to get even by lying in a case like this. You think we'll have any of that?"

"Sir, I don't really know. A recruit's kinda like a woman, you know? Who can tell what they'll do next?" He smiled. He disliked the officer's pretense of having a friendly conversation. It made Midberry feel that the lieutenant had him figured as a soft touch.

"You do know which recruits were in the area at the time, is that correct?"

"Yessir." He went to the desk and brought a list of names to the lieutenant.

"And you were there at the time?"

"Yessir."

"Would any recruits other than these six have had a chance to see what happened?"

227

"Just the ones that rack near Cooper, sir. The others shouldn't have seen anything."

The lieutenant looked up. "How's that?"

"Well, sir, the way they were lined up for drill, the manual of arms, sir, they shouldn't have been looking in Cooper's direction. A recruit's supposed to look straight ahead of him, sir, when he's drilling."

"Yes, sergeant, I know."

Then don't ask, Midberry thought.

"Just what did cause the incident, sergeant?"

"The accident, sir?" Midberry waited until the lieutenant finally nodded in agreement, then went on to tell his rehearsed story.

"There shouldn't be any trouble then," the lieutenant said. "Since this is an isolated case, it should be pretty clear-cut. With a platoon having a record of unexplained injuries, you see, the matter's a bit more complicated."

"Yessir." All right now, Midberry said to himself, spring Detar on me. And Klein.

"Staff Sergeant Maguire," the lieutenant said.

"Sir?" Midberry answered. Then he saw the lieutenant wasn't speaking to him. Maguire stood at the hatch. The lieutenant rose and stepped past Midberry to return Maguire's salute.

"I'm Lieutenant Hart from the provost marshall's."

Why hadn't he said what his name was before? Midberry thought. Or didn't J.D.I.s rate the full introduction?

"Sir," Maguire said. He went to the hot plate and switched on the burner beneath the pan of water. "Had to take my daughter to the dentist. I'd have been in earlier otherwise. She's got a toothache." Maguire turned to the lieutenant, stretched open his mouth and jabbed a finger toward the rear molars. "There. We were up most of the night with her."

Midberry wondered if the lieutenant had been able to keep his balance. He comes in here expecting to meet Iron Mike and instead finds a pot-bellied little character talking about his kid's toothache. Midberry wondered too whether or not Maguire was lying about the dentist.

"Coffee?" Maguire asked the lieutenant.

"I made him some already," Midberry said.

"No thanks," the lieutenant said.

Midberry burned under the lieutenant's sudden unawareness of his presence. He had been all right to talk to before Maguire had come.

"I wanted to get started early," the lieutenant said.

"Well, sir, you have the names of the witnesses," Midberry said. "You want me to call them in for you?"

"In a minute, sergeant."

"Aren't you supposed to have a partner working with you?" Maguire asked.

Midberry noticed that the 'sir' was conspicuously missing from Maguire's remarks. The lieutenant, however, either hadn't noticed the omission or was not about to call attention to it.

"Usually we do," the lieutenant said. "We're stretched a bit thin right now though. Seems there's been a lot of accidents lately."

"Got you humping, huh?"

"I believe your platoon alone has had three or four, hasn't it?"

"Oh yessir," Maguire said. "This place is no fucking country club, that's for sure."

"Sir," Midberry said, "you want me to call the witnesses in a bunch or one by one?"

"One at a time."

"Yessir." Midberry took the list from the lieutenant and went toward the hatch.

"I figure you'll want some privacy for the questioning," Maguire said.

"Yes," the lieutenant said. "I will."

"Well, we got some work to finish up here, but the head's clear."

Midberry looked at the lieutenant's face. He thought he saw it color slightly.

"You could use our extra chair here too if you wanna sit down. I'm sure Sergeant Midberry would be happy to take it in there for you."

"Sure," Midberry said. He picked up the chair and waited by the hatch. The lieutenant hadn't moved. Midberry felt certain this time Maguire had gone too far. The lieutenant was going to charge him with insubordination.

"You could have this place, of course," Maguire said. "We wanna do everything we can to cooperate. I'm sure though you understand, sir, we got a helluva lot to get done. 782 gear to be checked out and all. Gotta keep humpin, don't we, sir?"

"That's quite all right, sergeant."

"Cause I'm sure, sir, you'll be at it the whole day."

"Most likely." The lieutenant moved to follow Midberry from the hut.

"Most likely?" Maguire laughed loudly. "Oh, the whole damned day, that's a fact. I know. I been through these things before, y'understand. Twice last year. Not that anything was proved either time. Nope, both times, came out clean as a whistle. Course, you'd know that from my record, wouldn't you, sir?" Maguire grinned, then cut the lieutenant off before he had had a chance to answer. "Anyhow, good luck. Sir."

The lieutenant followed Midberry into the head without speaking. It was obvious the officer was furious. His lips were pressed tightly together and his cheeks were flushed.

The long, concrete head was lined on one side with commodes, the last in line labeled "VD ONLY," on the other with wash bowls and shaving mirrors. Midberry set the straight-backed chair against the blank back wall.

"This ought to be pretty private, sir. I'll see no one comes in till you're done."

"All right, sergeant."

"Anybody has to make a head call, an emergency I mean, they can use the one in the squad bay across from us." Midberry waited, but though the lieutenant looked at him, he said nothing. Midberry felt he was doing almost as well as Maguire. "I'll fetch those witnesses for you now, sir."

"Sergeant."

"Yessir?"

"Will the rest of the platoon be in the squad bay most of the day?"

"If the lieutenant wants them there, sir, that's where I'll keep'm."

"You think that would be all right with Staff Sergeant Maguire?"

230

"Oh, yessir."

"Then keep them in, would you?"

"Yessir. Anything to help, sir." Midberry resisted the temptation to smile. It wouldn't do to be too openly sarcastic. He didn't have a legend working for him like Maguire.

"I might just want to talk to some other recruits than the ones whose names you gave me."

"Yessir. Of course."

"It wouldn't look very good, would it, if the only recruits I questioned were the ones on your list. Or did Staff Sergeant Maguire make up the list?"

"Nosir," Midberry said. "I made it out. I thought it might give you some help. Kind of a place to start." That was the way to keep it, Midberry thought. Just trying to be helpful.

"I wasn't certain," the lieutenant said.

"Sir? Of what?"

"Whether Staff Sergeant Maguire did the list himself or let you do it, sergeant."

"Oh." Midberry could think of nothing to say. He tried hard, knowing from watching Maguire that one had to keep the initiative. "Sir, perhaps the lieutenant would prefer to call the witnesses he wants himself?"

"I'm sure you're capable of handling it, sergeant."

Midberry moved to the hatch. "Then I'll get . . ."

"I'll start with the men whose names are on the list. Have them line up in the passageway. I'll call them in one by one."

"Yessir." Midberry started out.

"And sergeant . . ."

"Yessir?"

"That chair . . ." the lieutenant trailed off, his hand cupping his chin.

"Sir?"

"Maybe it would be better over there." The lieutenant gestured toward the wash bowls.

Midberry hesitated.

"Would you put it over there, sergeant?"

Midberry moved the chair. He asked if that would be all, barely covering the bitter edge of mockery in his voice.

231

The lieutenant seemed to take no notice of either Midberry's tone or question. He rubbed his narrow chin for a moment. "Maybe the other wall," he said. "Near the hatch."

The little bastard, Midberry said to himself, the little bastard! But he moved the chair.

The lieutenant decided then that the chair would be best where it had first been placed. Midberry put it back against the rear wall.

"Sorry to be so much trouble, sergeant."

"Not at all, sir. Will that be all, sir?"

"You won't forget to call in the witnesses?"

"Nosir." Midberry waited to be told that would be all.

The lieutenant looked at him curiously. "Did you have something you wanted to tell me, sergeant?"

"Nosir, I thought the lieutenant. . . ."

"Well we'd best get started then, hadn't we?"

Midberry spun about and left the head. That was all right, he thought. Let the little bastard play smartass and strut, throw his weight around. Him and his pearl-handled six-shooter. What the hell good would it do him? None, Midberry thought. It would work against him here. The squad bay wasn't some swank officer's club. P.I. was a far cry from Quantico. Here, it would be precisely the officer's attitude and dress which would help him fail. The recruits would be suspicious of him. All marines were suspicious of an officer that seemed too fancy, all guidebook and glitter. That was the kind of man got troops killed trying to pull off a textbook maneuver in combat. At least, that's what Midberry had learned from his D.I.s. And that's what he and Maguire were teaching their platoon.

Maguire motioned to Midberry from the hut. "The general ready to proceed?"

"Right."

"Lemme see that list," Maguire said. "Better have Waite go in first."

"I thought maybe I'd put him last in line."

"Uh-uh," Maguire said. "It probably won't go so hard on the first few. Hearing the same story, though, the general will get tougher. First, Waite, then Adamczyk and

232

Brashers. After them, Logan, Taylor and Moore, however you want. They'll do all right."

"You wanna see Waite first?"

"You just tell'm to remember last night. And graduation."

Midberry nodded. "Sherlock says he wants us to keep the rest of the herd around too. He says he might want to talk to some of them. Some others than the ones on the list, that's what he told me."

"Cagey little fuck, isn't he?" Maguire said. He grinned, shaking his head. "Y'wonder sometimes where they dig up these characters."

"You catch the pistol grips?"

Maguire grinned again and Midberry laughed. It gave him a good feeling to know Maguire shared his opinion of the lieutenant. It made up somewhat to Midberry for the way Maguire and the lieutenant had excluded him in the hut. It was the closest he and Maguire had come to being real partners, equal partners, since the start. Maybe, Midberry thought, Maguire finally had come to trust him, or at least had realized that he had no choice but to depend on him. Like it or not, either one of them, they were a team. The lieutenant's being set against them made Midberry see just how much of a team they were. Maybe Maguire had seen it too. Midberry hoped so.

"I better go get Waite and the others."

"Right. Get back in here then and keep an eye on the hut, will you? I gotta take off for a while. 'Bout a half hour."

Midberry felt a twinge of fear at Maguire's dumping the situation in his lap. He asked where Maguire was going.

"Dentist," Maguire said. He glanced at his wrist watch. "Gotta pick up my kid a little after nine. Get her to school."

"Sure." So it hadn't been just a ruse! "See you later."

Midberry went into the squad bay and called Waite front and center. Pausing at the squad bay hatch, he reminded Waite of the night before and of the upcoming platoon graduation. "You remember this, too," he said. "What goes on here in the long run is for your own good.

233

Just like my telling Sergeant Maguire yesterday about what you said, that was to help straighten you out is all. Nobody here's out to kick ass just for the fun of it, understand. Now get on into the head and tell the man your story. Everybody sticks together and next week it'll all be over. Later on, you'll look back and see you did right."

"Yessir."

"And if the lieutenant asks you about your lip, you tell'm you were in a fight with another recruit was all. All right?"

"Yessir."

"He's waiting. Go on."

With Waite gone, Midberry told the other recruits on the list in what order they should line up outside the head. He gave them a brief pep talk, then sat on the rifle-cleaning table and watched the platoon busy itself studying guidebooks or cleaning rifles.

Why he should have thought Maguire's dentist trip was a trick, he wasn't sure. Because Maguire was hard didn't mean he was inhuman. If he had been some kind of a monster, then Midberry was certain he would've stopped backing him long ago. He saw a side of Maguire, though, that the recruits and the lieutenant hadn't seen. So why had he been surprised by the dentist business, his mind persisted in asking. And if Maguire was such an average family man, then why had he kicked Cooper in the nuts and made Detar crawl like a dog? But Cooper had been an accident. Accidents can happen to anyone, anytime. Detar? The job, Midberry thought. A tough job took a tough man. What did the brass know about training boots? Like Maguire said, all the brass did was set the quotas and proficiency levels that the D.I.s had to meet. If anyone was guilty for Cooper and Detar, Klein and the others, then it was the brass, all the way up the chain of command to the Commandant and maybe even further than that. After all, Midberry thought, a D.I. had his job cut out for him. The Corps had built a tradition that recruits had to be made to live up to. The D.I. didn't create the tradition or the image, it was there before he was. Look at all the people who praised marines for being hard and tough. Leathernecks. Devil dogs. With the help of God

234

and a few marines. *Semper Fidelis*. The movies and the books and the ad men who told the public what a marine was and what a marine could do. All the flag-flying and band-playing and applause and cheering, and then let a D.I. push a little too hard trying somehow, anyhow to shape his loose, civilian mob of recruits to the nearly impossible mold of a marine, a mold set up and case-hardened long, long before the D.I. had been born, and what happened? Then the brass suddenly and righteously decided that it hadn't meant for those poor American boys to be trained quite that hard. Then the same newspapers which during any and all wars ran front page pictures and stories of marine combat heroics, ran editorials condemning the sadists in charge of recruit training. Then the protected, gone-soft-in-peace, general public cried out in shocked indignation at the cruel methods by which innocent boys were being turned into the trained killers the public itself had praised for so many years. And whenever public opinion turned sour against the U.S.M.C., the brass beat the brush for a scapegoat and invariably, sometimes seemingly at random, came up with a drill instructor to be court-martialed as a public sacrifice. After that, everything went back to normal. Training went on the same as it always had, and the newspapers, the public and the brass patted themselves on the back for their alert service in the timeless cause of humanity.

Deep in thought, Midberry suddenly realized that Waite was sitting on his locker box, shining his dress shoes. He went quickly to Waite's rack.

"How'd it go?"

"Sir, all right," Waite said, standing to attention.

"What'd you tell him?"

"Sir, nothing."

"Nothing at all?"

"Sir, nothing except that it was an accident."

"What else did he ask you?"

"Sir, about my lip. I told him I got bit by a sand flea."

"What? He believe that?"

"Yessir."

"That was all?"

"Yessir. And he wanted to know how we were treated. Whether or not anyone hit us or tortured us."

"Tortured?"

"Yessir."

The lieutenant, as Midberry had suspected, seemed to have a flair for the dramatic. He probably thought of himself as a rescuing knight doing battle against the wicked D.I. for the sake of the recruits' honor and innocence. "What'd you tell him?"

"Sir, nothing."

"You sure?"

"Yessir."

"Good," Midberry said, patting Waite on the shoulder. "This'll blow over. We all stick together and we can get back to our job. You people are supposed to be learning how to be marines, not sea lawyers, right?"

"Yessir."

Although Waite did not return his smile—a recruit was not allowed to smile, Midberry reminded himself—Midberry thought he had probably appreciated the gesture of friendliness. Especially after his session with Maguire.

Midberry went to the table and sat, watching the platoon. He wondered how much Waite held it against him for telling Maguire. Maybe, he thought, he should have handled it himself. Yet he hadn't been sure how to go about it. He had thought that maybe Maguire, having more experience, would know a better way. Why shouldn't he have thought that? He hadn't been trying to dodge the responsibility. He took a tough problem to the S.D.I., that was all. It was standard operating procedure.

But Midberry silently cursed Maguire. Maguire had handled Waite's case the same as he did everything else. Yet what choice had he, Midberry, had? If he hadn't told Maguire, and Waite had run to the brass, then he'd have been derelict of his duty. Worse, it might have seemed he had thrown in with the recruits.

If Waite had listened to him in the first place, there would never have been any trouble. Could he help it if a recruit refused to take good advice? If the boy lacked common sense?

Midberry liked to think that being a D.I. was like being a teacher. He taught the recruits, so he hoped at least, more than the basic techniques of military drill. He felt he also taught them a way of behavior, a way of looking at things and at oneself as a man. Maguire aside, it was good for the recruits to learn to handle their bodies and to discipline themselves. And it was good for them to be taught the concept of duty. Especially that. If he had learned one thing of importance during his six years of service, Midberry thought, it was that a marine did his duty no matter what. Midberry might occasionally through his own weakness doubt that concept, but deep down he was certain it was one of the things necessary to be a man. It was when he went against his duty that he felt most lost and insecure. That in itself seemed proof to him of duty's importance.

That's what he had tried earlier to tell Waite. Over and over again, he had stressed the importance of doing one's duty. He had done his best to teach Waite how the concept of duty was the foundation not only of the military, but of government, business, society as a whole, even the basis of one's family. But like any teacher, the D.I. could not reach everyone. And it was only when he was certain that he had failed to make Waite understand where his duty as a recruit lay, that Midberry had gone to Maguire. Given the situation, Midberry thought he had done the best he could.

TWENTY SIX

The lieutenant disgusted Waite. The correct military manner, the rapid-fire questioning, the stagey attempts to befriend a poor recruit, everything about the investigator was disgusting. Waite was certain that if the lieutenant had a D.I.'s, rather than an investigator's, job, he would be a recruit's nightmare. All spit and polish, medals and military creases, guidebook and regulations. The lieutenant was the kind of officer who would correct a recruit's bearing simply as a matter of principle. He was the kind who swore that rigid discipline was the key to a happy, healthy unit. Waite doubted there would be much difference between the lieutenant and Maguire as a D.I. Except the lieutenant most likely would be more given to psychological, rather than physical, harrassment.

The lieutenant's attitude had made it easier for Waite to stick to the official story. "Help me clean this mess up, son. With your help we could put a stop to men like Maguire and the way they mishandle authority." Waite wished he could have believed it. But he felt sure all the lieutenant was interested in was captain's bars. Maybe even that would have been all right if Waite had thought for a moment his testimony would actually change anything. But he doubted the lieutenant would prove a match for Maguire. And what if he did win and get rid of Maguire? What about Midberry? What about the whole damned Corps? he thought. Who was going to change that? Not some rank-hungry first lieutenant playing detective, that was sure. How could he make captain if he took on the Corps?

Midberry came into the squad bay and told the platoon that the lieutenant was now asking recruits to take a lie detector test. Midberry said the recruits should know it was within their rights to say no. Under Article 31 of the Unified Code of Military Justice they were entitled to refuse such tests. And no matter what all he said, the lieutenant could not do a thing to them for refusing. The recruits said yessir, they understood, and Midberry hurried from the squad bay.

The investigation went on all day, the lieutenant calling in recruits at random. As soon as a recruit would return to the squad bay, he would be surrounded by those who had already been questioned, wanting to know if he had stuck to the story, and by those who had not yet been questioned, wanting to know what kinds of questions the lieutenant had asked. The train of recruits, the squad bay hatches swinging open and shut, continued until late afternoon. Maguire came in then to take the platoon to evening chow. He said the lieutenant would be back first thing in the morning. Of course for an officer, Maguire reminded the platoon, first thing in the morning meant around 0800 or 0900 hours, not 0430.

Waite saw the others smile. Aside from Maguire's joke, he knew they were glad to have to miss another training day. Waite, though, didn't feel at all relieved. He had been hoping the investigation would take only one day. All he wanted now was to get on with the training and be done with it, get it over so he could get the hell off the island.

After chow, Maguire and Midberry broke the ordinary routine and took the platoon to the Base Theatre. The film was "Around the World in Eighty Days" and the recruits, released momentarily from the tensions of training and of the investigation, laughed often and raucously at the antics of Cantinflas and at the crazily interrupted balloon voyage. Waite enjoyed the film and found it possible to relax and forget, so much so that he was jolted awake by the house lights at the film's end.

Later, he wished he hadn't slept in the theater. He had taken the edge from his fatigue and lay awake in his bunk, listening to the sighs and snores of the platoon. He considered getting up and talking to the firewatch, but was afraid to as Maguire had the duty.

One week more and he would have a week's leave. Waite wished the prospect of going home excited him. As it was, he would be glad to get off the island, but that was as far as his expectations went. What was there for him at home? No one seemed to have any real need of him. He had always suspected that, or known it maybe but pretended not to, but now his absence had made it so apparent he couldn't avoid it. The dry-cleaning shop was doing fine and Carolyn seemed quite content with her new fiance. Even the tone of his mother's letters suggested she was pleased with his being gone. He could have been mistaken. It could have been just the relief his mother felt that he was making some progress. Still, the feeling persisted. His brother had always been much better at clerking the store than he ever would be. Even with Carolyn, Waite had felt that he could be replaced with no great difficulty. And the past eleven weeks had proven his suspicions true. He was useless. His leaving had barely disturbed his family, fiance and friends' routine. Everything ran smoothly. Everyone did quite well without him.

But why should that annoy him? All his life he had kept himself free of entanglements. He was attached to nothing, therefore nothing was attached to him. It was very simple. And it was the way he had always told himself he wanted his life to be.

"You gotta think about your future," Jerry had told him, and Waite hadn't been able to hold back his laugh. "You ought to once in a while at least think about our future," Carolyn had said, and he had kept from laughing, keeping silent and obediently nodding his head. "What are you going to do with yourself?" his mother constantly asked him. Friends he ran into asked, "What're you doing? Got any plans?" On bill boards, bank ads warned him to "Plan Your Future Now!" and on the bus he sat staring at investment brochures entitled "Look Ahead." So he had enlisted in the United States Marines Corps. He had joined the branch of service, as a recruiting pamphlet put it, where a young man had an unlimited future. He had

240

joined because he had seen it as a way out; as a four-year break from the pressures at home that he commit himself to something. Himself? What self?

Waite sat up in his rack and dropped to the deck. He nodded as he passed the firewatch mooning out the window, but the recruit was too far away to notice. Planning his future, Waite thought. Dreaming of the days of glory as a corporal at Camp LeJeune.

In the head, Waite dropped his skivvie drawers and sat on the cool plastic commode seat. He squinted, his eyes pained by the bare overhead bulbs. Against the back wall stood the straight-backed chair he had sat in that morning, while the officer rattled off questions about Maguire and platoon treatment.

"Does Staff Sergeant Maguire hit you very often?" the lieutenant had asked.

"Nosir," Waite had said.

"Only once in a while."

"Nosir."

"You mind telling me then, private, how your lip got swollen?"

"Sir?"

The lieutenant sighed. "Look, son, don't play games with me, okay? You look like an intelligent young man. I'll treat you like an adult and you have the courtesy to do the same with me. Okay?"

"Yessir."

"You did know your lip was swollen, didn't you?"

"Oh yessir."

"Well. . . ."

"Sir?"

The lieutenant fidgeted in front of the chair. It seemed to Waite that the officer had to make a constant, conscious effort to keep from breaking out with what he really thought of all cowardly, crude, common, ignorant recruits good only for carrying rifles and answering questions like a bunch of ventriloquist's dummies. Waite wondered how long the lieutenant's determined friendliness would bear the strain of hearing the same carefully-rehearsed story. Would he wear down during the long afternoon and begin threatening recruits with the pearl-handled .38 tucked neatly in the gleaming brown leather holster high on his waist?

"Well," the lieutenant said with obvious patience, "just how did your lip get swollen?"

"Sir, I got bit."

The lieutenant raised an eyebrow.

"By a sandflea, sir. It swelled up. The lip."

"Then neither Staff Sergeant Maguire nor Sergeant Midberry has ever laid a hand on you? Struck you, I mean? Hit you?"

"Nosir."

"How do you explain that?"

"Sir, I don't know."

"Are you just lucky?"

"Sir?"

"Not getting hit. I'm sure some of the other recruits have been hit, haven't they?"

"Nosir."

"Come off it, son. I thought we were going to level with each other. We're both intelligent men, right? You're even. . . ."

"Oh, yessir."

The lieutenant cleared his throat. "As I was saying, you're even a squad leader. Third squad, isn't it?"

"Yessir."

"You see, I've looked into the platoon and I know a little more about you than you might think. I know for instance that you're a good marine, that you're squared away enough to be made a squad leader. Now they don't make dummies squad leaders, do they, private?"

Waite feigned embarrassment.

"So that means you're not one of the ones punished. But I'll bet you have a lot of fellows in the platoon, maybe even in your squad, that can't quite seem to get with it, if you know what I mean. Screw-offs, isn't that what you fellas call them? I'll bet they get hit often enough."

"Fuck-ups," Waite said. "That's what we call them all right, sir; fuck-ups. They fuck-up everything. Some of them would fuck-up a wet dream." Waite smiled. "That's a little joke of ours, sir."

242

"Yes," the lieutenant said. He returned the smile, weakly. "But these men must get hit once in a while, don't they?"

"Sir, the fuck-ups?"

"Yes."

"Sir, I wasn't sure which ones you meant."

"The fuck-ups," the lieutenant said. "Doesn't Staff Sergeant Maguire hit them?"

"Nosir."

"Never?"

"Nosir."

"What? Why not?"

Waite kept from smiling. "Sir," he said, "that's against the rules, isn't it?"

The rest of the questioning had gone the same way. Finally the lieutenant had given up and told Waite to get out and to tell the next man to step in. Waite had left, telling Adamczyk, next in line, that he was to wait there until his name was called.

Why, Waite wondered now, had he felt so driven to frustrate the lieutenant? For some reason it hadn't been enough to stick to his story, saying "Nosir" over and over again like a criminal pleading the fifth amendment. Instead, it had given him great satisfaction to play dumb and watch the officer trying to hide his increasing disgust and frustration. It had seemed to help Waite rid himself of the bitterness and self-disgust he had brought with him to the questioning.

Whatever the cause, Waite thought, he had done in his own way just what Maguire wanted. He had stuck to the official story. No recruit ever got hit or excessively punished. Cooper's injury was an accident and had been self-inflicted. He knew nothing about Detar. The same with Klein. Johnson? Quinn? The names weren't even familiar.

Waite rose from the commode and pressed the flush lever with a bare foot. No one could say he wasn't a good marine. He had followed orders. He had shown *esprit de corps*. So what that he had done it only out of fear? Fear, spiced with the hope for honors at graduation, was the motive behind every action of every recruit. Waite

243

had done well. Therefore, he would probably, even counting his temporary lapse of loyalty, be awarded P.F.C. at the end of the training. In fact, it was nearly certain. If he didn't get it for being squad leader, Maguire might put him up for it as a reward for keeping his mouth shut. Waite had heard of other recruits getting a stripe for less. He had done well. He could go home with a P.F.C. stripe and a marksman medal. His mother was sure to approve. Her son had finally succeeded in something. And he would have the stripe and the medal to prove it, had he any doubts.

Then where? Back from leave to Camp Geiger for infantry training. Shipped out from there to some infantry base where if he minded himself and stayed squared away he might in four years rise from P.F.C. to Lance Corporal to Sergeant; from fire-team leader to squad leader to maybe even platoon sergeant. He could then come home for good as a thorough success. He would have done well.

All right, Waite thought, so what was wrong with that? Klein, Detar, Cooper, they should've stuck it out, that was all. There were always some that couldn't make it. Was that his fault? What was he supposed to do, quit when he had it knocked just to show his heart was in the right place? What about his head? Bullshit. Let kids like Adamczyk swallow that line. Not him.

It wouldn't do anything anyhow. It wouldn't bring anyone back into the platoon and it wouldn't even stop Maguire from doing the same thing all over again. Even if Maguire did get busted, which Waite knew was next to impossible since none of the other recruits were willing to testify, even then he'd probably get rank again in a short time. He had too much experience for the Corps not to make use of him again in some sort of command. Anything a recruit tried to do about the situation then would be a waste of time and energy. It would. Because it took more than one man to change a situation like the one Waite felt himself up against. A single testimony was worthless.

Back in his rack, Waite dozed, slept fitfully and woke before reveille, his mind immediately resuming the struggle with the tangle of thoughts quieted for a while by sleep.

Maybe if he had told the lieutenant the truth, it might have encouraged some of the others and one or two just might have backed him. That maybe would have been enough. But no, the first man questioned, he lied and helped set the pattern that would last throughout the investigation. Helping to break down the lieutenant, he had helped keep Maguire in power. Everything was running along just as Maguire had expected.

Waite reviewed the men in his squad. Adamczyk, he was pretty sure, would still come along if someone else started it. But he was the only man he felt he could depend on in the squad. In the rest of the platoon he figured it was at least a fifty-fifty chance that Weasel and maybe Brashers, the tall skinny kid from Texas, would back him. They had taken hell from Maguire and would maybe want revenge bad enough to forget their fear. Then the ball would be rolling and there might be others. Waite did not know many of the recruits well. But then not many of the recruits knew each other well. They were not allowed to know each other well. They were kept apart by having to constantly worry about their own survival, by being pitted in competition against the other recruits, by having their success depend upon another's failure. Divide and conquer.

Wondering who he knew well enough to count on for sure, Waite felt his own indecision. Even he wasn't sure yet that he could go through with it. He disliked the lieutenant and even more he disliked the idea of testifying. It seemed somehow a betrayal, though he knew that it wasn't. Still, he would be called a traitor and a coward. And he most likely was a coward. For at the very bottom of himself, he was afraid. He wanted to hide, from the investigation, from questions, from himself. How could he ask anyone to back him up? For all he knew about himself, any resolution he made could be changed by reveille. Ask someone to follow him? Hell, he wasn't even sure where he was going.

At morning chow, Waite was silent and ate little. The others at the table passed whispered remarks about the lieutenant and about how much they hated to miss another whole day's drill out in the hot sun. They rolled their eyes in mock sorrow, and wolfed their eggs, fried potatoes and toast. Adamczyk asked for and got Waite's potatoes and Carleton and Moore, his eggs and toast. Waite drank his coffee and left the mess hall. He was the first recruit from the platoon onto the hard-stand. He stood at attention under the already hot sun, his solitary figure dwarfed by the huge stretch of vacant parade ground.

In less than a week he would march across this same parade ground to graduate. He would be a marine, not a maggot; a man, not a boy. And he would be free of all but the bitter memories of Maguire and P.I. He smiled to himself to think of Adamczyk the coward and Fillipone the bully, the rest of the mob too, himself included, being finally officially declared men. It made him think of Bert Lahr as the cowardly lion in the movie "The Wizard of Oz." He had loved that movie as a boy, had gone to see it a half-dozen times. Now he would get his chance to play the lion. Declared brave and given a medal to prove it. Waite laughed aloud, then checked himself as he knew Midberry was probably spying on him from one of the mess hall windows.

If he testified, the others would say he was chicken-shit. And all of them scared into buttoning up. And if no one backed him, then the Corps would shit-can him. He would be officially pronounced unfit, not enough of a man to be a marine. Or he'd be shipped from platoon to platoon, each D.I. getting in his licks for good old Maguire until he could no longer take it and would go over the hill. If no one backed him, he would fail. His intentions wouldn't matter, he would be a public failure. A hero, he remembered the Wizard explaining to the Cowardly Lion, is someone with a medal on his chest.

Other recruits began leaving the mess hall and walking out onto the parade ground to fill in ranks. Waite watched as Adamczyk came out onto the low stoop, picking his teeth. He walked toward the platoon with a low swinging step. Waite recognized the walk as John Wayne's and he would have laughed aloud, Midberry watching or not, had he not been hit squarely by the rock-hard thought that whatever he chose to do or not do, he would always

246

know. Like Adamczyk, no matter what front he succeeded in putting up, he would know. No matter what anyone else thought, he would know. No matter what the Commandant of the United States Marine Corps officially and publicly decreed, he would know.

As soon as Midberry had left the squad bay after calling the first recruit for questioning, Waite went to the head. "Sir," he said, "Private Waite requests permission to speak to the lieutenant."

"What is it, private?" The lieutenant only half-turned his head. It was obvious he had talked to Private Waite all he cared to.

Waite looked at the recruit seated in the chair. The lieutenant told him to go ahead and say what he had to say or get out.

"Sir, I would like to speak to the lieutenant in private."

The recruit was told to wait outside. When he had gone, Waite said he would like to change his story about the Cooper incident.

The lieutenant bobbed his head sharply and motioned Waite to the chair. "I knew it," he said, grinning tightly. "I knew someone here would have the sense to tell the truth. Don't worry, private, some of the others will open up now. It only takes one to break the ice. Go ahead. What about Cooper? And the others, Klein and what was the other's name?" The lieutenant seemed almost jubilant. His pacing revealed a new bounce to his step.

"Detar, sir."

"He's the one with the knee injuries?"

"Yessir."

"How did he hurt his knees?"

"Sir," Waite said, "crawling around in the head. Sergeant Maguire made him crawl like a dog."

The lieutenant snorted. "I thought as much," he said.

TWENTY SEVEN

Waite knew by the sidelong glances he got from the others that the word had gotten around. Taylor, the recruit in the head when he had asked to speak to the lieutenant, must have talked. He was pretty certain though that Maguire and Midberry didn't know yet. He would have been called into the hut if they knew. Well, he had done his part. Now it was up to the lieutenant and the rest of the platoon. All he could do was wait. Be true to his name, he thought.

Waite sat on his locker box at the rear of the rack, his back to the bulkhead, idly rubbing an oily rag against the barrel and receiver of his rifle. His bayonet, sheathed, but with the catch undone, lay at his feet. He knew that Fillipone and some of the others might decide it was their duty as loyal marine boots to punish him for not keeping his mouth shut. If they did come for him, he thought, then they had better come for blood because that's just what they'd get. They would find out quick enough who was chicken and who wasn't. Waite even hoped someone would try pushing him around. Anyone. He felt inside like a spring wound too tight. He was primed and ready, waiting for someone to set him off.

Adamczyk had been recalled to the head. Waite had told the lieutenant that either Adamczyk or Weasel might back him up. But Weasel had been in and come back and hadn't opened his mouth. Now, Waite watched Adamczyk return to the squad bay to be immediately surrounded by the recruits idling about the hatch. In a minute or so, Adamczyk emerged from the group and came to the rack, head down.

Even if he had told the lieutenant something, Waite thought, Adamczyk still wouldn't have been dumb enough to let the others know about it. No matter what, he would've told them he had kept his mouth shut. Waite figured there was still a chance Adamczyk had, or would, come over to his side. Though now, when Waite tried to get his attention, Adamczyk ignored him. He would answer none of Waite's questions.

Scared of everything, Waite thought. That was all right though. Adamczyk had only to talk to one person, the lieutenant. Waite could find out at evening chow whether or not he had.

But in the mess hall Adamczyk still refused to talk. He shook his head no to everything Waite asked him. The other recruits at the table, however, were talkative, passing remarks about chicken-shits and big mouths. Waite angrily bolted his meal and went outside to stand in ranks. He had been waiting only a short while when Taylor and Fillipone came out of the mess hall. Waite saw them talking and his body tightened in expectation. The two recruits passed him, however, and took their place in ranks without looking at him. A bit later, Adamczyk came out.

"You tell him anything?" Waite said from the corner of his mouth.

"No."

"You mean you told'm that goddam cock and bull story about Cooper?"

"That's right."

"Jesus," Waite said. "You really are yellow, aren't you?"

"Look who's talking," Adamczyk said.

"The big Bible-pounder, goddam Holy Joe."

"Look who's talking," Adamczyk said.

Waite asked him what he meant, trying to bait him into a fight, but Adamczyk clammed up, like a statue staring straight ahead.

But there was still a chance, Waite thought. Sister Mary, Scuz, any of the others. . . . Who could tell who might decide to get something off his chest once he was alone with the lieutenant. That's the way the lieutenant had said it would go, and his job was running investiga-

249

tions. He should know something about the way they went.

Back at the squad bay, the recruits were put to work cleaning their rifles. When they had finished, Maguire came into the squad bay and the platoon was called to attention.

Waite had been carefully watching the squad bay hatch since the platoon had returned from chow. As two full hours dragged past, he had felt his hopes sinking. Now, seeing the look on Maguire's face, he knew it was over. He had lost. They would all turn on him now. They'd go at him now like a pack of goddamned wolves. He was down now and he'd soon be out. But at least he had had the satisfaction of making Midberry and Maguire sweat it for a while. That was something.

Maguire announced what Waite had expected: the investigation was over. Tomorrow the platoon would get back to training. There would be no court martial and the platoon would therefore graduate on schedule. By the end of the week, Maguire told them, they'd be on the bus to Camp Geiger. The recruits, except for Waite and, Waite was quick to notice, Adamczyk, cheered the announcement.

"Insufficient evidence," Maguire said, grinning in Waite's direction. There were many recruits openly smiling and others were whispering, but Maguire seemed not to notice. "Seems there was only one maggot in this entire fucking mob that didn't have the guts to stick to his story. Wonder who it was?"

The recruits gawked, the squad bay going suddenly silent, as Maguire walked down the passageway to stand facing Waite.

"A maggot that can't stick to his story during one stinking little two-day investigation, he's just the kind of chicken-shit little prick gets into combat and gets his buddies killed. He's the kind runs out just when he's needed most. Be doing the Corps a favor to shitcan a maggot like that. Sure do wish we knew who was the one with the big mouth. Ain't that so, third squad leader?"

"Sir," Waite said, his voice fluttering despite his trying to keep it even and deep, "we already know."

"Oh we do, do we?"

"Yessir."

"Who? You mean everybody here knows who that chicken-shit is?"

"Sir, we all know who talked." He was going to say, 'who had the guts to talk,' but was afraid to aggravate Maguire any further. But he would not try to wriggle out of it either. He had seen Maguire time and again trick other recruits into lying and begging by dangling in front of them the false hope that the drill instructor actually didn't know what had happened. Maguire would have to find someone else to play cat and mouse with him this time, Waite thought. He knew what he had done. Maguire knew what he had done. And he would do it again if he had to, Waite thought. No matter how scared he was. He was not ashamed. And he would not allow Maguire to make a fool of him.

"Oh," Maguire said again, "we do, huh?"

"Yessir."

"Suppose you clue me in then, maggot. Who was it shot off his rotten mouth?"

"Sir, the drill instructor already knows."

"Oh no," Maguire said, his eyes widening in mock innocence. "No, I don't. You tell me."

"Sir," Waite said. "The drill instructor already knows."

The recruits murmured. Maguire told them to shut up. "Didn't I just say I didn't know," Maguire said to Waite. "Now you had best tell me, maggot. And you had best be goddam quick about it."

"Sir, the drill instructor already knows. I think private Taylor already told the. . . ."

Maguire punched Waite sharply in the stomach and on the chin. Waite slammed back against the rack frame, bounced forward to take a right on his cheekbone, then another in the stomach. As he pitched forward, Maguire chopped at his neck, missed, striking Waite's shoulder.

"Let'm alone," Waite heard Maguire say. He felt Adamczyk's hands hesitate slightly before leaving his shoulders. His ears were buzzing, but he did not think his cheekbone was broken and he was getting his breath back. He lifted himself onto one elbow. He was scared and wanted out.

251

But he was not going to let himself cry. Or beg. Or faint. Or lie. He would show them all that there was at least one goddamned man in the chicken-coop of a squad bay. He heard Maguire then telling him to get up and he wondered what chance he had of getting to his bayonet. He had put it back on the cartridge belt hanging from his rack right after chow, but had thought to leave the catch undone. The bayonet would slide out quickly, if he could get to it before Maguire realized what he was doing. Waite pushed himself to one knee.

Maguire grabbed Waite by the shirt and hauled him to his feet. "I said I didn't know who it was, maggot. You hear me? Now you tell me and I just might let you off easy."

The platoon laughed. Maguire grinned. "Hell boy, you got no cause to protect whoever it was shot off his mouth. He don't care enough about you and the rest of the platoon to stick to his story, does he? Why should you worry about him?"

The uneven chorus of laughter angered Waite. Maguire wanted to play comedian, did he? All right, Waite thought, fuck it. He was bound to be shit-canned anyway. "Sir," he said loudly, "I won't tell his name because I respect the man."

"Respect!" Maguire said. "Ho, boy! Respect what man, you raggedy-assed little fuck? What d'you respect him for, huh? Diarrhea of the mouth?"

"For his courage," Waite said. "It took. . . ."

Some recruits laughed. Maguire shushed them.

"Sir, it took courage to tell the truth even though he knew he'd catch hell for it. I respect him for that."

"Shit," Maguire said.

"Sir, he has guts. That's a helluva lot more than the rest of this platoon has."

Maguire stepped back, his hand out as if presenting Waite to an audience. "Y'hear that," he said to the platoon. "This maggot says you're all yellow!" The recruits booed. "That's what he says," Maguire went on. "You wanna argue about it, you can do it later. Myself, I sure as hell wouldn't like it somebody calling me yellow."

"We'll see who's yellow," someone called down from the far end of the squad bay.

"Maybe you can find out who it was talked, too," Maguire said. "Kind of kill two birds with one stone, so to speak." The platoon laughed again, and Maguire studied Waite for a long moment, his bugeyes cold and hard. "You think maybe your pistol-packing buddy will have your heroic young ass shipped home in a fancy coffin, huh?"

"Sir," Waite said, "I don't know."

"Oh you don't?"

"Nosir. I don't much care either, sir."

Maguire faked a right-handed slap, the hand stopping just short of Waite's cheek. Waite flinched. "Shit," Maguire said. "You scared or something?"

"Yessir."

"Bout now you wish y'would've kept your mouth shut, huh?"

"Nosir."

"Bull. That's all right. We'll see how much guts you got before tonight's over, understand?"

"Yessir," Waite said.

"I wanna see you in the hut soon's it's time for lights out, understand?"

"Yessir."

"You too," Maguire said to Adamczyk.

"Sir? Me?" Adamczyk tried to cover his fear and surprise. "Yessir."

When Maguire left the squad bay, Fillipone and a few others sauntered past Waite's rack making remarks about finding out who had the guts in the platoon. Waite, again with his back to the bulkhead and the bayonet at his feet, ignored them. He was biding his time. He figured he still had at least one chance. As soon as the area had cleared, therefore, Waite stepped to the front of the rack, took a firm hold on Adamczyk's arm and pulled him between the racks.

"Sit down." He motioned to the bunk. Adamczyk tried to argue and Waite roughly pushed him down. He took his seat then on his locker box.

Adamczyk saw the bayonet laying open beside Waite. "Hey, what the hell you trying to do?"

"I wanna talk to you."

"I don't want to hear it," Adamczyk said. He put his hands over his ears. "You got me in enough trouble now."

Waite picked up the bayonet. "You're gonna talk to me and you're gonna listen to me, or so help me Christ I'll cut you apart."

Adamczyk took his hands from his ears. "What?"

"You heard me."

"How could I hear you with. . . ."

"I'm through playing games, so shuttup and listen."

"Oh no. Not till you put that away."

"Shuttup," Waite said. But he saw that Adamczyk's attention was riveted strictly on the bayonet, so he sheathed it again. It would do him no good to threaten Adamczyk. He had to get him on his side, not scare him away. "All right. How come you didn't tell the lieutenant the truth?"

"You think I'm crazy? You're just trying to get me in with you. Why didn't you keep your mouth shut anyhow? How come you gotta make trouble now for everybody?"

"You know damn well why. Don't tell me you're not sick of the crap Maguire hands out."

"So?"

"Why didn't you tell him then? The lieutenant. That was your chance."

"Because," Adamczyk said. He thought for a moment, knowing he couldn't talk to Waite about duty or honor, and not wanting to admit how afraid he was of what Maguire would do to him if he talked. It was different for Waite. He was tough. How could he ever understand how it was for someone barely able to hang on. Adamczyk could hardly handle the everyday routine of training. He knew he wasn't up to taking on any extra trouble. He'd crack up. Just like Klein, he'd go looney.

"Because you were scared, right?"

"No. Because I had the guts to stick it out. Not like you, breaking down and blabbing just as soon as there's a little pressure. Don't. . . ."

"Come off it," Waite said. "Hell, we were both scared, all right? But I didn't break down under pressure and you know it. You know damned well it takes more guts to talk than not to."

"I don't know . . ." Adamczyk started.

"So what're you going to do now?"

"What do you mean?"

"You gonna stick with me or not?"

"What?" Adamczyk started up, but Waite pushed him back onto the edge of the bunk. "What in hell you trying to do anyhow," Adamczyk said, speaking quickly, his voice high. "We're in the same squad, that's all. I never said I'd help. We never made any deals. Hell, I told you I wanted nothing to do with it, remember? Don't you remember? I told you that earlier, a long time ago. I don't want anything to do with it."

"You're just gonna keep right on lying?"

"I'm not gonna keep on doing anything. It's all over. Done."

"Not yet, it isn't," Waite said.

"Not for you maybe."

"What about tonight?"

"That's your problem."

"Maybe not," Waite said.

Adamczyk waited. He bit at a fingernail. "What d'you mean?"

"Maguire wants to see you too, right?"

"So what?"

"What for?"

"How should I know! Don't try making it out to be something big, okay. He wants to see me, that's all."

"Oh hell," Waite said. "Maguire knows we're buddies."

"But we're not!"

"He thinks so though."

"Okay, so I'll tell'm we're not. What you do is strictly up to you. I got nothing to do with it. And that's just what I'll tell Maguire."

"Sure, sure. But you know how he is, don't you? When he gets something into his head, that's all he'll believe, right? He'll just think you're trying to lie your way out of it. That'll just make him madder."

"Lie my way out of what? I didn't do a damn thing."

"Not yet maybe. But Maguire'll want to make sure you

255

don't, so that means he plans to lean on you a little. Like he did on Klein and Detar." Waite touched his puffed lip and reddened cheek. "And me. That's what you got in store for you tonight, and you know it just like I do."

"It's not fair," Adamczyk said. He seemed near tears.

"You're damn right it's not," Waite said. "That's what I'm telling you. But that's Maguire's way. The only way to stop it is to stop him, don't you see? You could request mast, see the lieutenant."

"Oh sure."

"You could. Request mast. Maguire can't turn you down. Even if he tried you could go to Midberry. He'd let you, I'm sure of it. He might even help if he saw there was more than one of us and that he couldn't get out of it."

"I don't know," Adamczyk said.

"Look, let's face it. It's a rotten situation, right? You're gonna get your ass kicked either way, fair or not. So why not get it kicked taking a chance at nailing Maguire?"

"I said I don't know!" Adamczyk didn't know what to do and he didn't want to think about it. He was afraid of Maguire and he was afraid of Waite talking him into something. Why should he listen to Waite? Misery loves company, he thought. Yet turning in his mind were all the scenes of Maguire's beatings and harrassments. He remembered earlier bending to pick up Waite and hating Maguire for ordering him to leave Waite alone. Inside him, fanned by Waite's voice, he felt a bit of the fire he had had when he'd gone to see the chaplain. Then he had thought that with enough perseverance he could change the whole situation. Now, even as afraid as he was, Adamczyk was excited by the discovery that the possibility still existed. All that was needed, he heard Waite's voice saying, was one more man with guts.

"Maybe," Adamczyk said quietly, glancing about him to see if there might be anyone else to hear.

"Really? You sure?"

"What'd I say? I said maybe, didn't I. Maybe. I gotta think about it."

"What's there to think about? Just go tell Midberry you want to see the lieutenant. Go on."

Adamczyk bent his head, getting slowly up from the bunk. "Look, don't rush me, okay? Maybe means maybe. I'll think about it. I'll talk to you later."

During the rest of the hour before lights-out, Adamczyk sat on his locker box and tried to think. He wished there was someone he could talk to—ask for advice. Waite and Maguire and Midberry would be more than ready to answer his questions, but none of them would be objective. What he needed most, Adamczyk told himself, was objectivity. He had to forget his fear and anger, any emotional attachments, and try to see the situation just as it was. But whenever he tried that, the situation being what it was, he visualized Maguire knocking Waite down, Waite's body landing at his feet, and he felt a furious urge to punish Maguire not just for that, but for everything Maguire had done to the platoon. Like the time Maguire had caught him dreaming on guard duty, and the first six weeks always calling him "Doubleshit" and making fun of his religion. He had a fair chance now, Adamczyk thought, of getting back for everything.

Adamczyk recalled other instances of Maguire's cruelty, forgetting objectivity in an effort to stir up in himself enough anger for him to act without second thoughts. As soon as he began reviewing Maguire's actions, however, the flare of his anger was doused by chill waves of fear. Adamczyk was angered by Maguire hitting Waite that night, that was true, but deeper than that he was scared and his fear told him it could have been, would yet be, him instead of someone else. It was the same with memories of Cooper and Detar. If he sided with Waite, Adamczyk knew there was no telling what Maguire might do to him. He could get killed. He tried to tell himself he was exaggerating and that Maguire had a career to worry about and therefore wasn't about to kill anyone right after an official investigation. Yet Adamczyk could not rid himself of the memory of the wild look in Maguire's eyes. That and the realization that it was Maguire's career he would be threatening, paralyzed Adamczyk. Fear and frustration and, out of the mixture, a desperate anger strung his nerves out so thin and tight he thought

257

he'd scream. He felt on the verge of cursing not just Maguire but the Corps and even more so the government as a whole. Who was it anyhow that allowed a man like Maguire to have control over people's lives? What had Adamczyk ever done to have deserved Maguire as a D.I.? The entire situation was unfair; to be stuck through no fault of your own and with no choice in a situation where no matter what you decided to do, you lost. The injustice of Adamczyk's predicament frustrated his efforts to think clearly. He felt badgered, put upon. It seemed to him that just at the moment he had glimpsed a door opening to the outside world, the long blank squad bay walls had begun slowly and surely closing in upon him. He was trapped. His fear told him that he would suffocate or be crushed, that one way or another, before the night was over, he'd be dead.

TWENTY EIGHT

Midberry put the platoon to bed. Waite and Adamczyk waited before their rack at attention until all the recruits were quiet in their bunks, then went before Midberry out of the darkened squad bay to the hut.

In the passageway Waite asked in a quick whisper whether or not Adamczyk was going to help him. Adamczyk nodded.

"What?" Waite hissed. "Yes or no?"

"I said I would, didn't I?"

"No talking," Midberry said.

Adamczyk shook his head. His eyes shone.

"Just tell'm you wanna request mast," Waite whispered.

Midberry stepped in front of them at the hut's hatch. "I said no talking," he said. "You hear me?"

"Yessir," they said.

"All right, get inside. Hold it." He touched Waite's arm, holding him back. "You stay here."

Adamczyk and Midberry went into the hut and the hatch was closed behind them. Waite leaned close to the hatch. He could hear Maguire's voice, but could not make out the words. The muted tone, however, encouraged him. He was afraid Adamczyk would break if Maguire got rough. He felt that his only real hope was Midberry helping to keep Maguire in line.

The firewatch passed him. It was a man from his squad, Hammarburg. He acted as if Waite were invisible, passing him to go to the middle of the passageway where he pivoted at the red line marking the end of platoon 197's area and of his responsibility, and, back straight, eyes dead ahead, returned to the squad bay.

The murmur inside the hut grew louder. Waite began more and more to doubt his chance of winning. He wished he had thought to tell Adamczyk to play along until he got a chance to talk to the captain. That way Adamczyk wouldn't have had to face Maguire. Except Waite hadn't had much time. Didn't have much time, he thought; by morning he might already have been shipped out. He wasn't sure exactly what Maguire had in store for him, but he knew the D.I. wouldn't be fool enough to let a recruit trying to line up witnesses for a court martial stick around the platoon. So he'd had to act quickly. He'd taken what he saw to be his only chance. What was done, was done.

Half an hour later the hatch opened and Waite didn't need to ask any questions. He knew by the look on Adamczyk's face that Maguire had won. Adamczyk hurried past Waite and into the squad bay.

"Am I gonna have to come out there and drag your yellow ass in here?" Maguire called from the hut.

Waite stepped to the edge of the hatch, did a sharp left face and knocked loudly on the woodwork. "Sir, Private Waite reporting as ordered." Maguire told him to come in and he stepped inside and stood at attention before the desk. Maguire was leaning back in the desk chair. Midberry stood to one side and to the rear, his hands behind his back.

"Your buddy the lieutenant wasn't much help, was he?"

"Nosir."

"Wasn't that what Sergeant Midberry and myself told you?"

"Yessir."

"What the fuck's the matter with you anyhow, maggot?"

"Sir, nothing."

"Don't you have any brains in that ugly head of yours?"

"Yessir."

"You sure don't use'm much, do you?"

"Nosir."

Maguire leaned forward. He held a sheaf of typewritten papers in one hand. "Discharge forms," he said. He dropped the papers onto the desk. "You give me any reason I shouldn't shit-can you?"

"Nosir."

"You know how tough a dishonorable can make it for you outside?"

The surprise showed on Waite's face and Maguire laughed. "You heard me right."

"Sir," Waite said. "On what charges?"

"Charges! Hell, we got plenty of those. Refusing to obey drill instructors' orders, lying, fighting. . . ." He looked up at Waite's face, the left cheekbone showing a bluish tinge. "Won't have any trouble proving you been fighting, will we?"

"Nosir."

"And stealing," Maguire said.

"Sir?"

"Wood's money, remember? And my watch?"

Waite looked at Midberry, but Midberry would not return the look. Waite realized how open he had left himself. What a fool he'd been to think he could outfox Maguire, a man who had every possible angle figured at any possible moment, a man who lived by the angles. The lieutenant had told Waite that Maguire had slid through two other investigations without a mark on him. The lieutenant had claimed that was because no recruits would testify. But it wasn't that simple. Maguire got off because he knew how to play the Corps' game and always kept himself covered. The lieutenant was too simple to catch Maguire as he played by the rules in the book. Maguire though knew the real ones, the unwritten ones, and he played for keeps. That goddam phoney, Waite said to himself, thinking of the lieutenant with his easy assurance and his pearl-handled revolver. Yet he knew even as he cursed the lieutenant that it wasn't the officer's fault. Waite hadn't been forced to testify. It was his own decision.

"You still with us, maggot?"

"Yessir."

"There'll be a man here from Headquarters tomorrow to haul you and your gear over there till your discharge is processed."

"Yessir."

"Nothing you got to say, is there?"

"Nosir."

"Sergeant Midberry?"

"No," Midberry said.

Maguire got out of the chair and looked at Waite, his hands on his hips. "Well, you really fucked it up nice, didn't you? Had it knocked here, a squad leader, no trouble, and then you piss it away cause you gotta play the hero. Didn't turn out that way though, did it, hero? Any of the other maggots cheering for you now? Shit, they won't even talk to you, right? And you know why? Not cause they're scared. Cause they know you're yellow and they hate your guts for it. A good marine hates failure, boy, and that's just what you are, a failure. You're on your way out and ain't nobody gonna miss you. Not even as third squad leader you won't be missed, cause Adam-czyk'll make a better one than you ever did."

The bastard, Waite thought.

"What the hell you expect him to do?" Maguire said, grinning. "You want him to jump off a bridge just cause you did? Shit, that boy's got a head on his shoulders. He'll make a good marine yet."

"Sir," Waite said, "is that all?"

"Real gutsy, ain't you? Sure, that's all. Just make sure you're packed and ready to get outta here tomorrow, understand?"

"Yessir."

"Cause I don't wanna see your pussy face around here again. Not ever, maggot, understand?"

"Yessir."

"G'wan then, get the fuck outta here. You make me sick. Git!"

Waite did not salute or click his heels or pivot, but simply turned and walked from the hut. "Hey boy, you forget something?" Maguire called, but Waite ignored him, went quickly down the passageway, swung open the hatch and stepped into the dark squad bay heading for Adamczyk's bunk. The blanket was over his head and arms and pulled tight before he had a chance to duck. He tried to fight loose but there were too many hands holding and pulling him. A belt was wrapped around his legs, others around his waist and shoulders. He could hear the harsh, panting whispers to tie him up, get him down, pull him back between the racks. He tugged his right arm free and got it around his head before the belts were cinched tight and he was dumped to the deck. He hit on his side and pulled his legs up as close to his belly as he could. The first punches landed on his exposed side and leg and did not really hurt. But, the pitch of the voices rising, he was soon being struck hard about the head and stomach. He tried to crawl away, but someone straddled his legs and held him down. A blow caught him behind the ear and whirls of white light flashed in the blanket-wrapped dark.

"Chicken-shit!" Waite suddenly yelled, too furious and filled with hate to care any longer what they did to him. "Chicken-shit! All of you!" He grunted as the punches came faster and harder. He was glad that he had spoken up. The others had lied because they were afraid. He'd been like them once, obeying out of fear, acting brave out of fear, always afraid. Even when he had finally worked up the nerve to talk, he had been afraid he might lose, afraid of what Maguire might do to him, afraid he wouldn't be able to stick it out. He'd been afraid earlier that night when Maguire hit him. Afraid even a few minutes ago in the hut. But no more. He knew now they were all, Maguire and Midberry as well as the platoon, afraid of him. They outnumbered him and could beat him, they had official power and could shit-can him, but only because they were afraid of him. He'd gone beyond them. He'd told the truth when they'd feared to, he'd faced Maguire when they'd feared to. They were still afraid now—of him, of his difference—and his fear was gone. Almost gone. Going. Each punch took more away. What more could they do? They had tried everything they knew, yet had lost their hold on him. His fear loosened under the beating and slid away and what was left inside him was something solid, not the brittle hardness that passed for strength among the recruits, but a core of something solid and deep and whole.

"Chicken-shit! All of you!" Waite yelled, at the same time laughing and grunting at the punches. "Chicken-shit! Chicken-shit! Chicken-shit!"

TWENTY NINE

Midberry stood at the hut's single window. He stared out at the gray parade ground and the long chain-link fence guarding the road to the main gate. On the outside of the window screen, a small, blue-green beetle clung to the fine wire mesh. Midberry snapped a finger against the screen and the beetle fell back and down, then caught in mid-air, a green blur of wings carrying it from sight.

"How about that," Maguire said. "He makes seven."

Midberry was thinking that the Waite incident had happened so quickly it had caught him unprepared. He wasn't sure yet what to make of it. He certainly didn't approve of the way Maguire had turned Waite over to the other recruits for punishment. And though Maguire pretended to be innocent, Midberry was sure he'd arranged it. That was why Maguire had been so eager to take the duty and let him hit the sack early. That way he hadn't been around to interfere. Sometime, Midberry thought, he would have to call Maguire on that. He would, if he were to hold his own, have to let Maguire know in no uncertain terms that such incidents were not going to happen again. Not as long as he was the J.D.I., they weren't.

"You deaf?"

Midberry half-turned from the window. Maguire was holding a sheet of note paper out to him.

"Here."

Midberry took the paper. On it were written the names of the recruits who'd been shit-canned: Tillits, Quinn, Johnson, Klein, Detar, Cooper and Waite. Beneath the list of names Maguire had divided seven into seventy.

"Right on the nose," Maguire said. "Ten per cent."

"How about that." Midberry tossed the paper onto the desk. Maguire picked it up and looked at it again.

"What'd I tell you right from the start. One herd's no different than any other." He crumpled the paper and tossed it into the shitcan beside his desk. "Right on the nose." Maguire got up, stretched, took his cover from the desk and put it on his head, angling it forward and down so that it hid his eyes in the shadow of the wide brim. "Better get the herd to chow so we make the rehearsal on time. Don't wanna give some chicken colonel a sore ass waiting for us to show. You comin?"

Midberry shook his head.

Maguire went out and Midberry soon heard the recruits lining up in front of the barracks. He waited until the platoon had gone before he went into the squad bay to Waite's rack.

"How you getting along?" Midberry asked.

Waite lay on his bunk, a wet washcloth covering his face but for his mouth. His lips were puffy. He lifted the cloth. His left eye was black and the cheek blue and swollen. "Fine," he said.

"Sir," Midberry considered reminding him, but didn't. How could he enforce an order with Waite. The recruit had already been beaten. Now he was being shit-canned. On the edge of being a civilian again, Waite seemed beyond Midberry's reach. "Here," Midberry said, holding out a small paper bag. "There's some APC's in here and some band-aids. Thought you might be able to use them."

Waite didn't move. "No thanks," he said, laying the washcloth over his eyes and nose again.

Midberry stood looking down at Waite, feeling foolish still holding the bag of band-aids and APC's. "You won't be getting a dishonorable," he said. "I got it held down to an undesirable. Those are pretty common. Not nearly as bad as a dishonorable." Waite said nothing. "It might not seem too important right now, but it will later. You start looking for jobs, you'll see what I mean."

Midberry waited a few minutes in silence, trying to think of something else to say. He knew Waite held him at least partly responsible for what had happened. What good would it do now to try to explain how he, Midberry, had actually kept the punishment from being worse? And all the other things he had done, or at least tried to do; things that had been done for Waite's own good. The recruit had cut him off completely. Midberry wondered just what had happened to Waite. What had made him change so much in such a short time. Ten weeks ago he had been a thoroughly squared-away recruit, a squad leader, too, and a dependable one. Now he acted as if it weren't the least bit important that he had failed to make it through boot camp. It was something, Midberry thought, he would never be able to understand.

"A driver from mainside will pick you up after noon chow. You got all your gear together?"

Waite nodded, keeping his silence and Midberry left the squad bay without trying to say anything more to the recruit. He went to the hut and wrote his parents a letter letting them know that his platoon was practicing that afternoon for its graduation the next week, and that he thought the platoon had a good chance to walk off with honors in drill, besides the first place it had already taken in riflery.

Maguire returned with the platoon as Midberry finished his letter and the two D.I.s changed from their utilities into tropicals. Maguire stood checking his appearance in the full-length mirror. Midberry was surprised at how many medals Maguire wore. "Fruit salad," he said, laughing as he put his own tropical shirt on, a single good-conduct bar pinned over the left pocket.

"Shit," Maguire said, "you're just a kid yet. All you need's one good shooting war. You'll pick'm up then, same as me."

Waite folded back the washcloth and laid it across his forehead when the platoon came back into the squad bay. He thought it wise to keep his eyes open, though he doubted anyone would have the nerve to call him out alone, and the platoon as a whole was too busy changing uniforms for anyone to get together a gang.

Adamczyk stood at the front of the rack, carefully tying his tie. He purposefully avoided Waite's look. Finished with the tie, he busied himself with his tie clip, then with buffing his dress shoes once more.

Waite felt no more hatred for Adamczyk. Maybe the boy had done the best he could. He had been taught the clever, hard rules of the game not only by the D.I.s, but by his squad leader as well. And he had made his choice, to follow those rules. Now he was stuck with that choice. All Waite felt for Adamczyk was pity.

The platoon was not long in getting ready. Recruits were already standing in place before their racks when Maguire, Midberry close behind him, came into the squad bay to call them to attention.

Maguire quickly checked one file of recruits while Midberry checked the other. "All right," Maguire said when he and Midberry were satisfied the platoon was ready, "outside, single file, first squad lead off. Left, face. Forward, harch."

Waite lay on the bunk, watching the dress-uniformed recruits filing past between his spread feet. When the last one had left the squad bay, followed by the D.I.s, and the front hatch had swung shut, Waite sat on the edge of his bunk. He reached down and hoisted the packed seabag to stand it against the side of his rack. Outside, he heard Maguire call a right face, then a forward march, then heard the platoon, heels hitting the pavement in perfect unison, moving away. The sound faded and the squad bay was quiet again.

Waite looked down the long, empty passageway at the neat racks and perfectly-aligned locker boxes. The windows were spotless and the wooden deck had been scrubbed by unknown numbers of recruits until it was nearly white. Waite noticed that despite the incessant scrubbing and polishing, dust specks floated in the angled shafts of sunlight.

Being alone in the squad bay gave him a momentary twinge of fear. He asked himself whether he had really made the concrete move in his life that he believed he had. Maybe he was only falling back into his old pattern of cutting himself off from everyone. Yet the feeling of fear, and the doubt that the fear brought with it, soon passed. Waite sensed a freedom he'd never before known.

It was as if at the same moment he had opened his mouth to testify, he had come awake. Right or wrong, he had this one time finally refused to drift. That no one at home, any more than those in the Corps, would be able to see his being shit-canned as a victory, no longer mattered to him. It had been something that he had felt, for himself if for no one else, that he had had to do. And despite the aching in his head and throughout his body, he was glad he had done it.

And he knew now, though it would be easier considering his undesirable discharge, that he wouldn't be going back to work at the dry-cleaners. It was not what he wanted or needed. And he was finished doing what others wanted him to do.

That thought cheered him. He felt that his life until the past few weeks had been nothing but an extended dream. Now, his feeling of energy or interest, perhaps simple awareness, gave him confidence. No matter how tough his future might be, it had to be better than his past. And for that he was grateful to the corps. "The Marine Corps Builds Men," the recruiting poster had promised him and he felt now that the promise had been kept.

Waite got up and smoothed the wrinkles from Adamczyk's bunk blanket, he'd been too stiff that morning to climb back into his own, upper bunk, then hoisted the seabag onto his shoulder. He steadied himself, his head pounding, and walked from the squad bay into the harsh sunlight. He went slowly down the iron ladder to the curb and sat, his back resting against the loaded seabag.

Across the road on the parade ground, recruit platoons were being put through their graduation dress rehearsal. The official base band stood in formation beside the Mount Surabachi monument, brassily playing the Marine Corps Hymn. Waite could make out what he thought to be platoon 197's guidon. He watched the platoon execute a sharp column left and march, in perfect step, toward the empty reviewing stand. The platoon passed proudly before the stand and into the spreading shadow of the huge gray monument. It halted on command and stood, the recruits in ranks as rigid as statues, as the other platoons passed before the empty stand.

The two D.I.s in front of the halted platoon looked to Waite like Maguire and Midberry. The recruit in line directly behind the Junior D.I. would be the third squad leader. Waite squinted, but could not be certain whether or not it was Adamczyk and platoon 197. In identical tropical uniforms, identical platoon formations, behind identical scarlet and gold guidons, there was no way for Waite to distinguish one platoon from another.

An olive-drab jeep pulled into the curb. A skinny buck sergeant in tropicals sat behind the wheel. Waite stood. The jeep idling, the sergeant took a clipboard from the dash.

"Your name Waite?"

"That's right."

"Joseph L.?"

"That's right."

The sergeant took a pen from beneath his tie and made a check on a sheet of yellow paper. Waite noticed the man's cheeks were deeply pitted and that the pits had been caked over with a skin-toned cream. The cream gave the man's face a dead, pasty look.

The sergeant replaced the clipboard in its holder on the dash. He stuck the pen back under his tie and shoved the jeep into gear.

"Get in."

THE BEST OF THE BESTSELLERS
FROM WARNER BOOKS

REELING
by Pauline Kael　　　　　　　　　(83-420, $2.95)

Rich, varied, 720 pages containing 74 brilliant pieces covering the period between 1972-75, this is the fifth collection of movie criticism by the film critic *Newsday* calls "the most accomplished practitioner of film criticism in America today. and possibly the most important film critic this country has ever produced.

P.S. YOUR CAT IS DEAD
by James Kirkwood　　　　　　　(95-948, $2.75)

It's New Year's Eve. Your best friend died in September. You've been robbed twice. Your girlfriend is leaving you. You've just lost your job. And the only one left to talk to is a gay burglar you've got tied up in the kitchen.

ELVIS
by Jerry Hopkins　　　　　　　　(81-665, $2.50)

More than 2 million copies sold! It's Elvis as he really was, from his humble beginnings to fame and fortune. It's Elvis the man and Elvis the performer, with a complete listing of his records, his films, a thorough astrological profile, and 32 pages of rare, early photographs!

A STRANGER IN THE MIRROR
by Sidney Sheldon　　　　　　　(93-814, $2.95)

Toby Temple is a lonely, desperate superstar. Jill Castle is a disillusioned girl, still dreaming of stardom and carrying a terrible secret. This is their love story. A brilliant, compulsive tale of emotions, ambitions, and machinations in that vast underworld called Hollywood.

COAL MINER'S DAUGHTER
by Loretta Lynn with George Veesey　　(91-477, $2.50)

America's Queen of Country Music tells her own story in her own words. "How a coal miner's daughter made it from Butcher Holler to Nashville . . . it's funny, sad, intense, but what makes it is Loretta Lynne herself . . . a remarkable combination of innocence, strength, and country shrewdness."　　　　　—*Publishers Weekly*